The Fair.

Copyright 2016 Jovee Winters
Cover Art by Nathalia Sullen
Formatted by D2D
My super seekrit hangout!

The Fairy Queen

Cruel. Cold. Wicked. Just a few adjectives used to describe the most ancient of fairies—Galeta The Blue. But did you know, dear reader, that once upon a time, long, long ago, the Blue was the Benevolent Pink?

Few know the trials of the fae reviled by all, save for one. The ancient and wise Creator. Galeta is the Creator's daughter, and It will stop at nothing to save her. The truth of who the fairy really is may startle you. She's the heroine of all of Kingdom. A sad truth no one knows, not even the wee fairy herself. The journey to getting her back will be marred by pain, trials, and tribulations, and when it's over, Kingdom will never be the same again...

Chapter 1: Forward

Danika

In this life, none has been wronged more than Galeta the Blue. I'm sure you never expected to hear that coming from me. But there you have it.

If you've read my own tales, then you know the trial I myself suffered under her iron fist. And not just I was affected by what she'd done. The lives and stories she altered simply by being there were many.

The Man in the Moon, Miriam the Gray, Violet Wolf, Gerard, and more recently Fable of Seren, characters in some of the *Tales'* most legendary stories, but did you know many of their stories (their real ones) should have turned out far different?

A truth we have only just discovered. I won't go in depth with those for now, because for some of you it could shatter your concept of happily ever afters, and Kingdom is a world built upon them—a world that survives and thrives due to the most powerful magic of all...love.

Fate is an interesting character herself, for nothing is written that cannot be unwritten, nothing is set that cannot be undone. She helped turn what was bad into good. And she can help fix again what's been lost. If any fairy can do it, it would be her.

Though Galeta twisted much of what should have happened in this world, the happily ever afters prevailed. Some wound up as they should have; others never got the chance to meet. For a time, Kingdom was exactly as it should be. It was good. Not without its share of hurt, but happy and wonderful all the same.

Not everything turns out quite as we'd hoped, though. But we learn to move on, and eventually the sorrow merely turns into a "what if" on a cold, lonely winter's night when thoughts turn inward and maudlin.

I could hate The Blue, quite easily, but had she not cast the die as she had, my Alice and Hatter, Hook and Trishelle—why, even Rumple and his Shayera would never have been, not to mention so many more. A fact I only recently discovered to be true.

The path The Blue chose allowed those happily ever afters to manifest. So can you really hate someone when such joy was derived from the sorrow? Who knows—I'll leave that to you, dear readers, to decide.

Miriam the Gray, my oldest and truest friend, used to tell me a fantastical tale. A story of creation, of rebirth, and transformation. The story of how Kingdom came to be.

Of course I believed her—Miriam had the second sight. All Grays do. But it scared me too. I didn't want to believe it could be true, didn't want to think that a creature I'd pinned all my frustrations, rage, and fears on could be anything other than the conniving, twisted, and demented creature she'd become.

There is an old Earthen saying I'm quite fond of: "When a butterfly flaps its wings in one part of the world, it can eventually cause a hurricane in another..."

Basically, it's sometimes the smallest and most inconsequential actions that can cause unbelievable pain and catastrophe down the road.

I had no idea at the beginning of my tenure as godmother to the villains that life was anything other than what I'd always known deep in my heart to be true. That people weren't exactly who they appeared to be. I never really understood the degrees of layers or the fact that for some people, the truth of who they were was a lot like a tiny pebble rolling down a snowy hill.

By the time they reach the bottom, they no longer resemble who they once were. Galeta was that butterfly— she flapped her gossamer wings, and life altered forever. For the people. For Kingdom. But most especially for her.

I did not want to pen this forward, but mostly because it shames me. Reveals to me the painful truths of just who I am. I was willing to hate Galeta and pin all of my frustrations on her fragile shoulders, but little did I know that as I hated her there was another in a pantheon far away who knew The Blue for what she truly was—a heroine in her own right.

The path to pulling Galeta from the darkness and back into the light was not an easy one—in fact, it took many hands and many hearts, and in the end one would have to die so that another might live.

All I can say is this—be careful whom you judge, for you never know the heavy burden of the cross they bear...

~Danika Moon, one of the thirteen keepers of the true tales of Kingdom

Letter to the Audience

Galeta

I know very well there is nothing I can say in this moment to make you think kindly or differently about me. I've not been kind, good, or even simply decent. I've been none of those things; my sins have been shown for what they are.

All I can say is this... I wasn't always this way.

Once, I was good.

Once, I believed in the truths of what it meant to be a fairy godmother. What it meant to help bring about the happily ever afters to the denizens of this world. Once, I was even someone worth knowing. I didn't remember that until just recently, but I'll strive to never forget that again.

My sins are many.

There are no excuses for what I've done. Though I hope that by the end of this story you might think a little more kindly of me.

All I can do now is pen this tale as truthfully and unvarnished as possible and let you decide whether all "dark queens" deserve a chance at redemption and happiness.

Without further ado, I'll begin this tale as I have every other one.

Once...

Upon...

A...

Time...

~The Blue, one of thirteen Keepers of the *Tales*

The First Act

If you do not change directions, you may end up where you are headed~ Lao Tzu

Chapter 2: In the Beginning

Galeta

Ten.

And then one more. One that did not belong with us, and yet had been born of us. It was dark. Cold. Foreboding. I shivered; not wanting to study that one too closely and instead turned my thoughts toward the colors.

I felt the beat, the pulse of all my sisters' hearts in rhythm with my own.

Whoosh.

Whoosh.

Whoosh.

I opened my eyes and looked around.

There was nothing but void.

Darkness.

An empty stretch of black that swept out into infinity and was coated in hypnotic winking lights of purest silver.

Around me, my sisters too blinked their eyes. Our souls were one. We were powerful, but we were so very, very young.

I knew nothing save my name—Galeta the Pink.

Blurry colors soon began to take form.

Gold. Yellow. Green. White. Gray. Red. Purple. Pink. Orange. Brown. All the colors of the world we were to fashion.

We'd been created by a hand far greater than our own. Though It never revealed Itself to us, we felt great love coming from It. A being that rippled as large and never-ending as the cosmos surrounding us. That being told us what to do.

I looked toward my sisters.

I did not yet know their names, only their colors. One looked like a living flame of brightest orange.

Strange that I should know what flame was when fire had yet to be designed. And yet I did. I knew everything.

The people who would soon fill the world we'd create.

The magic.

The love.

I sighed as the rest of my sisters did.

The Purple was a breath of fresh air. Her skin was as black as the night, and her eyes as pure as the flowers she'd one day imagine into being. She smiled at me and held out her hand.

"Pink," she said softly, and I couldn't help but smile back, taking her hand in mine and squeezing gently.

It was odd, the sensation of touch.

But I liked it.

Then Green grabbed my other hand. She was a beautiful woman dressed in streamers of ivy and who had nut-brown hair that fell down to her ankles.

"Pink," she said to me too.

It was then that I noticed them all turning to me. Red. White. Gray. Brown. All of them looking toward me.

Suddenly I was surrounded by the lot of them, their hands all over me, touching me. It was then that I understood why. I was their conduit, the instrument of power. To harness their own gifts, they first needed to channel mine.

My energies pulsed like a bright wave; the blackness we floated in began to burst with color. Clouds of green, red, pink, and purple and every other color of my sisters.

The White's eyes turned milky as a smile tipped the corners of them.

"Galeta," she said, and then the others began the chant too.

Galeta.

Galeta.

Galeta...

My name echoed into infinity, and that was when I felt it.

The pull of power that came from our Creator through me. I closed my eyes and let them take of me, let them draw from me.

A bottomless wellspring of magic that poured from the crown of my head to the toes of my feet, and the more they drew, the more I had to give. It was effortless, and so easy that all I could do was laugh with giddy delight.

But as I felt the pulse of our Creator's magic wind through me, I also felt Its voice. I could not call It a him. Or even a her. The voice simply was. The voice had always been. And would always be.

Galeta, can you hear me, daughter?

I smiled happily, nodding. I was in raptures; I was who I was always supposed to be. The vessel of Its magic in its most raw and purest form.

And as the ten pulled from me, I fed them the blueprints for life. Down to the minutest of molecular structures. How to fashion a leaf. A feather. A heart that beat. The Creator showed me how, and I, in turn, showed them.

Do you like this life?

I hadn't had it long. But I loved it already. I nodded. Watching as the ten spun magic to life. As The Red created rivers of molten magma. As The Brown created fissures of earthen stone and rock, dirt, and seeds. As the White created strange, fluffy little pockets of water that she hung like gossamer threads in a darkened sky.

I love this, I answered It back. *I love the colors. I love the endless creation and life of possibilities. I love it all.*

I felt It smile, and my heart sang.

Do you know who you are? Who you really are?

Confused by that question, I took time before answering. Formulating my thoughts so that I'd not sound foolish to the Creator.

I'd just been born. I had no grasp of who I'd been, for I'd never been before. But I could peer through the veil of power and see deep into the future of where we were going.

I saw trees and hills, valleys, and rivers. And an explosion of life all around us. It was lovely... but something felt different too.

Blinking, I studied the pictures further. Peeling back the initial layers of beauty and studying the strata beneath. No, I did not only see one timeline, but two.

Side by side.

One filled with darkness. And the other with pain, grief, and sorrow but also joy.

At its center was a being. Like me and yet not like me. In the dark future, I was as I am now. Beautiful. Pink. Honorable. But I'd failed them all. I stood in a field of blood and bones. Weeping into my hands as a beast, a monster of darkness, consumed all we'd crafted.

In the other timeline, life was still beautiful. Still thrumming with power and love. And though there was pain and darkness, hope always endured. I lived in this timeline too. I saw myself. Though I did not know how I knew that, for I'd never seen my face before. But when I looked upon the stark beauty of that woman's features, I recognized my own.

Unlike the lush beauty of The Pink, the other creature was frigid. Cold. Still beautiful, but untouchable. Unapproachable. She snapped at those around her. Hurt the innocent. She knew the fabric of love and spit in its face.

This person was bad. Very bad.

And she was a color I was unfamiliar with.

It is called blue, The Creator said with a voice grown deep and soft.

What is this? I asked It in a voice far steadier than how I currently felt.

The beginning. The end. And all the parts between.

It made sense, and yet it did not. For I was as confused now as I'd been when I'd asked It my question. My lips turned downward.

Would you like to hear a story, my beautiful one? It asked gently.

I would do anything to keep my Creator happy. So I nodded, though I did not think I would like the hearing of this story. Both futures scared me.

Once, there were others. I've crafted many worlds. But always things end the same. In bloodshed. Death. Famine. War. Plague. Hubris brings my creations down.

Even though I knew I should never interrupt The Creator, I couldn't seem to help myself. There was such sadness, such longing in The Creator's words, that it moved my soul to tears.

Then why do you continue to create? *If the creation is so vile, why make more?* *Why not end your pain and simply let us kill one another off and be done with it?*

Can I be aught but what I am? I heard Its smile in Its voice. *You are my creation, and I The Creator. It is what I am. Who I am. I cannot be other than that. Nor can you. In you, Galeta, I believe I have finally found the one.*

Though I'd just been born, I understood. For I too had been kissed by the divine. I had been built for one purpose, to help breathe life into The Creator's designs.

But the thought that It believed me to be the one. I shivered. The one of what?

Its laughter echoed in the vastness of time and space.

You need not fear me, little one. For I come in peace. But I have a question to ask you. One that will force you to search yourself—

Search myself for what? I interrupted, feeling queerly ill at ease. I loved my Creator, having hardly even known It; I loved It and wished only to please It.

Its patience flowed through me. *I've shown you the strings of fate. Two paths. But only one choice. You can become The Benevolent Pink, as is your right, and I will not hinder you your choice.*

The Benevolent Pink. I smiled, liking the sound of it. I'd seen myself in that alternate timeline. Through all the years that led up to the wasteland of blood and war, disease and famine. Before the death of the universe, there'd been happiness. Love. But there'd been a great and terrible darkness too. One that spread like an illness, slowly but surely snuffing the life out of the creation. Twisting what'd once been good into something befouled and evil.

There'd been many, many, many good lifetimes in that alternate timeline. Joy. Marriage. Love. Births. But the inevitable ruin marched on, an insidious virus that spread its roots deeper and deeper still until there was nothing left and nowhere left to run.

Must it truly end that way? I asked with a thread of hope in my voice. *Is it not possible that different choices could be made? That perhaps this time your creation will not fall, but stand strong? Could we not surprise you yet?*

It sighed, and in that tone I heard the truth of it. The Creator had had this same conversation before. Through many worlds, twists, and incarnations of creation.

Others who had come before me, who'd believed this time they could be exempt. This time they could make things work.

9

Has it ever worked before? My voice was a mere reed of a whisper. *Have your creations always fallen?*

Always, It said simply.

I, trapped within a shield of magic and surrounded by my sisters, was the only one who knew. The only one who understood the gravity of the choices I'd been offered.

The Creator hadn't had to say it, because It had shown it. In the other timeline. Where I'd become The Blue.

It would not only be my color that would change, would it?

Again, I heard Its smile. *Ah, to be so young and already so wise. I was right when I made you, my little Pink. Pink, the universal color of love of oneself and of others. That is who you are, my child. It is why I crafted you as I have. Why I gave you the pure soul I did. And why I've chosen you to bear the great weight of this tragedy.*

I sifted through the alternate future. Seeing the twisted, macabre heart I would one day bear. The lives I would ruin. All the curses flung at me. The deadly, violent hate I'd induce in all those around me.

Everyone will hate me, I whimpered sadly, feeling as though my heart were being cleaved in two. I was pure. I was an innocent. I believed in the goodness of others and in myself.

Creation hates what it does not understand. It is true, dear one, that you will bear a burden unlike any other. But I will not abandon you, though it may seem that way at times. I will always be there. Guarding your every step. Watching over you day and night.

Clutching at my breast, I felt the steady beat of my heart and fought back the tears. *My own heart will turn wicked. I will become a vile creation. One I can hardly stand to look at even now. Why? Why would you have me choose that path?*

Finally, The Creator showed me the final truth It had been withholding.

My sisters and I had not been the only ones to be born this night.

A vision sprouted in my mind of unmitigated malevolence. Just a seedling now. A tiny ball of great and wicked power. But pulsing within its shell beat a rhythm of great darkness. Even from a distance, I could feel the slick coat of its power, the twisted wrongness of it covering my soul like slime.

Black ice skated down my spine as I curled my lips, trying in vain to shove the image away.

It is the curse of life, that there too must be death. One cannot escape the other. You and your sisters are that life. And that seedling is that death. As you create, it will sink into the soil, planting its roots far and deep, infecting all it touches. That evil will fill the waters, the land, until finally it will spill over into my people's hearts. And then, as I have many times before this, I will watch you all destroy yourselves.

I gasped, covering my hands with my mouth, staring at my sisters, who happily hummed beneath their breaths, oblivious to the portent of their eventual demise.

Can you not destroy it? Fix it? You are The Creator. All powerful and ever present. How is it that you cannot stop this? Why must there be suffering and hurt and hate? Why can there not be only love and goodness?

A brushstroke passed over my flesh, causing my flesh to tingle and my soul to tremble. It had hugged me in a compression of air.

I'd never known such a touch could be so pleasurable.

A hug.

What a simple and yet powerful gesture of love. One tear leaked from my eye. I did not want to do this. Did not want to change. Did not want that darkness.

I could change it, Galeta The Pink. I could make it all go away. But then, I've given none of you the chance to choose for yourselves whether to be good and decent or not. Life is built upon choices. Those that cause you to blossom, and those that cause you to wither. None of you would thank me for taking your choice to live as you would choose away. Believe me, I have tried. My creation flourishes when they choose to. Not because I've forced them to. Do you understand?

I did understand. Though I did not agree. Surely if they knew, if the creation understood that they could make it all go away now, that It could fix all their problems before they ever even began—

10

Then I'd have nothing but anarchy. A creation enraged that they can never be aught but this. That they have no choice. No minds of their own. That they are owned in every way and nothing they do matters in the end because their will has been stripped from them. Tell me, little one, would you like to always be told what to do? Even if the knowing would make your life perfect? Wouldn't you ever wonder if maybe there wasn't another way?

I paused to consider Its words.

If I were told to go left, would I not wonder what lay to the right? Would the curiosity not burn at me?

I imagined myself at a crossroads. Looking left and right. To the left, nothing but brambles and weeds. To the right, clear and open skies. And I knew—with a sinking heart, I knew—that even if It told me to go left, I'd see those clear roads and skies and turn right. Because that was how I'd been created to be.

To have free will. To want to be what I wanted to be.

And that was good. Kind. A leader.

I closed my eyes; my soul grieved so deeply that when I rubbed at the liquid escaping my eyes, I pulled my fingers away to reveal smears of blood.

It is good you should feel this sorrow. This pain. For it tells me that you understand, my Pink. You understand the sacrifice you will make so that all others might be free.

Swallowing hard, I studied the faces of my sisters. Wondering if I would feel for them as I did now. Or would my love turn to hate? Would my own heart be poisoned by that darkness, so that I no longer recognized myself?

But I already knew the answer. For I had seen the vision.

I would never be myself again. I would kill. I would hate. I would be all the things that darkness was so that creation could live free.

There will be another. The burden will not be yours alone.

For the first time, I felt hope. Pulling in several sharp breaths, I shook my head. *When? For how long will I be forced to endure this?*

I do not know, my Pink. The truth is, I've searched lifetimes for one like you. And it could be that I'll be forced to search lifetimes more for another.

I understood what it would not tell me. That for me to be free, another must die to themselves. There would be another like me. Someone pure and perfect forced to endure the cancer of creation all alone.

I could not allow anyone else to suffer this agony.

No, my Creator. No, I would not ask any other to be burdened by this grief. Take me. Alone.

The breadth of Its shock raced across my skin, causing my fine hairs to stand on edge.

You would do that, my child? You would shoulder the entire burden alone?

Tears ran freely now, so rampantly that a few of my sisters began to notice the obvious transformation in me. But still, they could not understand the agony of my position. They simply knew I cried.

I did not want to do this. No part of me wanted to carry this burden, but I loved It, and after seeing the utter desolation and devastation of the alternate timeline, I knew there was no choice. Deep down, I'd always known that.

Yes. I would.

Strong, warm pressure against my forehead caused my sadness to evaporate for but a brief time as I felt the first touch of my Creator's kiss.

Then let us not tarry a moment longer.

For a wild second, I reconsidered my brave words, wanting to tell It I'd changed my mind. But then I felt it.

A hand shoving through my spirit, shoving that darkness so deep inside me, I felt its shockwaves reverberate through every cell in my body.

Back bowing, spine cracking as the power rushed through me, I gasped, screaming to the heavens and causing my sisters to scatter. Breaking off the conduit between It and them. I was possessed. Taken over.

11

Sinking into the quagmire of so much pain. So much heartache and hate. Agony. Loathing. Murder. Wickedness. On and on and on, that darkness spread. I clutched at my chest, screaming in rage, begging the darkness to stop its spread, not to infect my heart. My soul. To leave just one piece of me... me.

But like pincers they sank in, rooting in deep, spreading, spreading, spreading... making me lose myself. Then my colors started to bleed through.

My sisters gasped.

The heavens trembled.

And finally I heard It say, *Never alone, my child. Never alone. I will save you. Only trust in me...*

Chapter 3: Somewhere The Creator Finally Stirs

?

Somewhere in time...

The Creator never moved from Its looking glass. Not once in the millions of years It had kept an eye on her. Galeta never knew she wasn't alone. The moment she'd taken the dark seed into her heart, she had changed. Just as she'd feared she would. Her connection to the giver of life had been severed.

Darkness consumed her. A petty need for vengeance and a thirst for mayhem. I watched as my Creator watched her. Studying the vastness of Its shoulders. The steadiness of Its gaze upon her.

Never blinking.

Never eating.

Never speaking.

The Creator had spoken a promise to Its child, one I knew It would keep. At some destined hour. Some appointed time.

For many lifetimes, I'd kept watch over It, knowing that someday my time in this great scheme would come. That I would finally witness movement. A flicker of life and awareness back in Its gaze when The Creator finally deigned to look at me.

Always, I lived in the background.

Waiting.

And then, after many lifetimes of wondering and doubting, I saw the first twitch of movement.

Heart stuttering powerfully in my chest, I grabbed hold of my royal-purple tunic and sat as still as a statue as The Creator lifted Its head. The movements precise and slow, ponderous, as though a great weight had settled itself permanently upon Its shoulders.

Then It turned, and I gasped. Witnessing the face of my maker for the very first time.

I trembled, body quaking with great and terrible fear at the power that rolled off Its form. He. She. It... The beginning of all things and the end of them too. Swathed in a cloak of night and stardust. Its eyes were the burning red of fire. And Its face was obscured by the blazing light of the sun.

Tears spilled from my eyes. Hastily swiping at them, I turned my face aside, no longer able to bear the weight of Its gaze peering through my soul.

I have found one, It said simply.

Staring down at my sandaled feet, feeling as though I might faint at any moment, I fought through the doubt and fears to find my voice. I'd seen images of that night between The Creator and Galeta. She'd spoken to him with awed reverence but as an equal too. Understanding, perhaps intrinsically, how very much The Creator loved her.

I did not feel that same depth of devotion from It. I was merely built for one purpose. To be Its go-between betwixt worlds.

My wings fluttered nervously behind my back as I bit down on my bottom lip. Once, long ago, I'd made the mistake of whispering instruction into The Blue's ears while she'd slept. Telling her of a child born to bear the seed of darkness. In her dreams, I'd shown her how to build the wee one. How to envenom her. I'd shown her all I could. Confident in the knowledge that I'd done a good work.

I'd been so sure... so sure I'd found the next vessel, and all I'd wanted to do was please my Creator. But the child—I'd simply known as The Heartsong—had eventually gone mad from it. The Ten, knowing the Heartsong would be unable to bear the burden of such great evil, had been forced to separate her from the fold. They'd taken

13

her outside of the place of magic, to one without it, where she could not give in to her darkness. The Gray had been tasked with the care and keeping of the little one. A charge that'd resulted in her eventual demise.

I'd ruined so many lives with my meddling. The Creator had fixed things as best It could. But there could be no undoing the damage I'd wrought. The lives I'd very nearly destroyed by my interference.

The Heartsong thrived now, through no part of mine.

My stomach sank to my knees.

A gentle caress of wind lifted the golden hair off my shoulders, like the sweetest of touches, and I trembled. *You must forget that now. You were young and inexperienced then. You did not know. Let it go, harpy.*

I swallowed hard, my limbs full to bursting with the song of Its voice. Like the strings of a harp being plucked by the hands of a goddess. I shuddered, hanging my head.

"Tell me how to fix this madness, and I will, my Creator. Show me what to do. Only show me what to do, and I will move mountains for you."

I could feel Its smile by the sudden brightening of the stars around us.

I know you will, little one. This, then, is how we shall play it. In a pantheon far away are two females. Goddesses, they call themselves...

The Creator's laughter shook the heavens, causing the worlds to tremble and new planets to be birthed. I'd never known my Creator could laugh.

My lips twitched in response.

They are bored with their long lives. I would have you go to the one known as Aphrodite and whisper my commands into her ear. Of a game. A trial, as it were. A contest of love. I care not. However they wish to play it is of no consequence to me. But as you whisper this idea into her ear, you must also make sure they include The Blue.

I shook my head, frowning prettily. "But won't they question the insertion of a fairy all of Kingdom loathes?"

The air grew suddenly redolent with the lush perfume of roses in bloom. The Creator was pleased, though I could not figure out why. I would not question it. For millions of years, I'd never seen so much life out of It.

That is the very point of these games, my beautiful harpy. Finding happily ever afters for those deemed unloveable. Blue's inclusion in the games would not be questioned. Every queen inserted into the games will be invaluable to the reconciling of Kingdom after the Blue's salvation.

I frowned. "What? Reconciling of Kingdom? What does that mean?"

Its smile was patient. *In due time, you'll know all. But for now, make sure that each name I gave you is placed into the games. The games are but a ruse for something far greater.*

Hm. I cocked my head, working my fingers through the tips of my thick, golden hair. Love. Between the sexes. Not that I'd never seen such, of course. I was The Creator's messenger; it was my duty to spy on the lives of creation as well.

And while I'd noted the pleasure the joining of bodies seemed to bring them, I'd never actively cared much. I'd been built for a greater purpose.

This one.

But I could admit, even if only in the quiet of my own mind, that something about these games made me truly curious for the first time ever. What made these queens in particular so important?

The Creator shook Its head, and I knew It would not answer me. It knew a future It would not tell me. Which meant, somehow, I played an active role in it myself. Obviously as Its messenger. If I knew the outcome, I could change the entire trajectory of the future by choosing a different path. I had to choose as I would have chosen had I never known this at all.

I nodded. "I will whisper to them of The Blue."

Yes, but not only The Blue. Her mate as well.

14

My brows lifted at that. High onto my forehead. Fairies did not mate. They'd been built to abhor the very notion of it. Of course, there had been that one... Dani something or other, but she'd been an anomaly. An irregularity not to be repeated.

The Creator, noticing my heavy frown, said, *You seem confused, little one.*

Feeling a very little bit braver, I straightened my spine and flicked my eyes up at the shining light of Its face. But, quickly, tears gathered at the corners, forcing me to look back down at the silvery pinpricks of starlight beneath my feet.

"I am. A little. I do not understand why a male belongs. Eros love seems to me to be a messy, tawdry affair."

It chuckled. And a beam of pure-white light raced across the heavens, crashing into a solitary, frozen chunk of a planet. Obliterating it into an explosive shower of dust and debris.

The power of life and death rested on Its tongue. I shivered. How foolish the creation was to not understand just how fragile their lives truly were. They lived simply because The Creator allowed it. Even the so-called gods and goddesses of the many pantheons owed their lives to It. But so few knew. Or even remembered that anymore. The Creator had been forgotten by Its creation.

And yet It had never forgotten them.

I rubbed at the fine, raised hairs on my arms.

Someday you will.

My mouth parted just slightly. What did that mean? Surely I would never. I would never leave It. My place was here. Beside It. For always.

But now is not yet your time. Now is Galeta's. A promise I made to her many eons ago will finally be fulfilled. The male child is grown. But he is jaded. Dark. And complex.

I was no Creator. But it seemed to me that perhaps if the male was to help fix Galeta, he should certainly not be any of those three things. He should be gentle. Loving. Tender.

The heavens pulsed with flashing streams of burning stars as It gently cupped my chin in Its massive grip.

Like calls to like in many ways, my golden harpy. Galeta's true soul will come for no other.

Well, I'd have to trust It on that. I certainly wouldn't know. But The Creator had been playing this game a long time. At this point, It surely knew what It was about.

"How am I to do this? What am I to tell Aphrodite?"

No sooner had I asked it than I knew. It'd shown me Its will. My lips tingled with the words I must soon speak, my tongue thick with the knowledge of what to do. My head filled with the images of what came next for The Blue, her chosen mate, and the mirror.

"And the new vessel?"

Its mighty shoulders heaved, causing me to fall off my precarious perch. My downy, white wings flashed open as I beat them heavily to regain my balance.

Is finally ready.

Oh, that was momentous news indeed. Soaring high on my wings, I glanced over Its shoulder into the looking glass of worlds. Excitedly studying the many exotic faces within, looking for the one that would bear the mark of the vessel.

I looked into the worlds of waters, the worlds of fire, ash, stones, skies, colors, magic, mundane... but could not spot the telltale spark of a carrier.

I frowned.

"Where is it?" I asked in confusion, still trying to suss out who it might be next.

I did not envy that creature the burden of its new life. And as often as I could, I would make certain to keep watch over it. To nourish it as I was unable to nourish Galeta.

Wondering why The Creator had still not answered, I glanced over my shoulder at It. Twin flames hypnotized me, and in their depths I read the great sorrow.

15

The vessel is ready—it simply doesn't know it yet. And until it does, you will not find it. But trust in me, my dear girl, that all is as it should be.

I shuddered, clasped my hands to my breasts, and moaned at the obvious sadness in Its tone. "Is it wrong that I feel terrible for the poor creature?"

That gentle caress of breeze whispered across my cheek, and a tear slipped from the corner of my eye, crashing through the mirror of worlds. There was a mighty roar, the birth of a new river. Though I did not know in which world. I'm sure it didn't matter.

My sadness was a crushing, bruising thing inside my chest. I'd seen the sorrow of Galeta's fate, and it crushed me to think that another innocent would soon bear the terrible knowledge and burden of such.

Understand, my little golden one, I would never force this burden upon the vessel. As I did with Galeta, so I do with it. The choice is the vessel's alone. But if it takes this burden from her, then know this—as I trothed myself to her, so I would to it. I also have learned a thing or two since then. The burden would be vastly different this time.

"How?" That last bit of news lit a tiny spark within me. Perhaps things wouldn't be so dire this time. Perhaps this new vessel might yet survive and thrive.

I felt Its smile as It said, *You will know all in time, my harpy. Your only task is to go amongst creation and learn.*

Clasping my fingers tightly, I asked, "Learn? Learn what? I know them. I watch them all day long."

Ah yes, it is one thing to watch from on high. But quite another to be down there and move amongst them as a peer. You are kind and sweet—

I beamed at Its compliments.

But you are young yet and know far less than you might imagine. I want you to watch the queens and their mates. Study them. Learn them. Understand what it is to be... human.

"Why? My place is here with you. Isn't it?"

It laughed, a sound that warmed me to my toes. I could never imagine a time or a moment when I would not be with It. I loved my Creator. Surely, It knew that.

Of course, I do, my child.

"Then why do I suddenly feel as if you are asking me to leave you?"

Never.

Wind brushed beneath my chin, calming me instantly.

But it is not enough simply to see—you must also understand what they feel. The love. The pain. The hurt. The hope. That is what will ultimately grow you, my sweet one. That is how you shall finally mature. Now, will you go and whisper my commands into their ears?

It was right, of course. It was always right. I felt the press of my powers grow within me. When The Creator beckoned, I answered. It was that simple. It'd tasked me with the whispering of schemes, and so I would do as I'd been bade.

I was a messenger. I would always be a messenger. The need to do my duty beat powerfully within my chest. My nails dug into my palms, and I wanted to turn, to rush into the fray of things and unburden myself, deliver the message to the Goddesses. But something held me fast.

A terrible feeling that I might not like what lay ahead of me.

My lips turned down, and sadness weighted down my bones. Something told me that I would not like this journey. And yet Galeta had borne this curse for far too long. Too much longer, and she'd die.

And no one would mourn her.

No one would ever know the great sacrifice she'd made on their behalf. And that darkness that rested inside her soul... it would be let loose. Freed into the worlds. Destroying all she'd sacrificed her life for.

But could I truly take that seed from her and plant it into another? Knowing the devastation it would wreak on the vessel's soul? I wasn't sure I could.

Have faith, my harpy. And know that this new vessel, if it chooses to accept the burden, will do so with eyes wide open. You would do nothing that it would not allow.

I trembled a little. The very last thing in the worlds I wanted to do was hurt another, but if the vessel agreed, then perhaps I'd suffer no regret from any of this after all.

I looked into Its eyes and saw nothing but love staring back at me.

Chapter 4: We're Going To Do What?

Calypso

"The Blue? Really?" I looked at the list of players Dite had handed me and shook my head. "After what she's done to just about everyone in Kingdom? I think not."

Dite, ethereally beautiful as ever and dressed in a gown of sheerest white that dazzled in the darkness of my caves, nodded. "Yes, Caly. She's got to be part of these games."

I turned to my lover, Hades. The man of my heart. I'd made my bubble butt howl with pleasure this morning. I bit my bottom lip as his eyes flashed with fire all their own. We'd need to harvest our next batch of carrots sooner rather than later—we'd gone through last year's crop already.

Even after all these years together, he was the only one for me. Dressed in his customary black suit-and-tie combo, he made crypt keeper look good.

His dark eyes scanned the parchment in my hands. But his own hands had wrapped around my waist, dragging me closer into his side.

I trembled at the heat that always simmered between us. That combustible mix of love, lust, and raw power. My waters churned.

Dite snorted. She might claim to find Hades and I disgustingly touchy feely, but as the Goddess of Love, I secretly knew she adored it.

Finally, Hades shrugged, looking to both Dites and me. "The match-ups make sense. Though I'm no fan of the Blue fae, I hold no animosity toward her either."

I sniffed. I hated the little cretin and couldn't understand why Dites was so insistent. But she was, and one thing I'd learned through the years with my BFF was that there were very few things Dite would ever give me pushback on.

That she did so now revealed the depth of just how important this was to her. Though I wasn't sure why or how.

"Six pairs, Caly. It's how it's got to be," Dite insisted.

I lifted a brow, shaking my head as I thrust the sheet back at her so that I could return my attention to harvesting glowworms.

They only mated once a year but made good stock for Linx's stews. I secretly thought she didn't want them so much for the taste as for how pretty they made the soups. But that was neither here nor there. What my hippocampus wanted, my hippocampus got.

Lifting a bucket, I plucked another furry little ball of neon-green fluff from out of the cave wall. It landed in the half-filled bucket with a plop.

"And you agree with this, Hades?"

I felt his nod behind me. "I do."

I sighed. "Well, then whatever. I guess I don't have a choice in the matter here. But just know this—that fairy steps one foot out of line, and I will personally cut her balls off."

Hades chuckled. "My dear Caly—"

I rolled my eyes, plucking up ten more worms. "I know she doesn't actually have balls, bubble butt. But you catch my drift."

Aphrodite squealed, rushing to drop a kiss on my cheek. Why my friend was acting as if I'd handed her the keys to Atlantis, I wouldn't know. But, for some reason, she was ecstatic. "Fine. Fine. You do whatever you need to do, Cals. There is only one thing. And don't get mad, because I know you and I know how you get."

Spine stiffening, I rotated slowly on the balls of my feet. Glaring at my best friend as the waters between us turned ice cold.

Dite shivered. And Hades stepped in close to me, wrapping his arms around my waist as he dropped his head onto my shoulder. His touch brought me not only warmth, but also comfort. Easing deeper into the strong cage of his arms, I felt my muscles slowly loosen and relax.

The waters immediately turned less hostile.

"Cals, that's not actually listening," Dite snapped, rubbing her arms forcefully to get her blood flow back.

"Well, what do you expect, Love? You know you should never start a sentence that way with me. I do not care for surprises, and considering that you've asked me not to get upset after I just looked at the list—a list including my granddaughter—I can only assume she's somehow to be a part of this charade. Am I correct in this assumption?"

I lifted a peaked brow. My tentacle hair undulated in the heavy currents with a flicker of displeasure.

Crossing her lovely eyes, she stuck her tongue out at me. "You're annoying. Hades, did you not sex her up enough last night?"

"I satisfied my woman plenty," he rumbled, and I shivered, because, oh, he had.

"What are we, two now? Get to the point, Dites. Talking of The Blue gives me migraines. Please, just put me out of my misery already."

"Fine." She held up her hands. "Fine. The thing of it is, I feel each queen should have a chance to work with a familiar."

"A familiar? Or her familiar? Like the Piper with those damnable rats of hers?" I shuddered thinking of those red, beady eyes.

"Exactly." Dite shrugged. "Although perhaps with a minor tweak."

My lips thinned. I was certain I wasn't going to like where this was going.

She looked at me as though expecting me to say something. But I kept silent. Dite shifted on her heels, flicking a glance at Hades.

If she was looking for an ally, she was barking up the wrong tree. Hades, at the end of the day, would always have my back. His arms squeezed tighter around me, proving my words correct.

"We need to swap familiars," she rushed out. "It's the only way to truly keep this fair."

Confused as to why she'd made such a big deal out of this, I said, "Okay?"

Nibbling on the corner of her bottom lip, she pressed on. "As in, Galeta will be needing Fable's mirror."

I glowered, and the waters that had calmed just seconds ago now rolled and pitched.

"Bloody hell, Cals. Stop it." Dite pursed her lips, glaring hotly at me. She might be a Goddess, but I was an elemental with powers far exceeding her own.

"Why?"

I would protect what was mine at any and all costs. I did not trust Galeta. I did not know her all that well, to be sure, but I'd heard enough about The Blue's duplicity and spite to make me wary of her. Not to mention my spies had spoken to me of Galeta's presence lately hovering around Fable's castle.

My granddaughter was recently wed to some stupid legger—which was too bad because the entire point of these games had been to find Fable her happily ever after, until I'd heard of her nuptials. Which none of us had been invited to. Yes, I was a little salty about that bit there. Now some Wicked Witch of the West something or other had taken up our sixth spot. Sounded dreadfully pompous to me, that title, but what did I know?

19

I'd not spoken with Fable in forever, and I desperately missed her, but I did not wish to intrude on her honeymoon. However, I was a grandmother and couldn't butt out completely. I'd set my spies within the tributaries surrounding their estate.

It was how I knew The Blue was meddling.

"I had a dream," Dite confessed softly.

Immediately, my waters ceased moving. "A dream? That's what this is, isn't it? You dreamt that Blue must be part of our tournament. Dite." I gently laid a hand against my dearest friend's shoulder, speaking gently. "It was just a dream."

When Aphrodite looked at me next, I couldn't help but shake at the depth of pain in her eyes.

"Caly, you don't know. You didn't see it. But as a Goddess, you know as well as I that sometimes our dreams are portents of things to come."

Blinking slowly, shocked by the depth of my friend's emotions, I studied her. Aphrodite was considered by many to be flighty and silly. A goddess consumed by nothing but sex and romance. But Aphrodite was far more than that. She was brilliant, empathetic, and the best friend anyone—be they god or mortal—could ever boast of having.

Yes, my moods were as mercurial and temperamental as the seas I called home, but my friend loved me all the more for them. Aphrodite had always understood me, and I loved her dearly for that.

Dites was family too. Not by blood but by choice. Which sometimes meant far more.

"I believe you," I whispered.

"You're not mad?" she asked, sounding slightly surprised and making me feel just a little ashamed for my earlier behavior.

"No, Dites, I'm not mad. I believe you. You are right—we are Goddesses. I know the truth of visions and how the Fates move through us with them. I will never question you again on this decision. You have my blessing to do whatever you need to do concerning The Blue."

Her smile was brilliant and made my heart ache just a little bit.

"I am sorry, Dites. Truly. Please know that I love you dearly and think of you as a sister. I apologize for my—"

Resting her hand upon my shoulder, Aphrodite squeezed gently. "It is forgotten already, my friend. Now, I shall go and finish making preparations. Have you and Hades finished building the arena?"

I nodded, and Hades hugged me tight. As though sensing I needed it. I did. Though I couldn't put a finger on it, I felt a sudden disquieting emotion. One that seldom manifested within me.

I did not trust Blue. I did not like Blue. But now that Dite had told me what she had, I felt as though I'd just heard the whisperings of Fate decree that it was so. That all we did now was far greater than merely a simple love match.

There was a vastness. Something... great. Mighty.

But as quickly as the emotion had come over me, it vanished. Leaving me reeling and perplexed.

"Hades, you fixed Mirror for Fable, correct?" Dites asked, pulling me from my strange thoughts.

He nodded. "Yes."

"Good. Then I would ask you to tweak it for these games, with her permission, of course."

"What would you have me do?" He sat up straight, and I could feel his body tense. Knowing my lover as I did, I knew that he was sensing the same disquiet I was.

"I'll tell you later. I must hurry with this. Time is of the essence today." With those words, she vanished in a shower of sparkling pink.

I turned to Hades. He looked at me.

"You feel it, don't you?" I asked a moment later, more serious than I'd ever been before with him in my life.

Now was not the time for games or sexual innuendos.

"The shifting of Fate?" he said deeply, and I shivered, rushing into his arms and dropping the basket full of glowworms to the cave floor, scattering them like marbles.

But I didn't care. I needed the strength of his arms around me.

"Something is going to happen," I whispered into his lapel, clutching him tight.

"I know, my angel. I feel it too."

Those words brought me no comfort at all.

Chapter 5: Abra Cadabra

Galeta

Present Day

I had the blood.

The stupid little girl had fallen right into my trap. It'd been so ridiculously easy to get Fable to believe I was truly her friend. Her fairy godmother. What a damned fool. As I tipped the green glass vial full of Brunhilda's cursed blood before my eyes, my insides raged with adrenaline and excitement.

The end was finally near. Gods above, after all the lifetimes of searching, I'd done it. My lips twitched, and heat burned behind my eyes.

My wings flapped unsteadily behind me. Button—my golden beast of a massive dragon—nudged me with his snout hard enough to cause me to stumble.

I smacked his nostrils hard, shoving a ball of power behind it. His eyes widened, and fire curled from out of the edges of his snout at the sting of my touch.

"Do not think to stop me!" I snarled at him.

Button and I had had this discussion far too many times to count, and I was over being talked down to about it.

Intelligent, golden eyes thinned, and the rumbles of his displeasure echoed through the high ceiling of my cave built of ice and snow. Long, colorless stalactites of hoarfrost hung like giant fangs from above. Beneath my hovering feet were razor beds of rime sharp enough to skewer anyone who might be foolish enough to follow me inside.

Button, being a fire dragon, was impervious to my ice. I loved nothing and no one. But for reasons I could not quite fathom, the damnable beast seemed to care for me. I'd found his egg last year, and curiosity and the desire to control a beast of such power was what made me take him with me and guard him until he'd hatched.

"Why are you so bloody insistent on doing this, Galeta?" Button's voice was a terrible rumble that shoved at my flesh with prickles of heat and power.

Curling my fingers around the glass vial, I shook my head. "You keep away from me, you mangy mongrel. Do not think to stop me. I've worked over ten lifetimes for this. My plans have finally come to fruition. I will not be stopped!"

Shaking his massive head as a rush of arctic wind howled through the large opening of the cave, he glowered. He was angry with me.

But my heart was too fixed and too cold to care.

"You've ruined her!" he snapped back, blasting jets of flame so close to my hovering wings, they tingled.

Jerking out of the way before he fried them to ash, I laughed. "Please, don't tell me you care a whit about that damned queen. She is nothing to us. Nothing to—"

"There is no us in this, Galeta," he rushed on, his demonic mask of scales glistening like golden flame. "You've made your position perfectly clear on the matter! I tried with you!"

Tossing my head back, feeling the caress of ice move across the frozen flesh of my form, I shook my head. "I never asked you to, damned beast! Go, then. Leave! I do not want you!"

My chest heaved mightily as I stared the magnificent creature down. Still awed, even after so long, at the scope and breadth of him. Even if I did not care for his high-handed ways.

22

We'd had this same argument in times past. And, always, his threats had been empty words. Button had tasked himself with being my keeper from the moment he'd opened his glowing eyes. I'd never asked him to. Never wanted him to.

I notched my chin.

Our stare-down lasted for an eternity and no time at all. And then his massive frame shuddered, and I couldn't help but frown just slightly to see the beast looking so broken of a sudden.

"You're right, fairy. You never did want me around. More fool I. I'll leave you now. But know this—it's forever. You do not want me, then I have no use for you anymore."

Digging my talon like nails into my palms, I didn't move. Hardly dared to breathe. Why were my ears ringing? Why did my chest suddenly ache so badly?

What was this happening to me?

Unaware of my inner turmoil, Button shook his massive head. "This is good-bye, creature. May you be damned in the next life."

Then, moving his massive girth with the sensuous glide of a king cobra, he turned and blasted into the air, pumping his colossal wings as he flew out of my shelter.

"Go, then," I whispered to his back, even as my clawed hand reflexively reached toward him as though I meant to pull him back to me. Realizing what I'd done, I curled my fingers into a fist and hung my hand limply at my side.

My heart wasn't shattering inside me. My soul wasn't quaking. Noise didn't ring in my ears. I wasn't currently reeling from the loss of the only thing that'd ever given a damn about me in this life.

I wasn't.

I don't know how long I hovered there, lost in the thoughts and the ever-growing din tormenting me. But when next I blinked, the sun had set and the sky was aglow with frosty pinpricks of silvery light.

Button had left me.

And something already empty inside of me fissured further. I clutched at my chest, frowning deeply.

There were moments, stolen bits of time, where I wondered about myself. About what I'd become. I'd only ever been a cold-hearted creature. Consumed by my lusts and darkness. But every so often a memory would intrude. Something I knew deep down I shouldn't know, and yet I did.

I hadn't always been this way. And yet I had, hadn't I?

I shook my head, confused by my own nonsense. The fissure inside of me spread, and I clutched at my chest as though it were a palpable, tangible thing.

I was black inside.

I'd taken what I wanted. Done what I wanted. Trampled on whoever and whatever I'd was necessary to get to where I was today. I was queen of the fairies. They might all hate me, but there wasn't a thing they could do to change it either.

But as quickly as the moments came, they vanished. Squaring my shoulders, I growled beneath my breath.

"*Bah.* He doesn't want me, then I don't want him either. Stupid bloody dragon." He'd kept me away from my work long enough.

Soon I'd be forced to return to that damnable forest full of frolicking, idiotic winged drunkards racing snails and singing high-pitched songs of laughter and frivolity.

I spit as madness and fury whipped through my bones, hardening that fissure that'd cracked. My anger was my salve. Sealing up the holes, closing the gaps, so that I wouldn't have to look too deeply. Wouldn't have to dwell inside the shadows.

My hands moved of their own volition once I'd gotten to my workbench. I snatched up glass vials of powder, liquid, herbs, tongues, eyes, flesh, darkness... I didn't need to look to know.

I'd been preparing myself for this moment for eons. I'd stumbled across a book of magic many lifetimes ago.

23

I'd outlived them all.

No one knew. They all forgot. All fairies knew we'd live long lives, unless fate or misfortune befell us. I sniffed. They didn't know, though, but I did.

I never died.

Always. Always. Always I was.

All the originals had died.

Except for one.

Except for me.

Tossing ingredients into the stoneware cauldron before me. Knocking over vials. Hands manic as I reached and tossed. I sniffed louder.

My vision grew blurry.

I'd killed them all.

One by one.

All the colors.

Ended their lives only to see them replaced by others. Couldn't kill the magic.

Jealousy?

"No, there was a purpose," I whispered wildly. Tossing in too much, too little, it didn't matter. "Doesn't matter. Must finish."

Couldn't see all that well. Why?

I sniffed harder.

Fissure burning. Cracking open. I grimaced. Clutching onto the workbench as my heart hammered painfully within me. Might not be returning to the fairy games tonight after all. My wings shuddered.

I shook my head.

No, Galeta, don't think about that, I cautioned myself. The moment had come. I wasn't sad. "What does the Mad Hatter say? Tick-tock. Tick-tock. Tick-tock."

Time waits for no man.

I trembled. Almost over. Almost done. Finally learned how to do it. A watery smile.

I frowned, my manic movements pausing as I reached unsteady fingers toward my cheeks. Turning my hand slowly. Eyes going wide. So much blood. Tears too?

I shook my head. No matter. "Press on. Forget, Galeta. Try to forget."

Snick.

Snick.

Snick.

The hiss of a blade slicing through a neck. The gentle give and tug of ending life.

A terrible sound echoing deep inside my cave. Like a creature dying from a mortal blow.

"Stupid animal," I hissed, sniffling harder. Bloody tears so blinding. "Can't see a blasted thing."

Don't do this, Galeta.

I paused, every nerve ending in my body going still. Button had returned. Mouth twisting into a blazing smile against my will. Twirling, wings beating rapidly, eyes scanning. Heart plummeting to my feet.

Not here.

My Button had not returned to me.

You're better than this. If you don't want to be this, then stop...

Ah, echoes of memories. Button hadn't returned to me after all. Fissure cracking further. Darkness spreading through my limbs.

Echoes of the past warring with the sounds of the present.

Button roaring at me. Screaming at me that I was foolish. Mad. Crazy.

I laughed, smashing my pestle down roughly on a dried bushel of nightshade. The sounds of my madness rang back to me through the crystal fangs perched just above my head.

So deadly.

So lethal.

Standing beneath them, arms spread, singing to the rafters.

Crack.

Snap.

Whistling death coming straight at my heart. Excruciating pain as the icy blade tore through me. Blood. Blood everywhere. Pierced directly through. Grabbing onto the hilt. Confused. Still alive?

"Why? Why? Why!" I screamed, the claws above me trembling. Groaning. Creaking. But it didn't faze me.

Because they couldn't hurt me.

Nothing could.

Hated everything! So much hate! Dying. Dying. Dying inside...

Smashing down on the flower. It was already powder beneath the angry ministrations of my hands. But I couldn't stop. So much fury. Rage.

Blackness clawing out of me. Seeping through my pores. Darkness raging, swirling within me. Roots gone so deep there was no escaping.

"Try to do good. But always do bad," I muttered. The wind picked up my words, tossing them back at me spitefully.

The night hated me. Memories crowding at me.

I shoved them back. But the tide was too high, too powerful. They crashed into me. Drowning again.

Gerard in love? I should let them have each other. Step aside. He will love her. I can see it... Betty, lovely girl. Poison spreading through my heart. Stupid, silly words. They can never be happy. Curse him. Curse him now!

Wetness streamed down my face, burning the ice of my flesh. That same wounded sound intruding on my chaotic thoughts. Pain. So much raw pain. I stilled, looking up. Where did it come from?

Icy claws stared back at me. The lonely howl of the wind behind me. Nothing inside with me. Nothing would ever come here. Even the most evil sensed the darkness that dwelled here.

Brows lowering, I jerkily tossed the ground flowers into the cauldron. And finally, finally... the blood of a dark witch. Snatching up the vial from the countertop, I held it up to my eyes.

Release.

I breathed. The madness ebbing just long enough to remember Button's words.

It's forever, Galeta. What you choose, it will be forever...

Maybe I shouldn't do this. Maybe I could find another—

A tidal wave of memories.

Curse the child. Two faces. One of madness. One of beauty. The Huntsman can never have her. Whispering dark deeds to the Sun. The Moon loves only you. You must destroy Danika to get what you want. Fields of lavender and blood. The tears of the innocent. Never let them know. Only do enough to make them believe in you...

Great evil stirred, and I smiled.

It had been fun.

You know you want more. You can never leave me, fairy... you need me.

"Need you," I whispered mechanically, clutching onto the workbench, dropping the glass vial to the icy floor beneath.

A caress of twilight. A forbidden kiss beneath a bloodred moon. Glorious madness...

"No!" I screamed, and in that one word I heard the cry of the wounded. That sound of an animal dying, it was me.

Blinking, shaking my head, I released the bench, searching the ground for the green vial. There it was. Heart hammering before the darkness gripped me again. I shot out my hand for it, calling it to me with magic.

"Almost over, Galeta. None will care. Almost done now."

It landed in my palm, hot, warm, and inviting.

Death.

This time true.

Scrubbing at the tears blinding my eyes, I uncapped the bottle and tipped it over, pouring all of its contents in.

A flash of fire shot up, scorching the icy claws, melting them instantly. Drowning me in frigid water. But I didn't feel it.

I never felt it.

A hovering shadow of a skull and crossbones wavered in neon blue before me, and I sobbed with relief.

This will end anything, Galeta. Why use it on you? Use it on others... Torture. Maim. Kill. Kill. Kill.

I didn't realize what I'd done until I felt the cold glass vial of death tucked into the hidden pocket of my gown. I blinked. The evil was controlling me again. Always in control now.

"No. End me. No more," I whimpered, voice tight and full of grit.

One more. Evil beguiled.

My fingers clenched. What could it hurt just one more time? My heart raced, and I tasted my pulse on the back of my tongue. Imagining death, blood, gore... My eyes rolled to the back of my head as a sound of longing crawled out of me.

Fight this, Galeta. A small, tiny sound. One I hadn't heard in weeks now. A female. So lovely.

My chest ached, and I shook my head. "Not strong enough anymore."

The brush of a breeze against my cheek. But not cold. It was warm. Like the kiss of light, it rushed through me, obliterating the ice in my soul. I'd not felt warmth in so long, I'd almost forgotten the taste of it.

Sobbing painfully.

Clawing at my face. So tired. So, so tired.

Kill more. One more time.

"Yes," I whispered, responding to that darkness.

Galeta, no. You're stronger than this. Millions of years you've fought him. Hang on, little fae.

"No. No... killing." Words being ripped from out of me. No control over anything anymore.

Kill...

Blood on my hands. So much blood on my hands.

Wings pumping, the urge to turn and seek out death so strong I could taste it. I needed it. Wanted it.

Fight.

"Can't." Turning. Going to kill something. Anything. Then I'd do it. Then I'd drink from it myself. Then it would be over.

Suddenly, three faces stood before me. Calypso. Hades. Aphrodite. Why? I shook my head. A dream? A nightmare? Not real. No one came here.

"Now!" Calypso cried.

Hades and Aphrodite lifting a massive gilded mirror rippling with power on its glossy surface.

I screamed.

The mirror crashed over me. Sucking me in. The sound of glass shattering.

Darkness.

Chapter 6: The Nightmare

Syrith

Fifty feet.

Forty.

Thirty.

The rugged terrain surrounding the castle of the Queen of Hearts drew closer as I hurtled like a burning star ever downward. Tucking in my wings. I felt the rush, the pull of wind licking at my flesh.

Adrenaline pumped like a drug through my veins.

Twenty.

Ten.

I heard the whistle of impending doom, and I smiled. It would be nothing. Quick, even. Just couldn't open my wings. I wondered if it would even hurt at all.

Only seconds before impact.

But then I thought of my mother, and I just couldn't do it.

With a roar, I spread my wings as my claws crashed into the ground, ripping up clods of dirt and roots. My massive shoulder thundered into the trunk of Mother's favorite haunted willow.

Ghouls howled, moaning in frustration. I'd wrecked their home. I considered an apology, but I wouldn't feel it.

Eyeing them with the empty, glassy stare I'd perfected in the last three years, I drew my wings back into myself. Shifting form and defying any of them to come at me.

The ghouls—blood-sucking parasites—kept to within the shadows of the haunted forest. Their glares hostile but none of them daring to approach me. I was one of the few denizens of Wonderland that could walk among them unmolested. Let any poor soul stray too close to a clawed hand, and they'd never live to see another sunrise.

When I felt the last monster slink back into its hole, I finally turned and headed for home. Kicking at rocks beneath my booted feet.

Shoving my hands into my pockets, I glowered at the sun, hating that the day should feel so bright and cheery when, inside, I was empty, cold, and lifeless.

Not wanting to be bothered by any of my parents' servants, I switched form yet again, this time to one of a rager monkey, gliding up the exterior of the castle walls as though I flew. Digging my dexterous fingers into any crack I could find, moving with the grace of a sleek cat.

But in this form, I was a dark, shaggy beast with glowing red eyes. Should any of the servants stumble upon me as I was, they'd faint dead away. Ragers had fangs the size of a large man's wrist and a thirst for blood rivaled only by my father's people.

I was just about to my window when I heard the murmuring of voices from the neighboring quarters. My parents' private chambers. They would not like me eavesdropping, but something about their tight whispers and heated conversation told me whatever they spoke of, it concerned me.

Frowning, I pressed tight to the stone and stilled as I listened.

"He is not well, Ragoth," Zelena—my mother and Queen of Wonderland—said. "Each day, he gets worse. I'd hoped after all this time we'd have our son back."

My heart clenched to hear my mother sound so broken. I'd never wanted to hurt her. But I could no longer pretend I was happy either.

"Well, what did you expect, Zelena? He lost the love of his life. He's handling things as best he can. The truth is, if I'd lost you..." Father's words were soft and scratchy. "I do not think I could bear it as he has."

I clenched my jaw, shoving down the memories trying to surge to the fore. Smothering them so that they'd not come to the surface and drown me in them again. To simply say I'd lost something didn't express the depth of my loss. The utter black hole that now consumed me because of it.

There was rage and fire in my father's voice. I could almost visualize him pacing as he tunneled his blunt fingers through his thick, wavy hair. Ragoth was a true dragon of the line Draconian. Not a born resident of Wonderland, he'd come from another world entirely. Olympus.

Once a keeper of Zeus's golden fleece, Ragoth was also a prince of his people and the current King of Wonderland.

Both he and my mother were beautiful. Powerful.

As I was their offspring, everyone had expected I should be the same. I was not. And never would be.

In a world bursting with madness and magic, it should have come as no surprise to them that I'd not be normal. Not be everything they'd hoped for in a son. In an heir.

My nostrils flared as I dug my nails cruelly into my palm. The pain helping only a little to clear my mind of the shame and desolation I now felt because of it.

I would leave—run away and never return—but for the two inside. I'd never meant to hurt them as I had. And yet I could not seem to stop either.

"I should never have encouraged him to come out as he did. I'd just hoped—" Her words caught, and I blinked back heat. "I thought that... that... she truly did love him back."

"Oh, my queen," Ragoth groaned. There was a shifting of fabric and then the sound of my mother's broken sobs.

"That he should suffer this. I never meant for this to happen, Ragoth, you must believe me. He is our son. I love him. Love him so desperately." Her words were broken and laced with heartache.

Breathing heavily, I turned my face outward. Looking at the vastness of my parents' kingdom. Wonderland. Beautiful madness, it was. But it would never be mine.

The twisted trees. The haunted forests. The demons that ran wild within. The denizens full of laughter and drink. Nothing serious. Nothing real here. All of it, all of it, nothing at all like me.

I did not belong to this place. Though I'd been born of it, I felt no pride in it. The insanity of this place had infected my mother's womb, had birthed an abomination. Only once had I ever shown my true form outside of these walls... only to *her*. I would regret my decision till my dying breath.

Shuddering, I closed my eyes, but the memories were too close, and no matter how hard I tried to forget, they would never let me. The look of shock on Seraphina's beautiful face. The revulsion where once there'd been love. The wound of her rejection had pierced me like a blade.

I'd thought there could be nothing worse than to have your intended's heart suddenly turn to hate. But there could. And there had.

To perdition with this place.

I would never rule here. I wanted no part of it.

"He needs more help than we can give him, Zel." Ragoth's voice was calm, steady. Echoing with the dragon's wisdom.

"But to him? To them? How can we hand him over like that? What could they possibly do for him?"

Going still, I cocked my head, trying in vain to draw closer so that I missed not one word now being whispered low between them.

"I feel the quiver of Fate in all of this, Zel."

"Yes, but to just hand him over, he will think we do not—"

A mist of black shadow suddenly curled from out of the casement, wrapping like tentacles around my body and clinging like dark leeches.

"Hades!" Zelena and Ragoth gasped at the same moment that a dark head leaned out of the window, pinning me with a steely, intelligent look.

I'd never seen Hades personally, but I knew of him from father's association with Olympus.

Olive-skinned, with deep blue eyes and a head of shaggy black hair, there was something almost feral looking about the Lord of the Underworld. Hades was predatory in his mannerisms.

"We have a visitor," he said simply and in the deep voice of what you might expect the Lord of the Underworld to sound like.

I notched my chin. Determined not to be cowed by Death.

"Come inside, boy," he commanded with a flick of his finger before disappearing back inside. So sure that I would do exactly as he'd said.

"Syrith is out there!" Zelena gasped. The rush of footsteps preceded her pretty face popping out of the window a moment later, taking up Hades's spot of just moments ago.

There was pain reflected in the bright blue of her eyes, and her hair, normally a striking shade of blond, was now dull, almost dirty looking. A testament to the fact that mother had been in agony for the past three years over me and hadn't been taking good enough care of herself.

Nothing in this world hurt me more than to see her pain. My heart clenched, but I bit down on my back teeth, trying to shove it away as I had everything else.

"You sat out there and listened to us, son?" A thread of wounded hurt trembled through her words.

Because of my ability to transform, I'd been able to listen in on my parents' private conversations for as long as I could remember.

Mother had often chastised me about it growing up. I'd promised years ago never to do it again.

Hurt reflected clearly back at me as her lips thinned. No longer able to abide her wounded gaze, I turned my eyes away.

A second later, Father joined Mother, and I felt his gaze burn right through me.

"Get inside, Syrith," he commanded with the hard edge of the dragon in his tone.

I waited until they'd disappeared back inside before crawling in. I didn't want to hurt them, and yet I couldn't help but glare at them. Blaming them in some ways for what'd been done to me.

Before that day, she'd not known. Seraphina had liked me well enough, and I knew that, given time, she'd learn to love me. I'd wanted there to be nothing but truth between us. True, we'd been a matched pair meant to join two nations as one. But I'd fallen hard and fast for the innocent-looking raven-haired beauty. Within the village, rumors floated around me. That I did not care for the company of others. That I was standoffish and even cruel.

I was none of those things. I'd blossomed by Seraphina's side, believing I finally had a partner. An equal in every way. It'd been mother who'd urged me not to keep any secrets from my future bride.

Determined not to show either of them how torn up I truly was inside, I notched my chin and stared at the one I cared nothing about.

Hades's eyes were cold, calculating. "So you are he?" he said only a moment later, without preamble.

"As you see," I growled. "Why are you here? Why have you come?"

"Syrith!" Zelena gasped. "Manners! We've raised you better than this."

Curling my fingers into fists, I glared at her. It was easier to hide the pain when I could focus on the anger. I wanted to tell her I was no child. Not anymore. And I hadn't been for quite some time.

"Do not look at your mother that way!" Ragoth snapped, standing in front of her, shielding her from my view.

The apology rested heavily on my tongue, but the words were stuck fast. I breathed hard, turning my eyes away. I was the royal heir to the throne of Wonderland. I had a duty to fulfill.

Once, I'd believed in honor. Faith. And becoming an even better monarch than even my parents. Not now, though. Not anymore.

"He cannot do this, Hades. I do not know why you've come, but I am sorry to say that whoever told you Syrith was your man was wrong," Zelena rushed on, clenching her fingers tight before her.

The dark lord lifted a brow, staring at me with the force of a heated beam. As though peering through my soul. The look of disdain on his lips heated my blood, made me want to punch him.

Hurt him.

And then he shook his head, as if finding me lacking. My nostrils flared, the burn of my magic tingling through my blood, wanting nothing more than to transform into something powerful, terrifying, something that would help me swallow the pain down deep with its violence.

Mother shook her head. And I knew she knew what I was thinking, what I wanted to do. She'd always known me too well.

I trembled.

"He is definitely who I've come for, Queen of Hearts." Hades's voice caused a stir of rumbles in the clouds above.

But I heard what he hadn't said. The doubt in his eyes was as clear as day. For whatever purpose he'd come for me, he wasn't doing it of his own accord. Someone else had sent him along. Whatever I was or wasn't to Hades, in his eyes, I was lacking. Just as I'd been to everyone else.

I bit down on my tongue, counting slowly to ten in my head.

"No." Zelena shook her head. "No. I can't allow this. Won't—"

"Zel," Ragoth grabbed her flailing hands, clinging to them gently. "My love, stop it."

Her tiny nostrils flared, and her blue eyes clouded with hurt and anguish.

"I'll go." I squared my shoulders. Ignoring my mother's gasp of shock. I looked at Hades, hating him with every fiber of my soul but wanting nothing more than to leave this cursed place. I didn't care where I went or why. I just needed to get away.

"Syrith, but—" Zelena shrugged out of Ragoth's grip, coming to me and yanking me to her.

I towered over my mother by several feet. In my true form and in the one I now wore.

Gripping her arms tight, but not to hurt, I looked at her directly. "Mother, I cannot stay. Don't you understand?"

Tears swam in her eyes, and she shook her head.

It was father who came to my rescue. Gently peeling my mother off my rigid form, he grasped and held her tight. Rubbing his hand down the back of her spine, soothing her despite her protestations.

Ragoth looked to Hades. "Watch over our son, Hades. It's all I ask. Bring him back home to us."

I didn't have it in me to tell my father I'd never return again. Not to this place, where the pain and the memories lived and breathed and haunted my every step.

Hades turned toward me. He did not answer my father. I think because he knew, as well as I did, that I'd not be coming back.

Gripping my shoulder, Hades squeezed, and instantly, we were travelling. Moving through a tunnel of shadows and darkness that pulsed and breathed around us.

I frowned. I'd never left Wonderland before and had no idea where the Lord of the Underworld was taking me.

It should have worried me; he was the Lord of the Underworld. I could potentially be going to my doom. But even that didn't frighten me. At least then there'd be an end to the pain.

"I'm sure you're curious."

"Not really. No."

Turning toward me with a lifted brow, Hades cocked his head. A look of curiosity crossed his features. "You are not at all what I expected, son of the dragon."

I jutted out my chin. "I get that a lot."

Inhaling deeply, Hades spread his fingers wide. "Look. I have much to say to you and not much time to say it. So listen and do not interrupt. We go to a game of sorts. A love game."

I hissed, twirling on him. He could not have said anything else that could have elicited this reaction from me. "No."

"Listen, boy!" This time when Hades gripped my shoulder, his eyes flashed with obsidian smoke, and ghostly hands reached out from within the tunnel itself. The echoes of haunting moans and groans causing my flesh to shiver. "You are young and know so very little. Do you honestly think you're the only one who's ever suffered in love?"

I jerked, wondering if my parents had spoken of it to him. "What would you—"

He scoffed. "More than you could know, you bloody fool. Let me impart a bit of wisdom to you, whelp—had it truly been real love, you'd not be standing here with me today. We are creatures of desire, creatures that cannot function without a purpose. Whatever you imagine Seraphina was to you, I vow to you she was not. You hurt. Then hurt. But do not enshrine her—the little fool does not deserve it."

"Don't you dare say anything against—"

He shook me, and the groaning grew louder.

"I am the Lord of the Underworld. You think I do not know her. I know her. Better than you. She was weak. Feeble. And unworthy of the idealistic pedestal you've set her on. Where I take you now, I need all of you in this game. Do you hear me?"

His growl caused the wailing moans to cease. As though they feared their Lord's fury. But I was empty, and death did not frighten me.

"You cannot force me to love another."

"That is not what this is for you," he said, still gripping my shoulder with hands now digging into me like claws.

I blinked. He made no sense. "What?"

A light drew closer—wherever we were headed, we were close.

"This is so much more than merely finding a soul mate, Syrith. For you, anyway. You've been tasked with something far greater."

Still confused but also intrigued, I shook my head. "What exactly?"

"You must save her. Save The Blue."

The Blue? I'd never heard of her. "Who is that?"

"She is a foul, hateful, evil creature who'd just as soon stab you in the back the moment you turn around. But that is not who she truly is."

More perplexed than ever before, I didn't know what to say.

"The others in this game must believe that you are nothing more than they are. Simply players in a quest for love."

"Why?"

His chest heaved as he took a deep breath. "I do not know all the particulars. All I know is the Fates' hands are in this. We must save her. And the only one who can is you."

That made no sense to me at all. I could barely keep my own head above water; how the bloody hell was I supposed to help anyone else?

"How am I to pull this off?"

The light drew closer, and now I could begin to see the hazy images of others just on the other side of the tunnel.

"You are a prince of your land. You know how to act. So do it. Be something other than yourself. During the day, you will trial just as they do. What no one else will know is that The Blue will not truly be a part of the games. She's been trapped. For the safety of herself as well as others."

I shook my head because none of this made sense to me.

"She is too unstable. Too uncertain. Completely unbalanced. To save her, you will brave not one but two trials. The love games, which will merely be a charade for you. A reason for your being here only. Your true trial will run during the night. When you enter the mirror."

I frowned, not liking any of this. "So I am to run around this game alone?"

"No." He glanced over his shoulder as his lips tugged down. "No. You won't. My woman, Calypso, has created a facsimile of The Blue. She looks and even feels real—that's because a part of her is. We were able to siphon off a sliver of The Blue's soul to fashion the copy. But understand, The Blue's soul is a terrible and dark thing. During the games, the clone will be alert and autonomous. Only once you step within the world of the mirror will she power down."

"I do not understand any of this."

Hades's jaw clenched. "Do or don't. It doesn't matter. Only know this—none can know what you're doing. If they were to learn it, they might try to stop you."

I frowned even harder. "Why would they care if I saved The Blue or not?"

This time he was the one to look confused. "I'm not sure, to be honest. I only know that what happens within that mirror will impact all of Kingdom."

I thought instantly of my parents and wondered just what in the blue blazes Hades meant by that.

"Chin up, whelp." He growled. "For it is now show time."

The tunnel widened, revealing to me the world on the other side. There were shrieks and groans racing through the winds. Trees towering as high as the clouds themselves, and a gathering ring of confused-looking men.

Hades shoved me out of the tunnel. I snarled, twirling on him. But the calculating God walked past me. Casually ignoring me, as though I wasn't worth the bother.

It wasn't hard pretending to be furious.

While I did not regret leaving Wonderland, I very much resented finding myself here.

Whoever this Blue was, I hated her already.

Chapter 7: And So It Begins...

Wringing my hands together, I watched as the god and goddesses explained the rules of the "game" to their charges. Hades had draped the men in shadows so that the women couldn't see them.

But my eyes were for Syrith alone. He'd played his part well. Acting the uptight and spoiled royal that all surely believed him to be.

Biting onto my bottom lip, I looked up toward the heavens, knowing The Creator's eyes were already on me.

I'd gotten everything set this far. Whispering into the ears of all three gods, letting them believe Fate was the one guiding their hand, when in truth, every step was ordained so far as the dragon heir and The Blue were concerned.

Peeking inside of Syrith's heart, I was worried, though, and I didn't mind admitting that. The boy, who wasn't truly a boy in years—but seemed it to one as ancient as me—wasn't the friendliest sort.

I'd not known of his troubles, which no doubt accounted for his attitude, but certainly this could not bode well for The Blue.

Be patient, golden one...

I heard the voice of my Creator, and instantly, my mind quieted.

"I am nervous," I whispered softly, my voice echoing like the howls of moans and wails in the breeze surrounding the glen.

Have faith. I heard Its patient chuckle, and I couldn't help but fidget.

"I'll try. But you know that's never been my forte. Can I just ask one question, Creator?"

Always.

"What if the replacement vessel doesn't show? What if nothing comes to save Galeta? I'm scared." The last part sounded like a shriek in the woods, causing several sets of eyes to widen and faces to turn and look.

I was not a ghost. But I was outside the realm of this universe. Unless I wanted them to see me, they wouldn't. Though for some odd reason, I couldn't seem to control the noise of my passing.

I'd been told before that my voice carried an otherworldly, almost ghostly quality to it. Rather off-putting to those around me, or so it was said. I thought I had a lovely voice.

The vessel comes, my darling. In fact, it is already there. It simply doesn't know it yet.

"What? Who? Can't you tell me?" I asked with excitement tinging my words, studying the lot before me with brand-new eyes, wondering which of the twelve it could possibly be.

A centauress to the front of me suddenly turned around, her eyes narrowing, looking at me head on. I knew she could not see me. And yet, for a span of time, I froze. She was half-horse, so perhaps her animal nature sensed what no one else could.

She was pretty enough, with a chestnut-brown flank and ropes of braids coiled high upon her head. Her fingers caressed the tip of her bow, and I shivered. Was she the vessel?

You know I cannot, It said softly, and I sighed. Because of course I knew. But oh, just for once, why couldn't life be simple?

Its laughter caused the tops of the trees to quiver. Even the goddesses now looked slightly baffled. A bit later, the women dispersed, grabbing up their men one by one. The centauress looked back once, but this time her eyes missed me completely. A perplexed frown had crossed her lovely features. And then she laid a hand upon the shadowed male before her and they were gone.

My lips turned down. I'd never cared before that none could see me. In fact, I'd thrived upon moving undetected between worlds. I wondered what it might feel like to talk with someone other than my Creator. To laugh.

Something about the centauress intrigued me. There'd been great wisdom in her eyes. More and more, it seemed she might be the one.

A wave of sunlight suddenly crested through the trees above. And I knew It smiled down upon me.

Explore this world, my child. Move between the peoples. Learn. I think you might discover you like it...

"I have my duties to The Blue first."

Yes, you do. But do find time to take care of yourself too.

The Blue and Syrith flashed away. I shook my strange and maudlin thoughts off. "I must go now."

But I sensed my Creator had already left. Squaring my shoulders, I turned and entered a realm of darkness and chaos.

Syrith

I know Hades told me that the fairy was simply a facsimile of the real thing, but the moment her hand had landed upon my shoulder, I would not have believed him. Would have thought a grand joke had been played at my expense.

"So you're to be my future lover," she sneered, rolling her eyes and giving me a look of perverse disgust.

I might have considered her passably pretty. Until she'd opened her mouth. She was pale. With big, bobbing blue ringlets of hair dancing around her shoulders. Clear blue eyes. And a rosebud mouth. But now all I saw was an unattractive and hateful fae who made my skin crawl.

"Never lovers, fae, make no mistake," I shot back.

Snorting, she tapped a star-tipped wand against one palm, giving me a look that made me wonder whether she planned to turn me into a newt. Her eyes were like drills boring into me. The evidence of her abhorrence for me was apparent.

She shrugged, causing her broad electric wings to flutter almost prettily. If the chit would just keep her mouth shut, I might actually learn to like her appearance.

"Here's the deal, male. I fight. You stand there and look stupid. Or whatever it is you do." She fluttered her fingers at me.

I clenched my jaw. "It is no wonder the whole bloody world hates you—you're an evil-hearted, callous, cold—"

"Frosty bitch, right? Have I covered it all, or was there more?" she asked with eyes twinkling like cut gems.

Fire raced through my blood. Irritation and annoyance beating at my skull. How was I to deal with this...this thing for the next month? It was impossible. She was impossible.

"Gods above, fairy, you really don't have a soul, do you?"

The leering, sarcastic grin stretching her lips suddenly faded. Her shoulders stiffened, and then she collapsed. I watched it all happen in stunned silence. Shamefully, I wasn't able to catch her before she fell. Maybe if I hadn't been so angry, I might have moved faster. Still, the sound of her chin cracking against a buried stone in the ground caused me to grimace in commiseration. That would hurt when next she woke, no doubt.

I still hadn't fully believed Hades when he'd told me that this Galeta was nothing but a clone. Not with the ugly looks and evil laughter coming off of her. She'd felt very much real to me.

But now she was nothing but a crumpled heap of flesh and bones lying before me, looking as dead as dead could be.

I studied her form. She was slight, as all fairies were. Almost doll-like. But there was nothing sweet or kindly about this fae. She had thorns and spines that pricked. She was god-awful to be around, and I felt absolutely nothing when I looked upon her other than an immediate revulsion at the remembered sensation of her touch.

The wrongness of her had coated my flesh in prickled disgust. Flicking at imaginary pieces of lint on my arms, I shuddered.

"How am I supposed to rescue you when I can hardly bear to be around you? Lover indeed," I scoffed.

"You're not to concern yourself with that one," a sultry, feminine voice said, causing me to twirl on my heel.

Calypso, elemental goddess of all waters, stared back at me with an open and honest look, a far cry from the haughty disdain she'd shown in front of everyone else at the gathering.

Of the three gods, she was the very last one I'd expected to show up here. Alone. Her moods were infamous, and her misandry for any males but her own was legendary. Of all the elementals, Father had warned me never to petition Calypso for anything save for only the direst of circumstances.

Dressed in a gown built of clear water that ran with movement from the sensual glide of colorful betta fish within, she inhaled deeply and then tossed out her arms as though to encompass our surroundings.

"Welcome to Nox."

I frowned. "Nox?"

This land was dark, not empty exactly, or even foreboding in the way the haunted forests surrounding Mother's castle were. There were large pines dotting the grassy terrain. A full, silvery moon that was so large it appeared to encompass nearly all of the night hung in the sky. And dark shadows of birds in flight circled above. Nox was macabrely alluring.

She shrugged, causing her octopus tentacle of hair to undulate smoothly across her pale shoulder. "Night. Perpetual night. This is your home for however long it takes you to fix her. The Blue is far too unstable to remain in day hours for long, so we've rigged the game for you both so that when she is in there, you won't be required to remain long. I'm sure my husband told you that your true test lies in here?"

Looking up at the pitch-black sky bejeweled with millions of stars, I nodded slowly. There wasn't much to Nox. Nothing to entice me to stay, at any rate. I looked back to the goddess.

She had her hands clenched and was giving me a strange look, one that chilled me to my bones because if I hadn't known better, I'd almost swear that she looked nervous.

But when was the water ever nervous? Calypso was said to fear nothing and no one. Even I had heard of what she'd done against Zeus to save Hades. She was an elemental. That meant she was an original creation. Coming before the Olympians and even the Titans.

Long after the world faded, she would remain.

Twisting her lips, she sighed again, and this time I knew I'd not been mistaken. The goddess really was nervous. I bit down on my molars. I wasn't sure I should have gotten involved in any of this.

"Aphrodite was supposed to be here for this. I don't usually speak with the males. I'm more inclined to drown you than save you, truth be told." She snorted as though tickled. I didn't share in her humor, which instantly caused her crooked smile to slip. "I'm failing miserably at this, aren't I?" Inhaling deeply, she shook her head and gave me a tight grin. "Anyway, this was what she told me to share with you. Follow this trail"—her fingers flicked toward her feet and I noted a glowing, golden path I'd not seen before—"and it will lead you to Mirror. Step through, and in it you'll find Galeta. Or at least we hope you will. What you will find within is a world within a world within a world. She could be anywhere. You need to bring her back. Make her remember who she once was."

I frowned. "And just who was she?"

Because if she was anything like this thing lying at my feet now, I wasn't sure I was the right man for this job.

Pausing for several seconds, Calypso's gaze turned unfocused and far away, and again that strange zip of foreboding skated down my spine. The goddess's nerves were palpable. My palms began to sweat.

"I don't know, Syrith. I truly don't."

"Then if you don't know, why are we even here?" The moment I asked the question, I knew the answer. She didn't know.

And even as I questioned all of this, something deep inside of me felt a tugging, a draw to move down that path. To do as I'd been bid.

My brows gathered into a tight vee. She shook her head but said no more.

Having rarely spoken to others in my life outside of my own family, I'd developed an ability to read the tiny micronuances of a person's countenance. More than nervous, Calypso was uncomfortable. Unhappy, even.

"You do not want me here," I said before censoring my thoughts.

The goddess lifted a sharp brow, her beautiful face scowling deeply for a second and making me wonder if she'd make good on her threat of earlier and drown me where I stood. But though her taloned fingers clenched tight, she did nothing other than stare at me.

After a heartbeat of time, she inhaled deeply. "I think I see now why you were chosen for this."

"Chosen by whom?"

"Fate. Or something more." Her pretty features dissolved into one of confused annoyance before she quickly shook her head and smoothed her face into a calm mask once again. "Anyway. It is of no matter what I think or want. All that does matter is that you must go now. We will not call the groups together for the first match until two nights hence, giving you enough time to hopefully find her. Do what you must, Syrith, to rescue that fae, for I have the very real fear that the fate of our world depends upon it."

Chapter 8: We're Not in Kansas Anymore, Toto...

Syrith

I stared at the man-sized mirror hanging suspended in the air before me. The looking glass was gilded, and the mirror itself shone with a watery blue sheen of pulsating magic.

The power pulsing within it was strong, and I was reminded of a tale from nursery books my maid had read to me long ago. Father had brought the book from a place called Earth.

They were the tales of Kingdom, but all of them twisted and changed. I'd been especially fascinated by the tales of Wonderland.

Because very little of the book's Wonderland resembled my own.

In it, Hatter had been mad and his Alice was no longer his Alice, but a golden-haired child who'd fallen first through a rabbit hole and then a looking glass much like this one now before me.

Alice's adventures had been both bizarre and unpleasant at times.

"Why do you tarry, boy?"

Turning at the sound of the dulcet voice, I stood frozen and gape mouthed, staring at a pale, lovely woman with large, downy wings tucked in tight to her side. Glints of gold edging the outer feathers winked even in the dim bit of light coming off the stars above.

"Why does everyone lately insist on calling me a boy?" I glanced down at myself, studying my long, lean, muscular form with a raised brow. "I can promise you, bird—"

"Harpy," she interjected.

"What?" I frowned, brows bunching.

Her smile grew radiant, and I thinned my lips. "Harpy," she said again. "I am a Harpy."

"Is that your real name?"

She shrugged. "I do not know. I think my Creator forgot to give me one." She laughed, and there was an appealing innocence about her.

"You're not from around here, are you?"

The grin that already stretched her features tight only grew brighter, casting its own radiant glow upon the thick gloom of night. "My, you're bright. How did you reckon that?"

Unsure if she was being sarcastic or not, I was slow to respond. "Um... well."

She leaned forward, almost on tiptoe, wings extending broadly and fluttering gently, and I could practically taste her expectancy. That hadn't been sarcasm after all, which begged the question, "How in the blazes have you gotten to be so old and still seem so young?"

She huffed, fluffing her gown as she shook her wings, causing tiny downy feathers to flutter gracefully down around her. "Rude, boy. I am not so ancient that I do not understand when I am being mocked."

She made as if to go, and suddenly I found myself stretching out a hand to restrain her. "I wasn't mocking you, Harpy. I apologize."

Huffing primly, she pursed her lips and eyed me speculatively for a bit before finally saying, "Well, I suppose maybe I lost something in translation. Anyway, my question is the same as before. Why do you tarry?"

I blinked; the creature was quite astonishing in an odd yet not altogether unpleasing way. She was innocent. But there was also a glow to her, one that felt older and far wiser than she appeared to be.

How was this Harpy even here?

"This is my realm," I said.

She shrugged again. "Not really. I helped create it."

"I thought the goddesses—"

"Pft." She rolled her wrist. "They only did as I bade them to."

I laughed, but when she didn't join in, I knew she was quite serious. "Who are you, Harpy, that you can command the gods? How are you even here?"

Smacking her lips a moment, she tapped a finger to her chin and made soft "hm" sounds beneath her breath, as though considering how best to answer.

Confused and more than happy to continue to put off the inevitable fall into that looking glass, I waited patiently for her to answer.

"Well, I suppose I can tell you part of what I am and why I'm here." Piercing gold eyes turned to me. And though she spoke in a young manner, I felt the weight of the ancient's stare move through me. This was a creature who'd seen things. Things I could possibly only imagine in my wildest dreams.

"As you no doubt suspect, I am here for her." She pointed her thumb over her shoulder. "And you."

"Me?"

She nodded deeply, causing her golden curls to tumble prettily around her slim shoulders. "Indeed." Leaning in, she cupped her mouth and spoke in a loud stage whisper. "You're the keys." Then her eyes widened, and she fluttered her fingers dramatically. "Don't ask how. But apparently you both are two snowballs tumbling down a massive mountain. It's bound to be fun."

When she grinned, she revealed her only imperfection. A slightly crooked front tooth that was oddly charming and made me grin despite myself. Talking to her was like speaking with a child, one far brighter than they should be, but still a child nonetheless.

"Indeed. Sounds promising."

She laughed. "I did not think I would like you, male. Truth be told, I rarely like you males, with all your belching and passing wind and—"

Snorting, I couldn't help but give a hearty belly laugh. "Gods, female, you're quite the peculiar one."

And then I had a thought. Had I already passed through the mirror without realizing it? Was I like Alice from the book, who'd begun to traipse through a world full of bizarre wonders and dangers?

"No." She shook her head. "You've not walked through the glass. What a foolish boy you are. If you had, you'd already be there, now wouldn't you?"

Her blink was full of innocence.

I, on the other hand, had just realized she'd read my mind.

She covered her hand with her mouth, eyes going wide. "Oops. Sorry. It tells me I have a terrible habit of doing that." Then she thumped a fist to her forehead hard several times, muttering beneath her breath.

Afraid she might be a bit unhinged, I grabbed her arm to stop her from hurting herself further. "If you promise not to read my thoughts again, then I think I can find it in my heart to forgive you."

Her smile was beatific. "Swell."

All I could do was nod. She was truly a rare bird, this one. "So tell me, Harpy, are you here for long?"

She'd still not answered a single one of my questions, and I had no plan to answer hers until she gave me something a little more concrete.

"I'm not. No. I mean, I'll be fluttering here and there, but you'll hardly even notice me. Nope, the truth is, male, I'm here to watch and learn." She touched the tip of her nose with her pointer finger, giving me a look that clearly said we were now in cahoots.

The thing of it was, I had no bloody idea what she thought we were in cahoots about. "Right," I said slowly. "You're to watch me. With her?"

"Well." Her eyes bugged, and her lips thinned. "I mean, if you start to sex her, then no, I promise to avert my gaze."

38

I was inhaling just as she'd said that, and now I choked on my own breath. Yanking her hand out of my grip, she thwacked me hard on the back.

"Goodness me, quite impressive to choke on your own spit, male." She giggled, and I felt the nerves in my head begin to pinch.

Taking a few steadying breaths, I nodded. Mainly because I didn't know what else to do. "I doubt I'll be sexing anyone anytime soon, especially her. I've met her once. She's the very last female in the world I'd ever fall in love with. But thank you for your consideration, Harpy. I appreciate your thoughtfulness."

"You're welcome." She nodded regally, and I realized she had no idea I had been acting sarcastic then. "And do not judge the fairy too harshly, boy. The one in the games and the one in the mirror are really not at all the same. Much has happened to The Pink to turn her into what you know today."

"The Pink?" I shook my head quizzically. "I was told I was here for The Blue."

She nodded. "That she is. Now. But it wasn't always so. You're here to restore The Pink to herself."

Rubbing my temple, I looked back at the glass.

Why go through all this effort for a fairy everyone hated?

I hadn't realized I'd spoken until she answered. Either that, or she'd read my mind. Again.

"Because you don't know her as I do." Her voice was tinged in sadness, an ache so thick and deep that even I felt moved by it.

Curious for the first time about the fairy that'd caused such a disturbance in the life of so many, I tried to peer through the veil of magic upon the mirror to the woman behind it.

"How am I to save her, Harpy? How am I to do the impossible?"

But when I turned, it was to find the space she'd inhabited empty. The only proof of her ever being there was a lone golden feather sitting by my foot. Lips twitching, I bent forward and snatched it up, pocketing the thing if only as a reminder that there were forces at work behind the scenes for a person the whole world had given up on.

Why?

It seemed the only way I'd get my answer was to step inside and brave the unknown.

Galeta

For days, I'd traveled this strange place. More lost than I could remember. Shivering and cold, and with no wand to warm me.

This land of perpetual gloom and no sunlight spread out toward infinity, mocking me with each step I took that there'd never be any getting out. I'd walk through one door, and ten others would appear, without rhyme or reason.

I'd long ago lost track of my path. In the beginning, I'd laid a trail of pebbles behind me, but it'd become quite clear that wherever the gods had thrown me, they'd not meant for me to escape.

Stepping across a rut in the dirt path, I winced when a sharp stone pierced the sole of my foot. Grimacing, I hobbled my way over toward a boulder large enough to use as a stool.

I could fly, but then I'd not be able to use my wings as a cape to help ward off the chilly air. It wasn't freezing, but it wasn't comfortable without my makeshift coat either. Sniffing back the annoying tears that'd been threatening for the past however many days I'd been trapped in here, I plopped down onto my hard seat and studied my foot.

Swiping at a bead of blood with my fingertip, I shook my head. At first there'd been rage. Rage at being trapped like a rabid animal.

I'd screamed.

I'd cried.

I'd run like a mad fairy headlong through door after door after door, sure that somewhere in this maze there'd be a way out. I'd been so persistent, I hadn't stopped until the lethargy of utter exhaustion finally took me under its wings and dropped me, literally, where I'd stood.

I'd come to, in what had felt like hours later, to a world just as gloomy and dark and void as it was now. There was nothing but doors and dirt. No life at all.

After the rage had abated, I'd sunk into a depression. Sitting on my arse for what surely must have been days, doing nothing but staring vacantly at the never-ending path winding like a snake's body before me in perpetuity.

Hunger clawed at my gut.

And thirst mocked me. My tongue was thick and swollen in my mouth, my throat parched and desperate for wetness each time I was forced to swallow.

But just as had happened to me many times before, I did not die. Though I lingered on in agony, I remained, doomed to an existence of nothingness.

Maybe they'd all grown tired of me. Of my antics. I'd never imagined this would be my fate. My end. Trapped in an enchanted mirror and destined to wander all the rest of my ever-long days.

Whatever had been done to me, one thing had been made clear to me lately. This mirror realm of magic had somehow dulled the madness within me.

I wasn't sure how. Only that I didn't sense the desperate psychosis of a fractured mind rising up in me. I could think. Reason, even.

I was free of the monster. But only in a small way. I still felt the beat of something dark inside of me, but it was neutralized somehow too. It was hard to explain it, but that was as close as I could get.

Tapping my fingers rhythmically on my jaw, I looked out at a world of nothing and pondered my existence.

Was this truly it?

How the Blue would end?

It seemed terribly anticlimactic, after all the lives I'd ruined and all the antipathy I'd fostered, that this should be how it would end for me. I could get up and keep walking, but what was the point? I'd been traveling this realm for days, weeks, months? And there truly was naught in it. Just the cold. The barrenness of life. And darkness.

So again, what was the point?

While I enjoyed the freedom of being able to think again, I knew I could not survive this existence much longer. But what could be done when one could not die?

"Not die..." I said, my words scratchy and thick. I'd lost my voice around day two or two million—I truly had no way of marking time in this place. With frantic fingers, I shoved my hands into the hidden pocket of my gown, yipping with pleasant surprise when my fingers caressed the green glass vial of infinite death.

Heart hammering wildly in my chest, I gently eased the potion out and stared at the rare spot of color in this otherwise grey place. In my confusion over being tossed inside the glass, I'd completely forgotten what I'd been doing in the first place when I'd been caught.

Smiling my first true smile in ages, I wet my lips. I knew it would hurt. A death curse was never fun, but I did not deserve an easy death. My end was close at hand, and yet a faint seedling of doubt began to stir in my heart.

I did not truly wish to die. I only wished to end my suffering.

And to an extent, it had ended the moment I'd been shoved in here.

My gaze flicked up as I realized I'd merely traded one hell for another.

"*Hello.*"

Every cell in my body froze at the unfamiliar call.

A voice.

A male voice.

The wind whistled.

I shook my head. "It's the wind. Only the wind. No one is here. Don't be silly, Galeta. Don't be—"

"Hello? Is there anybody home?"

The voice was deep and lyrical, mellifluous to my ears, and every inch of me quaked.

I sat on my makeshift stool, staring on in wide-eyed panic as not only did I hear his voice sing upon the winds, but the entire landscape began to alter.

What was once barren began to swirl, transform.

The empty stretch of gray twisted into tall, roughly hewn shapes of buildings. Trees sprouted from nothingness. And, somewhere in the distance, I heard the gentle gurgling burble of a brook.

The colors were still dark, still muted.

But there was life in this realm now.

"Hello, Galeta, are you here, fae?"

With a yip, I did the only thing I knew to do. I spread my wings and flew up high. Transforming from the woman size I was, into the miniature one more typical of my kind. Easier to hide that way.

I was just sliding behind the thick wall of a twisted gray-stemmed leaf when I saw him.

Gripping tight to the leaf shielding me, I couldn't seem to keep from staring at him in wonder.

This stranger who somehow knew my name.

He was tall. Broad of shoulder and trim of waist. But packed with muscle. The moment I saw his face, I knew why. He had sharp, angular features. A chiseled jaw lightly dusted with scruff. A powerful nose. Full lips for a male. And slanted, exotic eyes an unusual shade of green-blue that practically burned like fire in the night. His hair was longish, coming to his shoulders in wild disarray.

He was dragonborne. It was all in the eyes, in the predatory and unconsciously graceful movements of his body.

Dragonborne were as beautiful as they were deadly, and exceedingly rare in Kingdom.

In fact, I only knew of two. One a female hunter, and the other a male King in Wonderland. The King and Queen had had a child, a male, long ago. But I'd not given him much thought other than knowing a male heir had been born to the Heart clan.

Fairies noticed beauty, of course. We were the divine instruments that created it. But our hearts never hammered at the sight of it. Our pulses didn't beat like a drum in our ears. And our fingers didn't clench so tight, the knuckles turned a ghostly shade of white. I shook my head, commanding my hands to relax and to breathe.

The male's thick brows lowered, and he stopped walking, turning in a slow circle. Dressed in finely stitched clothing connoting royalty, there could be no doubt that this male was none other than Syrith, heir to the throne of Wonderland. He even wore his mother's colors of red, gold, black, and white.

I wet my lips, leaning forward on tiptoe. Why was he here? And how the blue blazes had he affected such a change in this deadened world? I certainly hadn't caused this life to bloom. I'd only been trying with no success at it for days. Suddenly he appeared, and it all changed.

Why?

"I know you're here, little fae. I see your life force beating as a golden thread in this dark realm. Show yourself."

My eyes widened. Why was he following my golden thread? He couldn't possibly be. Only those with the second sight could see the threads of life.

And yet, not a moment later, he looked up. At my tree. At the very spot where I hid.

I was in miniature, so he would not see me.

"There you are," he growled, and good gods, my knees suddenly turned weak and wobbly.

Mortified by my strange reaction, I did the only thing I could do.

I fled.

I'd just barely caught a glimpse of the little one, when suddenly she sailed off her perch, flying like a demon out of hell as she raced for a doorway, zipping through it in a golden shower of sparks.

"Damn bloody bugs!" I snapped.

It'd taken me half the damn day to trace her thread, and now she was gone.

Wondering why I'd ever allowed myself to be talked into this, I shifted into a hummingbird. Not the most manly of creatures, but they were fast. And speed was essential.

Picking up the thread just as I had before, I gave chase. Speeding through one doorway after another after another.

When I'd first stepped foot in this dark realm, I hadn't known what to expect. A forest, maybe? Thick with life and flowers. Instead, I'd found the landscape literally shifting around me. Twisting from nothing into images and pictures of towns, shoppes, glens, mountains, and massive bodies of water with no rhyme or reason for any of it.

Even now, the darkness was transforming all around us. The demonic little fairy zipped to and fro with no obvious route in mind other than to get away from me.

Glowering in bird form, which wasn't nearly as terrifying as it would have been in my true form, I pumped my wings just a little bit faster. If I didn't catch her, this chase could potentially go on forever.

Now, I wasn't sure why I had to be with her, but those were the terms of this bloody mirror, and I aimed to do my part. The sooner I finished whatever it was that I'd been sent here to do, the sooner I could leave this abominable place.

Galeta was just about to zip through another doorway.

Pumping my wings so fast that they buzzed, I caught up to her. Shifting in mid-flight from bird to man, I snatched her out of the air, caging her in my fist.

"Let me out!" she squeaked in a broken voice filled with grit, vainly pounding at my fingers with her tiny fists.

Heart racing from the chase, and more annoyed than I'd have liked, I shook my fist just a little. Careful not to crush her wings but letting her know in no uncertain terms that I was vexed.

"Relax, she-devil, and I might just do that."

"She-devil!" she shrilled in her teeny voice. "How dare you. How dare you, male. Release me at once!"

I'd already been lambasted once by her clone, and I'd be damned if I'd subject myself to another one of her tirades.

Fed up with this nonsense, I spoke in a gruff tone, allowing her to hear the dragonish burr—a heavy rumble of man and beast that was often enough to quell even the most prickly of opponents into silence.

"Run, and I'll catch you. Hide, and I'll always find you. Do you hear me, bug?" I lifted my fist so that it was even with my eyes, which stared through the fingers of my cage at her.

I wasn't able to get a good glimpse of Galeta; she was mostly tangled up in her large wings and gown of spun ice crystals. But I caught flashes of that same spiraled robin's egg–blue hair and glowing clear blue eyes that seemed struck from a pure vein of ice.

Shoving the hair out of her face with both her hands, she hissed at me. And I couldn't explain it, but I felt the queerest need to chuckle at her. Already, she'd annoyed me, and yet... and yet I could hardly explain my curiosity about this fae. After my talk with the harpy, I had to admit to a slight niggling of inquisitiveness.

Slumping her shoulders, she hid her face behind her wings as she mumbled, "Why have you come here, Prince? And who sent you? The Gods? Did they say why?"

I lifted a brow. "You know me?"

For a brief moment, I caught a glimpse of her face. It was just a flash. Rounded cheeks. Smooth ivory skin. Perfectly shaped lips. The same as the face I'd seen in the games... and yet down here all her features seemed softer. Prettier, even.

"You're obviously dragonborne. There aren't many of you in these parts. I did the math. What do you want from me, Syrith?"

My heart thumped just then to hear my name spill off her tongue. Her voice was high-pitched but also musical, as it was with all fae.

The Blue—and now I could completely understand the moniker, as she was many different shades of it—collapsed onto my palm. Her weight was so slight as to be hardly noticeable.

I wasn't much in the know when it came to fairies and their kind. Any creature born with magical abilities was not given a fairy godmother. As I was nearly all magic, I'd never personally encountered one before.

After my time spent with the clone, I hadn't been sure what to expect from the fairy in the mirror. Maybe part demon spawn. With pointed fangs. Evil red eyes. And the face of a hag, with a black and twisted heart. I'd wondered if maybe they'd dampened the clone a little. But this face and that one were the same.

The creature before me might have a dark heart, but she was hardly a hag. Finding myself more curious than I should be, I made a decision.

"I will release you on one condition."

"That I do not try to run?" she said with a husky chuckle. "Indeed. And should I try it, you'd strip me of my wings? Or maybe dip me in a vat of heated oil? Scrape the flesh off my meat? Perhaps cut off a finger or two—"

"Bloody hell, fairy, you've a twisted sense of humor." I shook my head, appalled by her blasé attitude when it came to torture. Maybe she truly was all the wicked things I'd heard about. And yet this little woman didn't vex me the way the clone had. There was something more real about her.

Different.

She laughed, and the sound reminded me of fluted bells. My flesh prickled.

I felt her shrug. "You cannot make threats to me I haven't made a million times before in a million different ways. I'm immune to fear, dragonborne."

That wasn't entirely true. She hadn't flown away because she'd wished for privacy. I'd smelled the fear encasing her. I'd frightened her somehow. But I was gentleman enough not to say it.

She sighed deeply, and in that note, I heard her humanity. This was a complicated fairy. I wasn't sure how I knew this, but somehow I suspected she and I might have more in common than one might first imagine.

But which of the two was real? The horrible creature above? Or the sad little one in here with me now?

"Fine, Prince. I shall not attempt to escape you again. Only release me, and I'll transform."

"Into?" I asked.

Tiny hands pressed into my fingers as she tried to peel them away from her. "Into? You say that as though I have multiple forms. I only have two. Big and small. You wish to talk, then let me go."

"And you will not try to escape again?" I shifted on my toes, because I did have multiple forms. But only one true one. I found myself wondering the most bizarre thing just then... What might she think if she saw it?

"My word means absolutely nothing, but if you must have it, then I shall give it. Aye, I shall not attempt escape again."

I chuckled. I couldn't seem to help myself. "And yet you just said your word means nothing. Goddess, you are a strange wee thing, aren't you, fae?"

She laughed.

It didn't last long. Only half a second, if that. But the sound of it rolled across my flesh like sun-warmed honey. Then her fingers were covering her mouth, and her breathing grew heavy, and I sensed a wave of embarrassment flow off of her.

Had she never laughed before?

She swallowed hard and then steadily said, "I will not flee, giant. I...I vow it."

Frowning, because I wasn't exactly sure what had just passed between us, I opened the cage of my hand slowly.

43

For a moment, she sat as she'd been. Her tiny doll legs poking out from beneath her crystallized gown. A rolling breeze feathered through the strands of her hair. Extending her broad, electric-blue wings, she caught the current and flew. Hovering with her back to me.

Every nerve in my body went on alert, waiting for her to run again.

But instead, she turned. Her chin was tipped toward her chest, causing her hair to shield her features like a curtain.

"Step back, boy," she said softly.

I cocked my head and growled, "I'm not a boy."

"Considering I'm as old as Kingdom itself, everyone's a child to me. Try not to take it personally, Syrith. I apologize for giving offense."

I opened my mouth, to tell her I wasn't sure what, but I wasn't given the chance, because a second later, I was forced to shield my eyes from the impossibly bright glow of fairy magic. Encased by light, she looked like an angel bathed in beams of purest white.

Squinting, I took two giant steps back as the power of her magic transformed her from a living doll into a human-sized female.

When the light dimmed enough that I could finally look at her, all I could do was study her for changes.

Galeta wasn't tall, coming only to chest height on me, but she was curvy in all the right places. Willowy, as most fairies were, she had nice-sized breasts, a slim waist, and long, lean legs. The ice-crystal gown glinted even in the gloom of night. The thick curls of robin's egg–blue hair now hung long and curly down to her waist. On the crown of her head she wore a crown of sapphires. The tips of her ears pointed out from the thick wave of curls.

When I got my first good look at her face, I forgot to breathe.

Features that'd looked doll-like and passably pretty were now mature and enticing.

She had the elfin features of her kind, with the small, rounded face and button nose. But she also had full lips, high cheekbones, thin brows, and wide, crystal-blue eyes. And her wings...they were a thing of beauty. Large and veined in black and neon-blue that shimmered with threads of lavender in between.

I was right—there were slight differences between the clone and this one. That fairy I could not stand. But this one—this one was beginning to fascinate me.

My heart trembled violently in my chest. I grabbed at it without thought.

The tip of her bright-pink tongue poked out as she licked at her bottom lip nervously.

"Why are you here?" she asked, and this time her voice was not teeny and small but robust and sultry. My blood heated in my veins.

"I'm here for you, Galeta," I said slowly, taking my time to enunciate each word.

"Why?" she asked with a slight shake of her head. "I thought I'd been damned to this emptiness for an eternity."

She turned to stare over my shoulder, but I was enchanted, entranced by the ethereal beauty of the fairy before me. She had fangs, but they weren't large and menacing. They were small and dainty and wickedly distracting. And when she wasn't hurling insults at me, it was easy enough to see that my initial impression of her being pretty was correct. She was pretty. In fact, she was more than pretty. I particularly liked her teeth.

Odd, I know.

As a dragonborne, I'd never been squeamish about fangs. In fact, I found them rather enchanting. Dragon mating was often fierce and violent. And I couldn't help but wonder if she liked to bite.

Only when I felt her hard, quizzical look upon my face did I realize I'd spaced out, waxing poetic about a pair of pearly fangs instead of answering her question. I jerked. Cleared my throat. And tried to recall what she'd said.

Her lips twitched, and I knew she knew.

I glowered.

Her grin only grew wider. "Why are you here?" she asked again, and I rather had the notion that she'd asked only to remind me.

Bloody hell. I ground my molars. "As I said, fae, I was sent. I'm here to help you."

Her brows dipped, causing a cute wrinkle to gather between them. I suffered the vexing urge to smooth it out with my thumb. I kept my feet glued to the ground and my hands tight to my sides.

"Help me how?" She tossed a hand wide. "Look around us, Prince. There's very little here of note."

I did look, and she was right.

Though the world had transformed some, it was still bleak. Still mostly empty. Although seedlings were shooting from the ground with the promise of trees. And the air was now thick with the scent of flowers. I sniffed, vaguely recognizing the perfume but not quite able to place it either.

In the distance, I spotted a thatched-roof hut that'd not been there before. And I could almost swear that curls of smoke wound sensuously above its chimneystack.

She bit her bottom lip. "How can you help me, male, when I do not know what I am doing?"

I wished I had an answer for her. But I felt as stumped as she.

"My orders were to find you. It's what I've done."

She chuckled, and again I felt my nerves twitch to life within me. What was this witchcraft this fairy worked upon me? For three years, ever since Seraphina's death, I'd felt dead inside. Empty.

Now, suddenly, I found myself curious with anticipation. Though I couldn't for the life of me understand why.

Her brows twitched. "You came all this way, just to find me. Did you not think it odd, male, that you were sent with no other orders? Did you not even think to ask what it was you had to do?"

She wasn't ugly in the asking, but my spine stiffened all the same. She couldn't possibly understand the ennui and weariness of my life, the emptiness of it. No, I'd not questioned much of this, because it hadn't mattered to me one way or another at the time. But now I suddenly felt decidedly foolish for not doing so and irritated with her for bringing up my shortcomings.

I opened my mouth, ready to shoot a nasty retort back at her, when she sidled up next to me and planted a tentative hand upon my bicep.

"Forgive me, Prince. I am tired and weary to my core. You do not deserve my rancor."

Then, with those words, she turned and headed toward the hut that now glowed with muted-gray warmth through its solitary window.

I watched her walk away, feeling stunned and even slightly disquieted. This was not at all the woman I'd met in the world outside of the mirror. The harpy was right.

Who was this Blue really? And why was she hated by so many? It was easy enough to see how the fairy outside of the mirror could be reviled. What I had a hard time understanding was how this fairy and that one could be one and the same.

Each step she took seemed weighed down and heavy, as though she were bogged down by the worry of this world, and against my will I found myself moving toward her. Following in her wake. I wasn't sure what I must do from here. All I knew was that I could not leave her alone.

?

"Well, what do you think, Creator?" I asked, looking up toward the heavens.

The threads of fate were shifting; already, I felt the restlessness of this world beginning to exhale in anticipation of what was to come. I wasn't sure what was coming—all I knew was it was going to be momentous.

The Creator did not speak to me, but a wave of shooting stars sailed across the liquid navy-blue sky, and I smiled to myself, knowing It was pleased. Humming beneath my breath, I went in search of a centaur.

Chapter 9: In Which Nothing Is the Same

Syrith

I wasn't sure what to expect when we entered the hut. An empty clapboard room with no furniture and nothing on the walls.

But there was a large hearth burning with a warm fire. Upon the mantel were several white vases filled with clipped gray flowers.

There was a comfortable-looking gray couch placed before it. A black-and-white threaded rug lay on the gray wooden floors. And beside it rested a table large enough for two with two gray bowls full of a dark, steaming liquid.

Beyond this room looked to be another. Or at least there was a closed door that I could only assume led to a bedchamber.

Galeta turned slowly on her heels, taking it all in. In this black-and-gray world, she was a vivid splash of color. I found my eyes always straying toward her colors, seeking her out, and I hadn't realized before just how pretty the color blue really was.

"What is this place?" she asked softly, finally turning icy eyes toward me.

I knew as much as she, but still I answered. "I suppose this is to be our home for however long we remain here."

Sucking the corner of her bottom lip into her mouth, she nodded absently. "This world is very gray, is it not?"

It wasn't much as far as icebreakers went, but I knew she was trying. "Ah, well. Color's overrated, I always say."

She snorted, lifting a brow and gazing knowingly at her own blue tresses as if to say, "Is it really?"

My lips twitched in response.

Still unsure what my purpose was here, I latched onto the only thing I could. "I'm starved. Let us eat, shall we?" I gestured toward the bowls of unappetizing-looking broth.

She shrugged, following my lead.

I took a seat, and she stood before me only a brief moment before pulling out her own chair and daintily perching on the edge of it. Her fingers flitted nervously upon the tabletop.

Never accustomed to being forced to speak so much, I found myself in unusual territory. The room was tense with our shared silence.

I took up my spoon, ladling out my first scoop of broth, and took my first taste. I'd expected it to taste as unappealing as it looked, but the meaty slide of richly seasoned soup was an unexpected surprise.

"Beef stock. This is good," I muttered.

She was on her second sip. I knew this, because I could not seem to pull my gaze off her. Galeta would not look at me, but she shook her head just a little.

"Not beef. It's vegetable broth with a hint of elderberry." Another bright but fleeting smile passed her lips.

My heart thumped.

I cleared my throat, pretending to suddenly take an interest in a polished knot of grain in the wood.

"Magic is clearly at work here."

She sniffed delicately. "You could say that again."

But she didn't sound happy about it.

I scoured my brain for conversation starters, but nothing seemed right. And more to the point, Galeta herself looked wan and exhausted. Her lovely skin was turning the same shade of gray that surrounded us everywhere.

We were on the last dregs of our soup when I finally worked up the nerve to speak. "You look tired."

She blinked and went stiff. The spoon that'd been midway to her mouth paused before gently lowering back down.

Apart from a few brief glances now and then, she'd not looked at me. Not the way she was now. Her eyes shimmered with unshed tears, and my brows lowered.

"I am at that, Prince. I think I should go find my bed."

I curled my fingers into my pant legs, not wanting her to go. But not having a good enough reason to keep her with me either. She truly did look dead on her feet. As though she'd not slept well in ages.

Standing, she nodded down at me. "Good night, then, dragonborne."

I watched her walk away and head toward the closed door. When she opened it, I noted that it was indeed a bedchamber and that it only had one bed. A small twin frame not nearly big enough for two.

"Oh," she said then turned and stared over her shoulder at the couch with a tight grimace, "only one bed. I could take the c—"

I stood and shook my head. "I wouldn't dream of it, fairy. You take the bed. I'll take the couch."

"But it's not very big," she said, her words sounding unsure. And I suspected she really did want the bed but was trying to be polite about it. I inhaled deeply.

"Nor is the bed. I'll be fine, fairy. Sleep. And maybe when you awake in the morning, you'll find the world to be much changed." My smile was tight.

Her eyes were haunted. "As you say, Prince."

And then she left, locking herself away behind the door, and the only spot of color in this world vanished with her.

I wasn't sure how it was possible to miss someone I'd just met, and yet I did.

Later that night, I heard her sobs. They were quiet and muffled. I'd been forced to shift into a cat so as to give me room enough to stretch out on the couch, but I was instantly alerted by the sounds coming from behind the door. Jumping lithely off the couch, I padded toward the door.

Wishing I could enter. Wishing I could somehow make her feel better. The fairy had demons inside of her. Big, menacing ones. I didn't often care about the plight of others. Especially not in the past three years, too consumed with my own pain and sorrow.

But I cared now.

Lifting a paw, I touched the door. Meowing softly, telling her as best I could that she wasn't alone anymore. Instantly, the crying ceased.

I waited, holding my breath, wondering if she'd open the door to me. But she did not.

So I curled up into a ball, settled against the frame, and tried to find whatever rest I could. I sensed this lull would soon end, and come morning we'd discover, one way or another, our true purpose for being here.

Galeta

I cried last night.

And I wasn't sure why.

All I knew was the hate and rage that'd sealed up the cracks in my soul were fading away, leaving me with giant, gaping, pain-filled holes that threatened to drown me.

48

I'd closed my eyes to sleep, and then suddenly it'd all come crashing over me and I'd not been able to stop. Until I'd heard him.

He'd meowed.

I'd known Syrith could shift forms—I simply hadn't known he had so many. But I knew the moment I'd heard that gentle sound that it was he trying to give me comfort as best he could. Here we were, perfect strangers, and yet he truly did seem to care. I'd not been able to sleep last night, but I had at least closed my eyes and rested a little.

Which was a sight more than I'd been able to manage in the past few centuries.

Sitting up in my bed, I stretched my tiny arms above my head, watching as the dark sun rose in the still-gray sky. He'd hoped that the morning might bring blooms of color, but it seemed we were doomed to this monochromatic world of darkness.

With a bone-weary sigh, I shifted form so that I was once more the size of a human and walked toward the water closet to take care of my morning necessaries. Oh, how I missed my wand. One flick, and my morning ablutions would be done without all the messy water and scrubbing.

Unaccustomed to doing so much by hand, I was already exhausted by the time I exited. I'd half thought I'd find Syrith still in cat form, but instead he was sitting at the table and eating again.

He looked clean, as though he'd bathed, but I knew he had not. Dragonborne were able to cleanse themselves using the mist of their breath. Like me, he was a burst of vivid reds and golds in an otherwise gray world.

His clothes were freshly pressed, his hair combed out. And his green-blue eyes sparkled like vivid jewels in his swarthy and handsome face. Again, my heart did that strange stuttering-beat thing. Causing blood to rise in my cheeks. I lowered my eyes toward the ground, unable to maintain his intense gaze for long.

"Sleep well?" he asked airily, and I frowned.

He knew I hadn't. He'd heard my shame last night.

"I didn't," he said. "Some blasted bird kept me awake half the night with its cawing and caterwauling. I've half a mind to roast it for tonight's supper."

He kept up with his mumbling narrative of nothingness, and I couldn't stop the spread of a smile that had begun to twitch at the corners of my cheeks. He was pointedly speaking nonsense to help me keep my pride.

Warmth fluttered through my belly.

"Come, then, fairy. This very strange table has again provided our nourishment for the day. Today I've been given a big fat juicy steak with mashed tubers on the side."

He moaned, patting his belly dramatically, and this time I couldn't help the short burst of laughter that spilled off my tongue.

"It's broth, Prince." I stared at the same bowl as the night before full of that same dark liquid.

He shrugged. "Ah, well, the power of imagination. Eat up, fae."

Deciding it might just be easier to go with the flow, I sat and picked up my spoon. And yes, it was broth, that same vegetable broth from last night, but this time instead of hints of elderberry there were wafts of wild mushroom. It was delicious, and I couldn't help but look like an uncultured swine as I set down the spoon, lifted the bowl to my lips, and drank it all down.

I sighed with appreciation when I'd swallowed the last drop. Syrith gave me an appreciative look. "Always did like it when girls had an appetite."

Snorting and feeling ridiculous, I wiped my mouth off with the back of my hand and shrugged. "I've never been aught but what I am, Prince."

"And that is?" he asked, sitting forward and planting his chin on his fist. Giving me open and frank attention.

Feeling suddenly small and overwhelmed by the dragon's presence, I wet my lips.

"Should we walk?" I asked, switching subjects.

There was a flicker of something that passed through his eyes, but then he nodded, giving me a tight smile. "As you wish, fae. Are you ready?"

He was still as polite as ever but more reserved, and I knew that somehow I'd done that to him, but I also didn't know how to undo it either. I wasn't accustomed to this person I was now.

I kept waiting for the darkness to crawl out of me. To choke me in its dark grip as it often would, but it'd been blissfully suppressed for many days now. The prospect of being forever imprisoned in a world of darkness had been horrifying, but suddenly, things didn't seem quite so dark or so depressing.

There still wasn't color or even much life, but there was a Prince who was awfully kind.

I stood. "I am."

"Good. So am I." Then, standing himself, he came around to my side and crooked his elbow. "Shall we?"

Surprised by his noble gesture but also understanding that as a Prince he'd been trained since birth to exhibit manners, I knew this was absolutely nothing other than courtesy to him.

"Indeed." I slipped my arm through his, shivering a brief moment at the scent of male and dragon that lingered upon him.

Dragons always smelled of clean smoke and ash. Enticing and heady all at the same time.

Together, we walked out of the hut. Last night a few trees had sprouted. And a town, even.

We both stared agog at a world we'd not expected.

The town was now full of people milling idly about, those stopping to chat with vendors at various stalls, and others to chat amongst themselves.

There were children running. Mothers squawking at them to slow down. And fathers looking bored and miserable as they shambled behind.

There were haberdasheries and milliners. Jewelry makers and dressmakers. Food stalls. Penned animals for sale and so much more.

Everything was still in shades of gray, but for some reason none of it looked quite as dark and depressing as it had the night before. Perhaps it was the sun.

"I'll be hornswoggled," Syrith mumbled, and I nodded.

"This is all very strange."

He grinned. "Let's go exploring. What do you say?"

He looked excited. I, on the other hand, couldn't contain the terrible zip of foreboding suddenly running down my spine. Something about this place felt strangely familiar. Horribly familiar.

"Galeta," he said in his deep dragon's voice, and I shivered, looking up at him. His hand squeezed mine. "If something does happen today, I'm right here. Do you understand me?"

I wet my lips as my pulse thundered like horses' hooves inside me.

"Come on," he said, gently guiding me toward the open market. I let him lead me at first but kept scanning the crowds around me. Looking for someone or something to come jumping out at me, to snatch me away, hurt me.

We walked through several stalls. And bless him, he tried to engage me in idle chitchat, but I couldn't relax. Couldn't stop waiting for whatever it was the fates would do to me.

At one point, a loud ruckus at a vendor's shop ahead caused me to shriek, jumping away from him as I waited for the monster to finally make its show. Instead, everyone turned to look at me with befuddled curiosity. And the noise...well, it'd been nothing other than a mule overturning a barrel full of iron scraps.

Syrith nudged me forward, taking my arm once again and leading me around, but I was on edge and anxious.

After an hour of this, he stopped, turned me around, and in the middle of the busy street grasped my face and forced me to look up at him.

"Stop."

My brows dipped. "What?"

"Stop this, fairy. You look as though you wait for a monster to come and feast on your bones."

I blew out a heavy breath. "I do not."

"Fae, if you could have seen your face when that mule kicked over that crate—"

I glowered at him.

"That." He pointed. "That look exactly. Will you bloody relax? There's nothing at all happening here."

I rubbed at my forehead. "Don't you understand, Prince? I'm being tested. Tried somehow."

"What makes you say so?" he asked with infinite patience, but it still set my teeth on edge.

And I knew it wasn't because of him, but rather my unmet expectations. I was waiting for the bogeyman, and he wasn't showing. All of which was driving me even more nervous and erratic.

He took my hand away. "Talk to me, wee one. What's the matter?"

I watched the people milling past. The faces I'd never seen and yet somehow seemed familiar all the same. The stalls. The vendors. The smells of leather and polished wood, of roasted meats and sweets.

My memory was long, and sometimes things got lost over time, but something about all of this felt disquietingly familiar. It wasn't in my head—I really had seen this.

"Talk to me," he said again.

I growled, shrugging hard. "I don't know, Syrith. I don't know, okay. But I don't like this. I've been here before."

"What? Here?" He spread an arm.

He sounded dubious, and honestly, I felt a little mad. I shook my head. "Not here exactly. I mean—" I sighed. "I don't know what I mean. Obviously, it wasn't gray like this, and..." I watched a child run by using a stick to move a wheel before him, and I frowned harder. "Just something feels familiar. I can't explain it."

Grunting, I turned my face aside, but he grasped my chin very gently and turned me back to him. Jeweled eyes studied me with fierce intelligence.

"If you say you've seen this before, then I believe you. Were there monsters there?"

"What?" I gave a nervous laugh.

"In your vision, were there monsters in this place before?"

Twisting my lips, I suddenly knew what he was getting at. "I know what you're trying to do, dragon. It won't work."

His cocky grin revealed a small scar above his cheekbone I'd not noticed before. The color was a pale white compared to the darker tone of his skin, and my fingers clenched as I wondered what the texture of that scar might feel like.

"I think it already has," he said in his husky drawl.

That was when I realized I was smiling.

Again.

Something I'd begun to do with some regularity in these past two days. I rolled my eyes. "Whatever. And to answer your question, no, there were no monsters."

Then he took my hand in his, twining our fingers together. And again I knew this meant nothing, so why did my heart suddenly feel as though it might beat right out of my chest?

"Then let us enjoy what is left of this day, shall we?"

He tugged, and again I followed, now feeling silly and foolish about the whole thing.

"Why are you being so nice to me?" I asked after a while of staring at diaphanous scarves printed with images of birds and animals. If I squinted really hard, sometimes I could even make out a flicker of color.

He glanced down at me from the corner of his eyes. "Are you not accustomed to kindness, fairy?"

I shrugged, deciding not to answer that question. If I did, I'd have to confess to my past sins. To the hatred I'd instilled in so many.

"It was just a question."

"Hmm," he said after a moment, but there was a look on his face now. One I couldn't quite decipher.

One I wanted to figure out.

But why?

Why was I suddenly so curious about this male?

We didn't speak again after that. Syrith pointed at a building, as if asking whether I'd like to go in or not. I shrugged, not paying much mind to where we were going; I was too busy wondering about this man who I didn't know at all but who seemed determined to save me from myself.

It was only when we passed the door's threshold and I looked up did all my prior feelings of anxiety come crashing down around me.

"Oh my gods," I moaned, staring at the racks and racks of men's top hats. "Oh my gods, Syrith," I croaked, "we have to go. We have to go now!"

"Galeta, what's—"

But I didn't give him a chance to finish. I yanked out of his hand, racing for the door, feeling my stomach heave as the memories came crashing down around me. I latched onto the doorknob, but it wouldn't turn. I tried harder. Yanking with all my might.

"Galeta, stop," Syrith cautioned, then his hands were on my waist and he was pulling me back, but I was wild, desperate, and clawing for a way out.

"The magic, fairy. Don't you see it? We can't leave. You must stop."

Through the blinding tears, I saw the dark stain of black magic gathering like a poison toward the door, the windows, and any other avenues of egress.

Tears streamed down my face as I twirled around, shaking my head no, because I knew exactly what was about to transpire.

"And just where is my gorgeous Hatter?"

That high-pitched, lilting voice turned my blood to ice and my heart to a chunk of stone. My eyes went wide as I watched an Asian beauty saunter up toward the cash register.

Dressed in a gown of sterling-gray taffeta with a cinched bodice, she had long black hair that tumbled gracefully down her slim back. I covered my mouth with my hands and shook my head.

From a hidden doorway, a man stepped out. Tall, devilishly handsome, and with peaked dark brows. His hair wasn't quite so shaggy. It was neatly trimmed, and in color, his eyes would have been a molten brown. His jaw was square and rugged, his features exotic and alluring.

His gaze was completely clear eyed and sane.

This was Hatter before the madness took him.

This was the Hatter before I'd interfered.

And this...was my monster.

Memories of my past exposed for all to see.

"My lovely Alice"—he held out his hand to her, and she took it—"to what do I owe this pleasure?"

Alice Hu—the original of the Alices—smiled broadly. "I've come to steal you away, my lover. Come with me."

Chapter 10: In Which Love Is Turned to Hate

Syrith

She'd frozen up on me.

I stared at Galeta gazing on in horror at Hatter and his Alice. I knew of both. Having been born and raised in Wonderland, I was familiar with the Hatter and his bride.

But something about this version of Alice felt different. A little off somehow. She looked exactly the same. But there was a gleam in her eyes, a curving of her lips that felt forced. Felt calculated.

The scene before us quickly shifted, transforming into another. Of two lovers rolling in a massive bed. Hatter and Alice nothing but a tangled heap of intertwined limbs and heady moans.

Uncomfortable with spying during something so intimate, I shifted on the balls of my feet, looking toward Galeta again. Tears spilled thick and heavy down her cheeks.

"What's the matter?" I whispered. "You look upset. But aren't they—"

Her lips thinned, and a look of anguished pain crossed her lovely features. "You don't understand, Prince. This isn't Hatter and *his* Alice. This is the first Alice Hu. The one who turned him mad with grief."

I frowned. I'd never heard of the first Alice. "What did she do?"

Galeta's face crumpled as she whispered, "She broke his heart."

I looked back at the couple.

Alice Hu looked happy. Giddy, even. There was a sparkle in her eyes. I knew the sparkle for what it was because I'd seen it in my mother's when she looked upon the face of my father.

Love.

The scene shifted yet again.

This time it was Alice and Hatter walking amongst a garden of singing flowers.

"Do you love me?" she whispered, stopping their meanderings as she turned him toward her.

When Hatter gazed down upon Alice, I saw the same sparkle in his dark eyes.

"With all my soul."

Her long lashes flickered, and a soft, sensual smile curved her lips.

"And you, Alice? Do you love me?"

Her dark eyes danced. "Run with me, Hatter. Run far and fast. Only run..."

The echoes of their laughter danced around us.

The scene shifted yet again, but this time only Alice stood in the room. A room full of clocks tick, tock, ticking. She was wringing her hands and pacing to and fro.

Galeta suddenly inhaled, wrapping her arms tightly around her. Jerked from studying the image of the woman before me, I looked at the fairy. Her face was stricken with grief, her eyes huge.

"Galeta?"

Her long lashes were clumped together from her tears as she looked up at me. "Syrith, please don't jud—"

Then a burst of color caught my eye, causing me to look up just in time to witness the transformation of the gray world into one brimming over with saturated shades of pigment. Lush blacks and blues. Deep greens. And passionate reds.

Alice was even prettier in this version, but my eyes were for the tiny fairy flitting before her. The vision Galeta smiled serenely.

"So you are the infamous Alice Hu sent to tame our Mad Hatter?" Vision Galeta murmured.

Alice's smile of greeting slowly slipped. "Excuse me?"

Galeta's clear blue eyes sparkled with gleeful anticipation. Her tiny fangs poked out from beneath her cocky grin. "Oh, dear me, did I give away the happy ending?"

Her tone was wicked and cutting and full of terrible laughter.

"What? What are... Who are..."

Rolling her eyes, Galeta flitted forward. Until her feet were able to touch down upon the woman's shoulder. "Oh, come, come, Alice girl, use your words. Think before you speak, and all that twaddle."

She waved the wand in her hand, causing twirls of blue magic to spark in the air. Alice glanced sharply at the little woman perched on her shoulder.

"What in the hell are you talking about, demon spawn?"

Galeta snorted, touching a light hand to her chest. "Demon spawn, am I? Has that imbecilic Danika been getting into your ear? Don't you know, dear child? Or has she fooled you too?"

I didn't trust the avarice in vision Galeta's eyes, and an uneasy feeling slithered through my gut. Apparently Alice felt the same, because she shook the tiny fae off her shoulder, taking several steps back.

"Know what?" she demanded, her small hands clenched tight to her sides.

Galeta brushed at her ice-spun gown and chuckled. "Temper. Temper. And why should I tell you now? I only came to do a good deed. To save a woman from a fate worse than death."

"What? Death?" Alice's eyes grew huge in her now-pale face.

"Mm. Truly." Galeta nodded. "But since you don't seem inclined to hear me out, best if I should—"

She was turning, as though to leave, but Alice's hand shot out.

What Alice didn't see, but I did, was the sudden spiteful gleam glowing through the wee fae's eyes. I bit down on my back teeth, grinding them hard. Beside me, I felt the real Galeta go ramrod stiff.

"No, wait," Alice whispered. "Please, tell me what you've come to say."

The wee fairy tilted up her chin, sniffing delicately as though offended. "I really shouldn't now. You're a terrible girl, but"—a slow grin stretched one corner of her mouth—"I just can't seem to help myself. I know something about the Hatter, Alice. Something dreadful. Do you not wish to know to whom you'll be wedding yourself?"

Alice's words were stiff and fearful as she said, "What do you know?"

Galeta shook her head, causing her ringlets to bob. "What I'm about to tell you, you can never tell Danika. She'd never believe you. She's so blinded by her love for her bad boys that she cannot see beyond it."

Alice's eyes searched the wee fairy's. "I vow it."

The Blue nodded. "Your Hatter is positively mad."

"No." Alice shook her head. "No, he can't be. I just spoke with him this morning."

The fairy flicked her wrist, silencing Alice's protests. "Oh yes, my dear. Quite. It's a slow disease of the mind but a disease all the same."

"But surely Danika—"

"Like I said"—the fairy shrugged—"she's too blinded by love. You could never have children, Alice. Not sane ones, anyway. You'd be fastened forever to a creature too mad to endure."

"I don't believe you."

The fairy grinned. "If hearing doesn't convince you, then perhaps seeing would."

With a flick of her wrist, a bubble appeared between them. And an image coalesced within.

And there was the Hatter, sitting on a chair in the middle of an empty field, quoting Edgar Allen Poe's "The Raven" as rain poured down upon him. His face was blank. His hands shaking. And his eyes burned with madness.

Alice gasped, covering her mouth with her hands. "No. This is a lie."

"Is it, Alice? Is it really?"

"But my Hatter—"

The fairy rolled her eyes, bursting the image within the bubble. Her face contorted into one of anger. "Let us not pretend that he is your anything—you wanted his power."

Alice sucked in a sharp breath, trembling hard. "Lies!"

At that, Galeta tipped her head back and let roll a cackling laugh. "Now that's the pot calling the kettle black, isn't it?"

Those words echoed like a ghost's wail between us, and all the color began to once more leech out until the world was nothing but a canvas of gray.

The scene faded, leaving us standing alone in an empty stretch of field. With no people and no laughter.

I stared at the back of Galeta's head. Her shoulders were moving, but no sounds came out of her. I knew she was crying.

With a start, she turned on her heel and fled back to the safety of the hut. I watched her go, trying to reconcile the double-crossing fairy with the haunted woman running away from me.

I couldn't even understand what it was that I'd seen, but I knew whatever it was, it wasn't good.

Galeta

He came into the hut hours later, his eyes hooded and thoughtful but also distant and nowhere near as warm as they'd been only this morning. I didn't know Syrith, but he was all I had in this place. The thought of him hating me too, it made me feel sick and empty.

I'd sat before the fire, staring into black flames, not moving, and reliving what I'd done all those years ago. It wasn't as if Hatter's life was the only one I'd ruined, but seeing the images again, reliving them one by one, I'd been ashamed of myself.

And not just for what I'd done, but because another had been there to witness my shame. I looked up at him, silently awaiting his reproach, knowing he had questions I wasn't sure I wanted to answer.

These were my memories. My past. They didn't involve him.

And yet somehow Syrith was tied to it now. Whatever this magic was at work here, he'd been the one to activate it.

Why?

He was as quiet as a field mouse as he took a seat on the opposite side of the couch, a stain of life against the relentless wash of gray.

The muscle in his jaw twitched as he bit down on his back teeth, and the silence in the room was deafening.

No longer able to look at him, I turned back to watching the fire. Seeing but not really seeing. My mind was consumed by the past. By what I'd done.

Hatter's wasn't the only happily ever after I'd ruined, but he'd been one of the first. One minute stretched into two. Three. Four. Until finally I couldn't handle it anymore. Fidgeting on my bum, I could no longer bear his crushing silence.

"I'm sure you're wondering what it was you saw back there," I said, voice almost robotic, eyes staring blankly ahead.

I felt his movements. His body sliding around until he faced me full on. "What did I see back there?"

It would be so easy to snap at him. I might not have my wand on hand, which helped me to focus and channel my powers, but I could still hurt him if I cared to do so.

I could turn his skin to wood, his heart to stone, his mind to mush. Not as if I hadn't done it before. To others before him. Nameless faces down through time who'd annoyed me in some form or fashion.

I remembered the stark terror in each and every gaze seconds before I'd snuffed the life from them.

Looking down at my hands, I gave my head a minute shake. How could anything like me ever hope to find redemption? Be forgiven?

Did I even want forgiveness?

The idea was a startling one. I'd never cared before.

But without the hum of darkness being an ever-present burden inside of me, I found myself tired and weary, found myself opening up Pandora's box and allowing those memories I'd kept caged for years to slowly leak out.

Something like me deserved death, surely.

"Talk to me, fairy. Tell me what it is you did."

His words were low, cajoling, as though he spoke to a wild and frightened beast. It was only when I twirled on him that I realized why. My nails had tipped to claws, and I'd shoved them through my thighs, causing beads of blood to well up and stain the pale blue of my dress. My fangs were out and exposed, and I knew I wore a mask of violence and hate.

With a grunt that sounded torn from the lips of a dying animal, I yanked my claws out, wrapped my arms tight around my middle, and rocked for a moment. The sting of the cuts helped to ground and focus me.

"Galeta," he said again slowly. This time daring to lay a hand upon my upper arm but not moving it. "Sometimes talking helps."

"How would you know?" I hissed, yanking away from his burning touch. I could handle hate, could handle antipathy—it was what I'd learned to deal with all my life. What I could not handle was his gentle kindness.

What did he possibly want from me? No one was ever kind to me just because. There was always something required in return. Tit for tat.

The gentle mask he wore slipped for a moment, and I was ready to crow. To pump my fist in exultation at being right. That he was just the same as everyone else. I'd see his fire, his fury, and I'd bask in it.

But that wasn't what he showed me.

What I saw was pain.

So much so that it pricked my already raw and shriveled heart.

Buttons had cared for me because he'd known nothing else. I'd raised him from a wee hatchling; he'd viewed me as a mother. I'd quickly dispelled his love for me, as I had all others who'd ever thought to try. In the end, his hatred of me had been as complete as everyone else's.

But Syrith seemed unfazed by my rage and stony silence. If the darkness rode me, I'd wrap myself in it. Use it as my armor as I always have. But the darkness was dormant. Sleeping. And all I was left with now was an unrelenting well of shame and fear that threatened to consume me.

"You're wrong, fairy. You think you're the only one who's suffered in this life, but you're wrong. We all suffer in our own ways. Perhaps my own sins are as grave as yours."

I snorted. I knew what he was trying to do. Bond with me somehow. Create a connection, a tether that would keep me tied to him, make me want to "share." To slice open my heart and let the befouled sins of my past flow down around his feet so that he might stare at them, might somehow *commiserate* with me about them.

"I don't need nor do I want your pity, dragonborne. I am who I am."

I notched my chin, daring him to defy my words. To tell me I was still able to be saved, to be spared this nightmare.

His brows lowered. "Are you truly that far gone, fairy, that you cannot see this for what it really is? I'm trying to bloody help you."

I'd never known that such soft words could carry such a massive blow to my chest. I cringed, gripping the edge of my icy gown tight.

"I've been alone all my life. And I don't intend to change now. Leave me alone, Prince."

His face twisted up into tight, angry features, and it was awful. To see him do as everyone else had done. But this was what I was good at.

Being alone.

Being angry.

Being prickly and rude and mean. It was my armor. My shield. And I didn't know how to be anything other than this.

My smile was grim. "You might say you want to help me, dragon. But, in the end, you'll see me just as everyone else always has."

"And how is that?" he snapped, and I flinched.

My fingers twitched as I imagined running them down his slightly whiskered cheek and tracing the sharp planes of his handsome face.

Cold. Indifferent. Indomitable. All those thoughts floated to the top of my head, but in a moment of perverse honesty, I muttered, "As nothing at all."

His beautiful blue-green eyes widened at my raw frankness, and I gasped, realizing what I'd just said, what I'd done. Slapping my hand over my mouth, I shot up from the couch and transformed instantly. Still glowing, I flew to my back room. Slamming the door shut behind me and burrowing deep beneath the mussed sheets.

I didn't stop crying all through the night.

Harpy

Hidden within the background of this realm, I watched Galeta flee, leaving a stunned-looking Syrith sitting frozen on the couch. His eyes were downcast and hooded, but I could read his heart. His thoughts.

He was confused. Angry. And something else, though I couldn't quite put my finger on that emotion. It was clouded and difficult to decipher. But he was bathed in shades of soft blue. Curiosity. Pain, maybe? I simply couldn't tell.

"This isn't at all how things should go. I'm failing, Creator. I'm—"

My daughter has lived in darkness for so long, she has lost her way. Worry not, little golden bird. I have chosen correctly, sending her this dragonborne. It will not be easy cracking open her armor, but if anyone can do it—

"It would be the dragon," I said softly, finishing my Creator's thoughts.

I felt Its smile, and I shook my head. This was my biggest assignment yet—I could not fail It, and yet I feared I already was.

"But she is so tortured, Creator," I pressed on.

Is not the butterfly proof enough that one can go through a great deal of darkness and still become something beautiful?

I hung my head. It was right. And I would have to trust Its judgment. "But if the seed is not taken from her, then all of this is for naught. Isn't it, Creator?"

Deep down, I knew the answer to this question, but I desperately wished It would tell me otherwise.

A brushstroke of phantom wings grazed my cheek, causing me to shiver. Then It was gone. I shook my head, sick and disquieted to my soul. Even here, in this place full of powerful magic, Galeta still fought the darkness.

Where was that replacement? Why hadn't it shown itself yet? It wasn't that I didn't trust my Creator. I did. With my whole heart. But if the vessel were really here, surely I'd have sensed it by now.

No?

Frowning, I twirled on my heel and swiped my hand through the air, opening a rift between realms. I'd been visiting the centauress of late.

It wasn't that I hadn't taken notice of the others, but something about the she-horse called to me. Some certainty that she must surely be the vessel.

Stepping through the realms, I moved into the centauress's temporary domicile. I'd given the goddesses very specific designs for each habitat, knowing that to thrive and open up to their future mates, they'd need someplace that felt like home.

Even the barren land of Baba Yaga had been designed with purpose.

The centauress—whose name was actually Tymanon—was designed to make her feel as if she were back in her world of Olympus. The grass of the plains was lush and ripe, filling the night with its earthy, nutty scent. Pale moonflowers waved in the gentle breeze. Apple, pear, and dogwood trees bursting with pretty white petals dotted the landscape.

I'd taken to watching Ty—as I thought of her—the past few days. Not really studying her male, since he was of no importance to me. But wondering what it was about her that'd called to me.

And the quiet, vain hope beating in my heart that she might be the replacement.

I'd not said hi to her, but merely watched her interactions in this world. The pretty brunette of mane and flank stood upon a hillock alone, practicing her archery. Nocking an arrow into her bow, letting it fly, and just as quickly replacing it with a new one.

In the time it'd taken me to walk up the short hill to her, she'd released her entire quiver full into the mound of dirt with a makeshift bull's-eye painted upon it. Grabbing her arrows, she dusted off the dirt, checked that her arrow tips were still in good-working fashion, and nodded to herself, as though pleased by her progress.

When the Creator had given me the list of names to be brought to this realm, I couldn't understand why Ty was on it. She was of Olympus and not of Kingdom at all, as the rest of the queens were.

Rubbing my arms gently, I frowned. I'd been drawn to this startlingly lovely creature almost against my will.

"Whoever you are," she said in a dulcet voice, "I know you've been watching me. Now tell me why, or you shall surely die."

Then, in a move I'd not seen coming, she'd nocked her arrow, twirled, and had it aimed unerringly in my direction.

Eyes wide, I held up my hands. It was entirely possible I could be injured—I simply wasn't certain and didn't want to risk it. Remaining hidden seemed pointless now.

So I popped into existence and said jerkily, "Do not shoot, centauress. I merely watched. I am sorry. I will go now."

But the moment I appeared, a tiny frown line appeared between her brows, and the arrow that'd been pointed directly at my heart—though I knew she'd not seen me—was now sheathed, her weapon harmless. I'd never even seen her move.

I clutched at my chest, my heart wildly beating inside. "Gods, you're deadly, aren't you?" My laughter was weak with relief.

Slipping her bow over one shoulder, she shook her head. "Who are you, creature? And why have you been haunting me?"

I blinked. In the short time I'd come to know Ty, I'd learned she was an honorable creature, and I trusted her. She was prickly. But that wasn't always necessarily a bad thing either.

Maybe I'd tell her just a little.

"My name is Harpy. I think."

"You think?" Her light-brown eyes sparkled, as though I amused her.

Which caused me to smile. "Aye. My Creator forgot to name me."

"Then"—she shrugged—"Harpy it is. Why are you here?"

"I don't know." I flitted my fingers along one of my downy feathers. I always molted when I was nervous, and I was nervous now. Already, I'd lost several feathers to this strange realm.

Her eyelids drew together to form slits. "Do you harass everyone else, or have I been the only one to receive this dubious honor?"

I chuckled weakly. "I wouldn't call what I'm doing harassment. I'm simply trying to learn what it means to be human."

She laughed. Tossed her head back, which caused her thick braid to undulate behind her. "And you'd come to learn that from a centaur." Knuckling tears from her eyes, she shook her head. "Harpy, you're a strange little thing, aren't you? I've decided I won't kill you. Centaurs aren't exactly known for our humor, and yet you've given me quite a laugh tonight. I like you."

I snorted pleasantly.

"Come. You must be famished. I was just about to have my evening cup of fresh cider. We can sit and chat until I weary if you'd like."

"Your man won't mind?"

Her smile turned soft at the mention of him, and I could see that my Creator had been right in his pairings.

"No, Petra will not be a problem. He's already abed. It was why you caught me target practicing."

I nodded. "Well, all right then. For a while."

She turned, walking steadily toward a shelter large enough she'd not need to lower her head to walk through. I studied her animal form. I did not know enough about horses to know what any specific parts of her were called, only that she was pretty in both forms.

Upon entering the hut, she pointed toward the glow of a warm fire. "Sit," she commanded.

I nodded, watching a moment as she reverently put away her weapon for the night. By the time I'd sat on the log before the flame, she was working on crushing several apples between her hands.

My brows rose at the strength she must possess to be able to turn the hard fruits into soft pulp. Juices ran from between her fingers into twin stoneware mugs.

Glancing to the left of me, I noted the bundled form of her Petra and smiled softly. Last night, I'd watched him gift her a single, solitary, and perfectly shaped rose. I'd thought it'd been nothing special. Except for the fact that Ty had seemed both startled and terribly pleased by it.

Even now that rose was threaded through her hair.

Love was a strange thing.

"Here, take and drink." Ty shoved a mug at me.

I nodded my thanks and took it from her. Then I took a small sip and made a noise of gratitude. It was actually rather good.

Fruity.

Pulpy.

Very sweet.

Forgoing a log, Ty knelt on her forelegs, slowly lowering her big body to the ground, and studied me with intelligent eyes.

Feeling nervous and fidgety, I sipped at my drink. I'd not had a thing to drink in over a thousand years, and I'd nearly forgotten the pleasures of it.

"Why am I really here, Harpy girl? Who I somehow doubt to be girl at all," Ty asked with a lifted brow.

Eyes going wide, I stared at her pretty equine features. She had big teeth, like her ancestors. But everything else was uniquely feminine and soft. Which helped to soften her overall appearance, which was actually somewhat masculine. Especially her arms and torso.

"I suppose I do owe you an answer now." I tipped the mug toward her with a small grin, but she didn't share one back.

I sighed.

"You see," she said slowly, setting her now-empty mug down beside her, "I've had time to study these 'games,' and something has become abundantly clear to me. I do not belong here. Nor does Petra. These are games

59

for the Dark Queens, of which I am not one. I'm not going to say I'm necessarily the sweetest centaur of the bunch, but I am certainly no queen."

My brows lifted. Perceptive horse, she was. Wetting my lips, I tasted the hint of fresh apple upon them. Having been drawn to the centaur the past few days, I could only imagine it was because she was the replacement.

And if that were the case, then she'd need to know a little bit.

I decided to use my free will and trust my gut. "No, you're right. You aren't like the rest of them. You're intelligent. Keenly so. And you do serve a future purpose."

Her nostrils flared, and she paused for several moments, as if trying to scent out a lie in me. After a moment, she nodded. "Hm. I'm not surprised to hear this."

I'd always known of the intelligence of the centaurs, but I'd never imagined them to be quite so perceptive. "What might that purpose be?"

I shrugged. "I'm not truly certain. Only my Creator knows, but It assures me that in time, all will be made clear."

"And I'm to trust this Creator whom I do not know, am I?"

She tipped her chin forward, and I shook my head. "But you do know It, Tymanon. It is in all things. The colors. Life. The smile of a child. All that lives and breathes is because of It."

Her full lips tipped at the corners. "My people have a name for that. Would you like to know what we call it?"

I nodded. "Very much."

"Father sky."

Smiling, I nodded softly. "I think It would like that. It is a rather robust being, at that."

She snorted, which sounded more like a neigh. "I'm sure It is. So you've been sent here to learn more about me, or more about yourself?"

I opened my mouth, ready to correct her, when I was brought up short by that question. "What do you mean, more about myself?"

Turning to stare into the flame, she flicked a little kernel of something off her finger into the fire. Immediately, the sparks leapt high, turning from orange to a bright yellow.

But rather than answer my question, she said slowly, "The very first day, I felt an awareness of something watching me. But not just me, watching the dragon Prince too. It was you, wasn't it?"

Her eyes were piercing, and I knew she'd know if I lied, so I said nothing instead. She nodded, as though that were answer enough.

"These games, they aren't." She frowned. "I've studied my opponents. Many of them believe this place truly is what it seems to be. But none of us have been sent here just to find our true loves. Not that we won't, Aphrodite chose well, of course. Though I'm hardly certain I'll be spending my life soul bound to a satyr, however, that is a different story entirely." She snorted, as though amused, then flicked her wrist, growing serious once more. "But there is so much more to what is happening here than merely discovering our mates. None of us matter. None of us are important enough alone to be anything of any great importance in Kingdom. So why would the gods go through such trouble to create these games of 'love?'" She finger quoted. Looking at Harpy with a piercing, intelligent gaze. "You know what I think, Harpy, we were each chosen for a very specific set of skills. I've had ample opportunity to study my opponents and one thing I've found to be constant. Together, we are a force to be reckoned with. Are we not?"

I could hardly feel my toes. How did this creature know so much?

More and more, I was becoming certain that she was the replacement I'd waited so long to find, but on the heel of that thought came another. If she was the vessel, this strangely brilliant creature before me would be no more.

What a sad thought.

"Do you really believe these games aren't simply games? That perhaps you're looking far too deeply into matters?" I asked, leaning forward, eager to hear her answer.

"No. I do not. When I study my opponents, time and again I return to the fairy's domain, and do you know what I see there, Harpy?"

I swallowed hard and shook my head.

"Nothing. Nothing at all. Why is that?"

This creature was far too smart to fool, and yet I could not tell her everything. Right now, she had her suspicions and her certainty that all wasn't what it seemed, and she was right. But if she was smart enough to figure that out on her own, she was certainly capable enough of trying to change the course of destiny.

"I do not know—"

She held up her hand. "Do not lie to me, Harpy, for I would know it, and then I'd have more questions of you."

Her eyes twinkled, and I sensed she was not angry with me. "Why do you seem happy?"

"Because a centaur loves nothing more than a grand journey, and barring that, working out a good puzzle. Keeps our minds engaged. And aside from Petra, I find this entire place wholly tedious."

I flicked a glance at the soundly sleeping shadow. "I am glad you like your mate."

One of her brows lifted. "I never said he was my mate. Though I do find his mind stimulating."

My Creator was always right. Petra and Ty would eventually fall in love, I was certain of it, even if she wasn't yet. She shrugged, swiping a hand through the air.

"Anyway. Tell me, little one—what have you learned studying me?" A thin brow lifted high, as if daring my honesty.

"That you are quite smart and that I would do well to keep my thoughts to myself."

Her laughter rang through the night.

Chapter 11: Gods, You're a Nasty Lil' Demon, Aren't You?

Syrith

I stayed curled up in a bowl of fluff the entire night through, sitting guard at her door. I'd not been able to sleep for many hours after our disquieting conversation. I'd seen a flash of the she-devil I'd witnessed in the clone in the above realm. I'd seen a curl of hate flicker through her blue-eyed gaze.

Felt the sting of her rage.

But unlike the creature above, I hadn't felt disgust for her. Only pity. It would be so easy to hate Galeta, so much easier than trying to get beneath the armor to the terrified and delicate creature beneath, who with one powerful gust of wind could easily snap in half.

I'd come to a conclusion last night.

Galeta was prickly because she was terrified. Scared of her own shadow.

I knew a thing or two about that myself.

For years, I'd shut down after Seraphina's death. Cursing at anyone or anything that would dare intrude upon the sanctity of my isolation.

Not because I hated them, but because I'd hated myself.

I swallowed hard. I'd maybe only slept an hour or two. And though I could hear the gentle beating sound of her heart, indicating she was finally asleep, I still heard the broken whimpers and quiet sobs. Even in her sleep, she was haunted.

I wasn't sure why I cared so much. Very little had pricked my curiosity as of late. But something in me recognized something in her. We were broken, both of us reeling from deep pain. We were similar, she and I.

Stretching out my tired and achy limbs, I called upon a transformation. This time my true one. She was well asleep, and I knew she'd not catch me as I really was.

At least once a day, I was forced to take on my true form. I didn't have to walk around in it long, but after so much shape-shifting, if I didn't change, my body would literally begin to meld and re-form into twisted amalgams of everything I'd ever shifted into.

It was quite uncomfortable for me. Which was why I forced myself to do it, though I did not care to.

She could walk out and catch me. She was a fairy, after all. She could even wink herself into existence right before my eyes, so fast that I'd not have a moment to re-form into something more appealing and less macabre.

Mother had always loved me as I was. But I remembered Father's shock, even the curl of his disgust at the sight of me as a newborn babe.

Yes, I was dragonborne, but I was also a creation born straight out of Wonderland's twisted womb.

In this form, I was both phantom and flesh.

To an unobservant witness, I would appear to have no head at all. Simply a walking body and neck. But if they could peer beneath the dark magic, they could see me. The real me.

The face I wore in my day to day was my true face, only more substantial. I could see. I could taste. Touch. Feel. But it was rare that others could see me.

Rumors had floated through Wonderland for many years now of a creature born of madness. The Headless Horseman, it was called. A creature so vile, so wicked, that it would eat the souls of the living. That the only thing one would see before their death was the mad red, glowing eyes of the devil himself.

It wasn't true.

My eyes were neither red, nor did they glow. I was simply not fully corporeal at times. There'd been a few times in my youth when I'd dared to go out in public as I really was, always terribly careful to hide my condition from the censorious eyes of others.

But no matter how careful I'd been, I had been spotted, and the legend of my wickedness had grown. So much so that when I'd finally dared to reveal myself to Seraphina for who I really was, she'd opted to end her life by drinking a vial of poison the night before our wedding. Her note to me had said only one thing.

I could never bear your children...

I shuddered as those words sliced through my heart like blades, bleeding me all over again.

With a growl, I shifted to a fully corporeal man and caught the tantalizing whiff of breakfast steaming on the table. Glancing over, I noted that our bowls were full of that same strange broth once more.

This was the start of day three.

And I'd managed to accomplish nothing with Galeta.

Soon, I'd be forced to return to the above realm, to that awful clone that made my flesh crawl with revulsion. Bathing myself in dragon steam, I cleaned up quickly then took a seat and ate without tasting.

The broth was good, as always, and kept me surprisingly full, but my mind was a jumble of thoughts.

How long would I be forced to remain in the outer realm? How long until I could return? And just what in the bloody blazes did this asinine game entail?

I was halfway through my bowl of soup when I felt the press and pop of displaced air.

I'd halfway expected it would be Calypso returning to spirit me away, but instead I looked into the golden eyes of the harpy. She looked sad. Innocent. And curious.

"I saw your form, boy," she said without preamble.

Instantly, I stiffened, ready with a snappy retort. But she held up her hand, quelling my words.

"Prince of dragons and monsters, you are." She cocked her head, staring at me in a way she hadn't before. As though intrigued but not sure why. Then she gave a tiny shake of her head.

"Why are you here?" I asked, staring at her hard as I tried to make sense of my new reality.

She'd told me she'd be watching. But she'd been so silent, so invisible, that not even the keen senses of my dragon had picked up on her. I did not like being surprised.

"I'm learning, boy," she said slowly.

It was on the tip of my tongue to snap at her that I was no boy. I hadn't slept well last night, and I was in a foul mood, but the way she spoke, as though she were deeply confused about something, I couldn't seem to get the words out.

"And what have you learned?" I asked into the thick silence hanging between us.

My words caused her lashes to flicker and her gaze to meet mine. Surprise filtered through their golden depths, as though she'd temporarily forgotten I was even there at all.

The quiet stretched for another long pause before she haltingly said, "I-I am not certain."

I opened my mouth, ready to ask her another question, but she was gone. All traces of her. Even her scent of lilac and patchouli was no more. Frowning, I stared at all the empty crevices, sensing she was still very much here, but unable to accurately pinpoint where.

A moment later, the air tightened again. And this time it was the goddess come to fetch me. Except this time it was Aphrodite and not her cohort, Calypso.

The Goddess of Love was as beautiful as ever. She wore a cloak of long blond hair only. Not a stitch of clothing encased her form beneath, but the hair slid easily into place with each step she took, keeping a fair bit of her covered while also revealing tantalizing glimpses of toned flesh.

Stardust swirled beneath her eyes and upon her cheekbones. Rosebud lips the color of deepest blood and ivory skin as pale and flawless as an exquisitely cut moonstone, sonnets had been sung over Aphrodite's beauty. Wars had been fought.

And though I could admire her beauty, I was not moved by it as others might be. My father was of the house of Draconian. Draconian blood ran through my veins. Making me nearly immune to the pulse and power of the Greek pantheon.

She was beautiful, but that was all she was to me.

"Dragonborne," she said deeply, inclining her head in greeting.

Of all the gods of the pantheon, Aphrodite had always been one of my favorites. She had every right to be vain and petty, and yet she was not. She was kindhearted and loving. Very different from her proud father.

"It is good to finally meet you. I regret I've not had the opportunity to do so until now. Forgive me."

It was impossible to remain vexed around anyone as lovely as she. Aphrodite was also one of the few in the universe who knew what I really was. I highly doubted that her coming to me now was a coincidence.

Blue eyes the color of deepest silk gazed back at me. "You know why I'm here, surely?"

I nodded. "To escort me to the outer realm."

"Indeed." She nodded, causing her hair to tumble and undulate like a gentle wave around her trim shoulders. "I bestow this honor upon no other. But your father was always a favorite of mine, Headless Prince."

Full lips tipped up at the corners, and I found myself responding in kind.

"This I know. He speaks of you often."

She accepted my words with a graceful sweep of her lashes. "We haven't much time, Syrith. I come to tell you what to expect today. The clone has been manufactured to act as she would were she Galeta in truth."

"Why all the smoke and mirrors? Why didn't you make a clone of me too? Why must I leave this place?"

Her sparkling eyes turned distant and reflective as she said, "To be perfectly honest with you, Prince, I'm not sure. But I have this feeling in my heart that everything we know and love will change. Maybe your being with the clone is required? I simply don't know."

To hear Aphrodite speak of the heart was no small matter. It was her power, after all. There was none in existence who knew or understood matters of the heart as she did.

"Then why do this at all?"

Now that I knew Galeta better, I genuinely wanted to help her. Fix her. Mend her. She was broken just like me. It made me feel a bond to her because of it. But changing everything, I did not relish the sound of that.

Again she shrugged. "I only do what my heart tells me to do, Prince. And in this, I am helpless to stop it. This must happen, and you are the key to undoing all this pain."

"For her?"

I wasn't exactly sure what I meant by the question. As a dragon, I had a tendency to ponder matters into the ground. It was what my kind did. Think and think and think some more; trying to analyze all angles of a matter, trying to discern every possible position of every possible outcome. It was the curse of my kind, I supposed, but we did not come to be known as the wise ones for no reason.

Her pretty lips thinned. "And others."

"Who?"

She shook her head, sighing deeply. "That, I do not know. And though I wish we had more time to tarry on this matter, we must go now. There are games to play."

Aphrodite sounded weary to my sensitive ears. But then she plastered on a bright smile and shook her head. "Come, Prince. Time to place that surly mask back on and play the game."

I rather thought she wasn't speaking to me so much as herself, but I pretended not to notice and nodded instead. "Aye. Let us go now."

A portal of revolving colors opened up before us, highlighting the depressive bleakness of this realm all over again.

She grinned, as if noticing my thought. "It will not always remain so, Prince. After you."

Glancing one final time at Galeta's closed door, I clenched down on my back teeth and stepped through, and Aphrodite followed close on my heels.

"Your first match will be against the centauress. The clone believes, as all the rest do, that this is a match to the death, or a stalemate at the very least. The clone is wicked, and she will take those words to heart. She will try to kill anyone or anything that comes against her. Do not trust her. But also, stop her where you can. The Fates have decreed that only two will die in these games. And I was told that Galeta cannot end the life of any. You must make it appear as though you're helping and not hindering her."

I wasn't sure how I was to pull off this coup, but I'd do it. Somehow. I nodded. "You can depend upon me, Love."

She smiled. "I know. Unlike my friends, Hades and Caly, I know your soul, Syrith. And I know deep down you're a good man—you've simply forgotten your way."

I snorted with humor, but the sound wasn't a funny one.

She laid a gentle hand upon my shoulder, causing me to look down at her. She nodded. "I'm serious, dragon. Seraphina was never good enough for you. Though you gave her your heart, she'd never truly given you hers back."

I flinched, the words stinging me to my core. Her look was sad.

"I'm sorry to cause you more pain, Prince. But I thought you should know that."

Gnashing my teeth together so hard that the world echoed with the sound of it, I shrugged as if it didn't matter.

But it was no easy thing to hear that I'd been the only fool to fall.

Ahead, lights gathered and colors swirled. We were reaching our destination.

"I have designed the setup so that you will always reach the fighting realm before the others. As neither of you have a familiar to guide you here, I've stepped up to be that guide."

We popped out on the other side, into a world full of jagged rocks and spires. The mountain was a strange color of rusted reds and deep, veined purples. The sky a clear shade of blue that reminded me somehow of Galeta's eyes.

Once, I would have called this place dull, but after days of living in gray, this was an oasis of life. Galeta would have liked it here.

"Thank you," I said to her. She nodded then snapped her fingers.

A second later, the lifeless Galeta clone appeared by my feet. Looking exactly as she had two days ago. Her chest did not rise with breath.

"Remember my words, Syrith," Aphrodite said. "And now I'll leave you. The centauress comes soon. Subdue them as quick as might be. Once you do, I'll cover this realm in a blanket of darkness and whisk you both away from the prying and intelligent eyes of that horse who is entirely too smart for her own good. Returning you to the mirror and the clone to her place. May the gods be with you."

She vanished, and the clone rose.

There was no jerky turning on. The clone was simply not aware one moment but aware the next. Twirling on me, she gave me a haughty, calculating look.

"Still here, dragon?" Her words were practically spat at me. "I thought I'd have run you off by now."

"Impossible to do, fae. I do not scare easily," I said.

Rushing to my side, until her fist suddenly gripping her wand pressed into my chest, she hissed, "Nor do I. Stay out of my way, and I might let you live."

I lifted a brow. How was it possible that I could vehemently hate this Galeta as I did and yet still wonder about the one I'd left behind?

They were both part of the same whole. And yet...I hoped she slept true now.

The air displaced once more. And I knew without looking up that the centauress and her mate had finally arrived.

The centauress was pretty enough. With supple brown fur on her backside and a shiny black tail, she was a fine specimen of horseflesh. Her female form too was lovely. She had full breasts, a long, elegant neck, and lovely features. Her teeth were blunt and white and looking a little more horsey than human, but she was beautiful in her own right.

A thick braid of brown hair crowned her head. Across her chest plate was a brown leather strap that held her bow and quiver full of arrows strapped tight to her back. Standing beside her was an equally handsome-looking man.

He had dark hair, rather shaggy, with the tips of it reaching his shoulders. He was bare chested and wore no pants. But then, satyrs rarely did. His legs were as hairy and shaggy as the hair crowning his head. I lifted a brow at the strange pairing. Interspecies romances were severely frowned upon by centaur herds.

But who was I to cast aspersions? There wasn't another in all of Kingdom quite like me.

The centauress withdrew her bow and gripped it fast in her hand. She and the satyr stood several hundred yards away from us, both looking at us with intelligent and keen eyes.

She spoke first. "This day we must fight. But I bear neither of you any ill will. Remember that."

Her voice was steady and sure, reminding me of the majestic grace of a prized stallion. This was an honorable creature. But she would fight. And so we must too.

"I bear you ill will, horse-faced bitch," Galeta chewed out beneath her breath and then shoved me back, hissing at me once more to keep my distance and not get in her way. I rubbed at my temple. This was going to be a long bloody exercise in patience for me today. Never something I'd excelled at before.

The clone taunted the pair with crude gestures and then twirled her star-tipped wand in the air.

I stood there, watching dispassionately, wondering what kind of mask I should be wearing today. That of the spoiled Prince or perhaps an angry beast matching the fury of the fae beside me. So deep in contemplation was I that I didn't pay attention until almost too late to realize that Galeta had conjured a spear of dark magic and was now aiming to throw a direct hit to the centauress's chestnut-colored flank.

"Bloody hell," I bit out.

Making a quick decision, I shifted. Into my dragon form. I was a large beast with red scales that gleamed like magma in sunlight. I was also graceful. Elegant.

Not the clumsy oaf I now suddenly was who stumbled around like a clod on massively taloned feet and stumbled into the wee fairy, knocking the spear from her hand and shattering it upon the earth.

"Damn you, bastard!" Galeta snarled, and I was certain she would have loved nothing more than to have ended me herself.

But the centaur was letting her arrows fly with uncanny precision. I howled as one sharp-tipped arrowhead pierced through the narrowest sliver between scales to the tender skin right above my brow bone. Blood instantly filled my eye.

Growing angry and disgusted by the entire ordeal, I found that it wasn't difficult to pretend to be a beast.

I defended Galeta as best I could while also preventing the nasty she-devil from enacting death curses. Once, she'd gotten to within the final word of a curse before I was able to "accidentally" trip over an exposed chunk of rock in the ground. My broad tail whipped out haphazardly, tossing the wee fae high into the sky.

She screamed, confused for a moment and nearly falling on her head before she spread her wings to right herself.

Death glared back at me through cold, frosty eyes. She knew. I knew the clone knew what I was doing. Dragons weren't clumsy. Yet, several times now, I'd very nearly fallen and taken her out.

The satyr was nowhere to be seen. The men didn't have to fight in these games. In fact, it was rather better if they didn't, since killing one of us immediately eliminated the female from the games.

The centauress had ordered her satyr to hide from the very first moment Galeta had conjured a spell. But the female was a warrior and had held her own just fine. True, I wasn't actively trying to kill her.

But she didn't know that.

Which was probably why I was currently stuck with dozens of arrows all over, looking as though I'd been covered in porcupine quills. There was even an arrow embedded deep into my left nostril, causing a strange fluttering whistle to escape my nose with each breath.

I was escaping another volley of arrows and trying to dig a particularly irksome one out of my spine plate with my back foot when I realized that Galeta was no longer by my side.

Frowning and immediately worried, I looked left and right for her, ignoring the continuing irritation of arrows finding their mark. I was a bloodied mess and would bruise tonight for it.

Anyone worth his or her salt knew never to enter into a game of war against an armed centaur. It was a foolish endeavor, even for a dragon with hide as thick as mine. I would not die, but this was far from pleasant.

Thankfully, the centauress hadn't tipped her arrows in poison; otherwise, I'd be singing a very different tune.

Then I spotted the clone. She was rushing out from behind a boulder some twenty yards away from me. Rushing the centaur with a blade crafted of red stone that gleamed like fire-dusted rubies and aimed directly at the centaur's heart.

It would be a deathblow.

I shook my head and looked at the centaur, who'd been looking at me. Her brows dipped, and I saw the intelligent creature begin to piece the puzzle together.

In one fluid motion, she twirled, nocking an arrow and aiming it unerringly at the clone's head.

I would never reach her in time in this current form, but transforming so many times in one day wasn't a good idea. After a while, my bones would stop responding and I'd twist into a thing of horrors.

But I had no choice.

Calling down a transformation, I became a jabberwocky. A Frankenstein's monster–type thing of feathers, lizard, and snake. Reaching out with my long neck, I head-slapped Galeta away at the same instant the centauress released her arrow.

I had no scales to deflect it this time.

The arrow sank deep into my neck, causing me to gasp as hot blood spilled from out of my vein. Alive with pain, I reacted, and using a broad, clawed foot, I slapped the centauress away too. Using more power than I otherwise might have because of the shock of my injuries. She fell hard, knocking her head upon an exposed boulder. In an instant, the satyr was beside her, but his eyes were for her alone.

Gasping for breath as each pump of my heart caused more blood to hemorrhage out of me, I held onto consciousness just long enough to gather up the clone's slight form and drag her away from the eyes of both centaur and satyr.

Then I collapsed against the mountainside and awaited Fate's hand.

I recall little of what happened next, other than that a terrible and thick darkness descended over the arena. Soft hands caressed the side of my neck, and then the power of a god pushed through me.

"You've done well, dragonborne," Aphrodite whispered. "Now rest. When next you awake, you'll be safe. Only shut your eyes...and dream."

Chapter 12: In Which a Fairy Begins to Let Go...

Galeta

I walked around the hut, and even the grounds surrounding it, later that day when I'd finally deigned to stir. Looking for Syrith in order to apologize for my abominable behavior the night before.

He hadn't deserved my rancor. But the shock of witnessing the past had been terrible to bear, and I had done what I'd always done—I'd retreated into my shell. Into my armor. Pushing people away because I couldn't handle feeling the press of their judgment upon me.

I didn't know how to be anything other than what I'd always been.

Cruel.

Alone.

Isolated.

But I'd felt his presence on the other side of the door all night. Again keeping watch over me. I'd wanted to get up and go to him.

I simply hadn't known how.

But when I'd finally been brave enough to leave the isolation of my room, he was gone. And so here I sat, at the table, staring into a bowl of now-tepid gray broth and fearing I'd lost my only ally in this place.

"I can't do this anymore," I whispered tightly. I'd been all alone, and then he'd found me and brought life with him.

I hadn't liked it. A part of me had even resented his intrusion into the sins of my past, but now that he was gone... My throat squeezed tight, and my face crumpled. I didn't want to be alone either.

How was it possible that I had any more tears left to cry?

And yet the burn of them continued to trek down my face.

Reaching into the hidden pocket, to the vial of death I kept tucked tight against my breast, I gently fluttered my fingers across it.

Pop.

Whirling in my seat, knowing the marker tunnel travel left behind, I watched as Syrith's body collapsed like dead weight upon the steel-gray couch.

With a cry wrenched from my soul, I jumped to my feet. Rushing toward him.

"Please don't be dead. Please don't be dead." I whispered the mantra over and over again.

My heart was a fluttering beat of hummingbird's wings inside my chest when I finally got to him and saw his chest rise and fall with breath. Collapsing with relief, I felt my legs give out beneath me, and my upper half draped over him.

And this time when I cried, I wasn't even sure why.

All I knew was I felt such a massive wave of relief that it shook me to my core.

Burying my face in his chest, I inhaled his heady fragrance of smoke and ash and male, trembling as I realized that the thought of him dying or being gone for good had affected me far more than almost anything else ever had before it.

I was sniffing into his shirt, staining it with my tears. I needed to get myself together, needed to move off of him and compose myself. That way, when he awoke, I wouldn't look like the blubbering idiot I had now become.

"Why do you cry, fae?" His deep voice cut like ice through my thoughts.

Stiffening, I jerked off his warmth as though scalded and gasped, staring at him wide eyed as though he were a snake ready to sink his fangs in me.

His dusky skin was pale. And his jewel eyes a little duller. There were dark bruises on his face and chin and neck. Whatever he'd been doing, it hadn't been a walk in the park for him.

My heart quivered as his long fingers brushed stray curls of thick hair out of his eyes.

He tipped his chin in expectation, and I knew he was awaiting my reply. No doubt he'd expect me to run off like a frightened, stupid bunny, same as I had last night. I steeled my nerves. I could do this. All I had to do was try. I'd thought I'd lost him. Now he was back. I couldn't lose him again.

"I-I..." I cleared my throat. "I grew worried when I could not find you this morning. Where did you run off to, dragon?" I rushed through my words, petrified out of my mind that he would not answer.

He blinked, looking shocked that I'd actually answered him. Scarlet rose in my cheeks. Twisting my lips, I stared down at my hands. I'd released my claws without realizing it.

What was happening to me to make me so unhinged?

Sheathing my claws, I squeezed my eyes shut and forced myself to take deep, steadying breaths, feeling my nerves settle just a little after that.

Syrith's warm touch made me open my eyes. He had laid his large, calloused palm over mine. I looked up and drowned in his electric blue-green eyes.

The press of his skin to mine, it was thrilling. It was also terrifying. My wings shivered.

"I had matters to attend to this morning. But I am fine, little fae. Do not worry over me."

I bit my bottom lip at the gentle tenderness of his words. I'd never been so open with anyone before, and though I craved this intimacy, I was also unsure of how to deal with it.

Pulling my hand out from under his, I curled my fingers one by one and placed it on my lap. My other hand tingled with my desire to reach over and touch his hand again. That maybe by somehow doing so I could feel the sensation of his touch burn through me all over again.

I remained still.

His eyes drilled into my hand for several long seconds. Then he looked at me.

Wetting my lips, I rocked back on my heels, feeling the desperate urge to turn and flee. To get away from him. From this weirdness tugging between us.

I'd once helped curse another fairy for feeling as I now did.

Danika Moon. I'd despised her weakness. Her need for love. She was a fairy godmother. All knew fairies couldn't fall in love; we simply weren't wired that way. We were built with the desire to bring love to others but not for ourselves. The fae were never more content than when we drank, danced, and frolicked with our animal familiars. That was our life, our purpose. To have fun and perhaps aid in the happiness of others now and again. But no more.

I'd been so angry with Danika for wanting more than that, that I'd—again—been instrumental in destroying her joy. For several hundred years, I'd kept her separated from her lover—the man in the moon.

If I could do that to her, what right did I have to expect any sort of happiness of my own? I should leave and not entertain this folly anymore. But instead I forced my limbs to obey my brain and not my heart. I sat. Gathering my knees beneath me and tucking the hem of my gown between my thighs, rubbing my arm with that same hand he'd touched, I spoke.

"I was wrong last night, Prince."

He went still. "About?"

Deep as liquid molasses was his voice. It pierced through me, resonated somewhere inside of me. My stomach flipped. I knew what was happening to me. I'd witnessed the first bloom of romance in its many varied forms through the ages.

"I should not have said the things I did. I am...I'm..."

I looked down at my knees, unable to finish saying the words.

His finger slid under my chin, and it was suddenly terribly hard to breathe.

"Say it," he commanded gently.

I wanted so desperately to unburden myself with someone. To share the pain of my past. This morning when I'd thought him gone, it'd wounded me. Revealed a raw truth.

I liked Syrith.

Fae and humans were so different. We didn't think as they did. We were born to do a task. Bring about joy and happiness to others. But I'd always been different. Always intrinsically wrong.

Most hated me. But they didn't know how I fought my own urges either. Up until recently, I'd been able to mostly control that darkness within me. I'd do wrong, but I'd do just enough good not to make anyone question or poke too deeply.

My sins were so great, though. How could anyone bear to hear them and still think kindly of me? What if I told him all?

What if I shared?

Would he still look at me like this?

As if he saw me.

Not the façade, but the scared woman beneath?

It went against every part of me to apologize. It wasn't who I was. Even if I felt the sting of regret, it never lasted long. I'd simply wrap myself deeper in rage, shoving out the maudlin, weak sentiments until I no longer felt them. Until I was hard and frosty again.

But this place wouldn't allow me to do that. I'd been stripped bare here. I was vulnerable, and it hurt. It really, really hurt.

I closed my eyes.

"You can tell me anything, Galeta."

He made to move away, but I clamped my fingers around his wrist, holding him fast. I might look slight, but I was strong. And though I didn't know how to say it, his touch grounded me. Helped clear the fog of pain and memories.

"Why?" I asked with a slight shake of my head. "Why are you so kind to me, Prince? Why do you care?"

He sat up, and I finally opened my eyes. What I saw scrolled on his face was the same pain I'd seen the night before. Heat burned behind my eyes. But I would not cry. Not in front of him.

"You think I don't know pain, little one, but I do. Keenly. Even after years, I still wake up with nightmares from it. Whatever you've done, whoever you think you are, you don't have to be that here. Look around you, Galeta." He lifted an arm, encompassing the whole of the room. "You're safe. Though your memories may beat at our door, there is nothing here can harm you."

"You?" I said softly. "You could."

He shook his head then swiped up a tear I'd not felt fall. "But I won't."

I wanted to believe him. But I couldn't understand this either. Life was give-and-take. Nothing was given for free. Not words of kindness. Not compassion. And certainly not truth.

"I don't understand you at all, dragonborne."

A lopsided grin stole across one corner of his full mouth. "That's okay, fairy. I don't often understand myself either."

I laughed at his unexpected frankness. Which caused him to pause, looking at me strangely. As if he'd never seen me before now. His look was raw and honest, and I squirmed beneath it.

"I'm sorry." I didn't think about what I was going to say. It simply poured out of me. And I held my breath, waiting for him to mock me. Tell me I was worthless. Nothing.

"As am I."

I swallowed hard. "Wha... Why would you—"

He would leave me now. Tell me he'd satisfied his curiosity and leave me alone in this foreboding and dreary realm. I just knew—

"I'm sorry that you believe yourself to be so unworthy of friendship, Galeta. I'm sorry that you've been so wounded by this world. And I'm sorry for what I'm about to do."

I frowned, shaking my head, so desperate to keep him with me that I resorted to begging. "Don't leave me now, Prince. I could not bear to be alo—"

But Syrith didn't move anywhere but closer to me. Swooping in, he stole my words and my lips. His touch was soft, exploratory, and so bloody gentle that it was almost a whisper of velvet.

The kiss didn't last long, but my entire world had just been rocked on its axis. Stars exploded behind my eyes. Blood rushed through my ears. And heat filled my bones.

When he pulled back, he rested his forehead upon mine and murmured like a brushstroke against my lips, "You can hate me, fae, but I nearly died this morning, and I knew I'd never forgive myself if I didn't do this at least once."

Syrith

I waited for her slap. Her hiss. Her hate. Every nerve in my body tensed and expectant.

Instead, what I got was a dewy-eyed look, and then she pounced. Pressing me back against the couch in her fevered need to kiss me again.

I hadn't been sure what to expect. I'd been gentle. Galeta was anything but. She stood up on her knees, leaning forward so far, her hands pressed into my chest. Her kisses were unpracticed and hard but all the more charming because they were so artless and naïve.

As Prince of Wonderland, I'd been made love to by beautiful women aplenty in dark, quiet corners. Nobles desperate to gain my hand and my title. Most of the women were adept in the art of seduction and had made my body tingle with need from one strategically placed kiss. But none of it had been real. All of it had been with the sole desire to gain the throne, and I'd known that. It was why I'd only once dared to give my heart to another.

I didn't think I could ever feel alive again.

But my body burned beneath Galeta's touch. Igniting in a passion and fury of raw, primal need I'd only ever felt once before. Never, however, with such fervency.

A sound of raw desire vibrated between us, and I knew it was our song. Hers and mine. Our need creating a melody of panting breaths and unspoken words.

I could only follow where she led me, willing to go now to any depths to save this female. When she pulled back, I was the one trembling.

Liquid blue eyes stared up at me with surprised shock. No longer quite so icy or pale blue, they now seemed to glow a deeper, brighter hue. Even the robin's egg-blue of her hair seemed pale, the corkscrew curls now softer, flowing prettily around her shoulders.

She touched the tip of three fingers to her mouth, and I knew what she felt, because I felt it too. The burn of her remembered touch still singed. I trailed my tongue along the inside of my lips, tasting her sweetness of tart berries.

"The first Alice Hu," she whispered brokenly, "she was foretold to be Hatter's great love."

I blinked, confused for a moment as to what she was talking about. But then I realized she was opening up to me, telling me what had happened yesterday. I waited. As long as she'd need, I'd wait.

"I planted the seed of doubt in her heart, Syrith. I told her lies."

Frowning, I gave my head a slight shake. "You told her the truth. That Hatter would go mad. Even I know of it."

"No." She sighed softly, clasping her hands before her almost like a shield. "No, he wouldn't have. He was as sane as you and I. What I showed her was an alternate version of history. One in which she'd left him, though she didn't know it. Hatter's madness was caused by her loss. By my machinations. The Alice with Hatter now, she wasn't the one The Gray had destined to be his original match."

I heard her pain, and I wanted to ease it somehow. "He may have suffered greatly, Galeta, but he found his great love. None could see this Alice and Hatter together now and think he suffers. He adores her. So who's to say that your interference wasn't also destined somehow? That maybe the Gray got it wrong?"

Her eyes flashed to mine. "What?"

I could tell by the note of shock in her tone that she'd never once entertained that idea as being a possibility. Being gentle, I thought of a conversation I'd once had with Mother several months after Seraphina's death. I'd thought her words nonsense then. Too wrapped up in my anger and depression to try and understand what she was trying to tell me. That, or I simply hadn't wanted to believe it was possible. But a part of me was finally beginning to grasp the truth.

"If you love something and you let it go and it doesn't come back, did it ever truly love you?" I was pricked by my own words, and my thoughts strayed and my heart shook.

Always, I'd blamed myself for her death, and I knew a part of me always would. But if I expected Galeta to believe my words, then shouldn't I at least try to do the same?

Were Hades and Aphrodite right? Had Seraphina never really loved me at all? Had any part of her ever cared?

"Do you really believe that, Prince?"

Yanked from my dangerous thoughts, I looked back at the pale fairy still kneeling before me. Seraphina had been the greatest love of my life. I'd never wanted another woman before or since, not with the same depth of longing. I'd vowed after Seraphina's funeral that I would never again fall in love.

But staring into this fairy's eyes, I felt something unavoidable inside of me shift. A fissure that'd been wide and fractured now didn't seem such an impossible hurdle to overcome.

I wasn't going to say I loved this fairy. But what I was ready to own up to was that I knew I was finally ready to let Seraphina's ghost go. And that maybe, just maybe, I didn't need to be alone all the rest of my days.

"Yes, little fae, I do."

We went to bed that night with soft looks between us. Neither of us had felt up to leaving the safety of our hut. We'd shared dinner in silence. But the silence hadn't been tense.

It'd been warm, full of stolen glances and questions.

And when she'd gone to bed, I'd stood sentry at her door. She didn't cry once.

Opening lazy eyes, feeling as though I'd slept twenty years rather than only a few hours, I stretched out tired muscles and moaned appreciatively.

I couldn't remember the last time I'd slept better. Ready to take care of my morning necessaries, I was just about to turn, when a spot of color snagged my eye.

Whipping my head around, I stared at the fire in dazed wonder. Flames, which had once been black and gray, were now burning ruby red and deepest gold.

Everything else was still in shades of gray. But the fire glowed. I shook my head, wondering if I still dreamed. But when I walked over to it and reached a hand inside, the warmth of it licked and danced across my flesh.

The door behind me opened not long after. I glanced over my shoulder. Galeta looked not at me, but at the fire.

"Is that—"

Awed wonder caught in her throat as I nodded. "Aye, love, you're changing things."

Blue eyes, far darker than I remembered them being, looked back to me. She was changing too. I wasn't sure how, but I knew it deep in my marrow. Something had happened last night.

72

Now we only had to figure out how to keep it happening.

Chapter 13: I Killed Them All...

Galeta

I was afraid to step out the door, to confront whatever might be thrown at me.

Syrith walked toward me, stopping only when he reached my side.

"Have you counted all the grain in the wood yet?" he asked deeply, sounding completely serious, but I knew he teased me.

Giving an exaggerated eye roll, I shook my head. I'd slept decently last night, the first time in years for me, but I still felt sleepy and muddled. And not quite ready to be teased yet.

"You tease, and yet I am not certain I can handle what awaits me out there."

My fingers clenched, my nails digging sharply into my palm as my heart began to race.

His hand slipped into mine. He didn't look down at our joined fingers. Didn't draw attention to his actions. He simply let me cling to him.

Biting my lower lip, I stared without seeing at the door. "What if I can't do this?" I whispered so low, I wasn't sure I'd actually intended him to hear.

But he was a dragon and clearly heard me. "You brought color into that flame, Galeta. You, not I. Not anyone else. You can do this."

I wasn't certain I was making myself clear here. "But what if I don't want to do this, Syrith?"

He moved until his entire body faced mine, his boots scraping the tip of my bare toes, causing me to shiver at the intensity written upon his thick brows.

"I do not know the rules of this Mirror, fae. I do know that you and I have a life to return to. We cannot remain in this place forever."

"But what if I can?" I pressed on. Maybe it made me a chicken, but I didn't care right now. I suspected what awaited me outside these doors was more of the same. Visions, memories of the past I couldn't erase. Proof of my misdeeds. "I'm safe here. Protected. Sheltered."

His fingers clenched mine, cutting through my frenzied and fearful thoughts. "You are a fairy. The great and powerful Blue. You were created to bring life to our realm, our world. Look at that fire, Galeta. Tell me you do not crave the colors."

I wanted to pinch my eyes shut and drown out his words, but I did as he asked. I looked at that fire, shielding my heart in a thick wedge of rime. Telling myself not to weaken, not to give in to the wisdom of his words.

But as a moth to flame, I drowned in the beautiful snap and curl of rubies and gold. He was right; I did love color. And this place, this dreary, awful landscape, made me feel dead inside.

I hadn't realized a tear had slipped down my cheek until he swiped it up with the pad of his thumb.

"I'm right here with you, Galeta. I will not leave your side. Whatever comes at us, we can weather this together."

As he'd said, he had a life to get back to. I wasn't sure what awaited him in Wonderland. His people. His family. Perhaps even a new love. I squashed the sudden twinge of hurt that flared through me at the thought.

Fairies did not fall in love.

We weren't built that way.

Once, I might have cursed him, told him he couldn't leave ever, that if I stayed, so would he. But he was right—he had a life, his peoples to return to. I had nothing. No family. No Buttons. No one.

"Come, fae." He squeezed my fingers once more. "This doesn't have to be so bad. We know what's coming now. We know how to protect ourselves."

He was saying "we," but he really meant "you," and I knew it. Still, it was easier pretending we truly were in this together. I nodded softly, and he flicked at a curl that'd landed on my shoulder.

My hair had lengthened during the night. Well, lengthened wasn't really the right word. It had softened. The impossibly tight and slightly ridiculous corkscrew curls had relaxed a fair bit, so that now I appeared to have soft waves rather than ringlets. Feeling oddly self-conscious about that, I glanced down at the floor.

Syrith was right—I was changing, and I wasn't sure whether I liked it or not.

"Are you ready?" he asked me in that deep voice of his that always seemed to turn my knees to putty.

My throat was tight. My pulse fluttering. My stomach a queasy, sick mess. I was so far from ready. He opened the door.

Light blasted my eyes. I winced, covering them with my hand. Curiosity had made me wonder whether there would be spots of color outside too, but it was just as depressingly gray as ever.

That same path that'd led us into the Hatter's old world awaited me. But this time there was no busy city square or people. Ahead lay a fog of thick clouds glowing with random bursts of lightning.

He tugged, and I dug in my feet, my wings flapping erratically with my need to shove that door shut, race back to my room, and hide from the world.

"You're not alone today, Galeta. Trust me."

My eyes locked with his. Several seconds passed. He didn't move. Didn't say anything else. Only waited on me to decide.

Taking a final shuddery breath, I forced my feet to move. The moment I crossed the threshold, the safety of our hut vanished.

Gasping, I twirled, searching frantically for its landmark.

"The same happened the last time. You're okay, fae. You know what this mirror plans to do now. We follow the path, we find that memory, and we return home."

My gaze snapped to his at his mention of home.

More specifically to "us" returning to it.

He nodded, causing a thick lock of dark hair to slip over his eye. I didn't think. I simply leaned up on tiptoe and brushed it back with fingertips gone cold as ice.

His mouth parted just slightly. I still hadn't pulled back. My cold fingers tingled from the heat of his flesh, and I swallowed hard.

"You promise you won't leave me?" I asked unsteadily.

"Never."

Harpy

I clapped my hands, causing a rumble of thunder to roll through the thick clouds before them. But neither of them heard, locked in the intense gaze of love's first bloom.

"Creator," I whispered, "you were right. She is changing, and all because of him."

No, my golden one, it is not he, but she.

I frowned. "But you said—"

Wind whispered through the long length of my hair. *I said he would open up her eyes. But the change can only come from deep within one's own heart.*

That made sense, I supposed. But watching the two of them together, witnessing their shared moment of intimacy the night before, I couldn't help but begin to grow curious about it all.

I understood love of one for another. But I was learning that I'd never truly understood the love between partners. The magic inherent in that kind of union.

Galeta grew stronger because of Syrith's belief in her.

"The land changes, Creator. As does she. I begin to believe that she might yet overcome the seed of darkness."

Yes. In here, where I've dampened that darkness. But were she to ever leave, she'd become worse than ever before. The darkness still lives on within her, harpy.

I sighed, wringing my hands nervously. "But that is where the vessel comes in. Where is it? You said—"

Worry not, golden one. The vessel comes even now. But the journey is not quite done yet.

The thought of the vessel choosing not to accept the dark curse made my chest ache. Seeing the hope spring alive in Galeta's eyes, the promise of love in Syrith's, I'd never wanted to see a happily ever after more than I did now.

If anyone deserved one, it was she.

Suddenly, fog obscured my vision, and I knew that it was the Creator's doing.

"What—"

Some things, little one, should not be shared with others. And you still have a task to do. Do not forget why you've been sent. Soon, Syrith will be forced to meet up with another dark queen. You must prepare that realm and make certain that he does not nearly perish, as he did last time. The Prince must be protected at all costs. It is imperative now more than ever. The land rumbles, and destiny cries out to me. Galeta will restore balance once more but not without him by her side.

Glum to my very core, because things were just beginning to get interesting between the fairy and the dragonborne, I nodded dutifully. "Aye, my Creator. I shall."

Syrith

We walked together, arm in arm. She was quieter this time. Not quite as fearful but still alert, still slightly on edge, awaiting whatever came next.

Now, having spent so many days together, I found myself growing exceedingly curious about the woman I'd been sent to guard.

Our path wound through a deep forest. The fog floating ever before us, moving as we did so that we could never quite reach it. But the deeper onto the trail we went, the darker the clouds became.

A balmy zephyr blew, bringing with it the sweet scent of honeysuckle in bloom. Her lips tipped up at the corners.

"I love flowers."

Blinking, I looked at her. Galeta intrigued me, but she'd given me very little of herself in the short time we'd known one another. Rarely speaking unless I spoke first. The fact that she did so now so shocked me, I latched onto the first thought that popped into my head.

"I'd imagine all fairies do."

"No." She looked at me, and my heart skipped a beat at the sparkle in her deep-blue eyes. "Not like me."

Curling one hand over hers, I rubbed her knuckles lightly. "Tell me more about yourself, Galeta. I fear I know very little."

Giving a self-conscious snort of laughter, she lifted her brows. "I'm an open book, Syrith, or didn't you know that?"

I paused, realizing she'd just teased me. "Did you just—"

Biting onto her bottom lip with her cute little fangs, she gave a one-shouldered shrug. "Hush. I know not of what you speak. I've a reputation to uphold, beast."

My cheeks hurt from grinning so broadly. "Your secret is safe with me."

For the first time since we left the hut, she seemed far more relaxed. Expelling a deep breath, she gave her head a tiny shake. "You wish to know more about me. I'm sure I don't know why, but I shall endeavor to answer any questions you might have."

"Why the sudden change of heart?" I asked, eyelids narrowing at this rapid turnaround. Not that I didn't enjoy it—I certainly did—but I wasn't altogether sure I should trust it either.

Galeta had walls a mile high. Even in our short time together, I knew one thing with a certainty—she didn't let others in. Was it possible I might become the exception?

Why did my stomach suddenly feel knotted at the thought?

Fluttering her free hand around, she said, "There's nothing else to distract me at the moment. Perhaps talking would help ease my panic a little."

I hated that she was still so scared, but I understood it too. If the situation were reversed, I wasn't sure I'd want another privy to the darkest parts of my past. Squeezing her arm just a little tighter, I grinned.

"Then this is an opportunity too good to squander. So let me see, which question should I ask first?"

She groaned. "Why do I suddenly regret my decision?"

I chuckled. "I promise it won't be so bad, fairy. Okay." I nodded quickly. "I thought of a question. Why do you think you love flowers more than others?"

Her shoulders visibly eased at that question, and I was glad I had started out with something simple and easy.

"There are parts of my past, my beginnings, that I do not recall." She blinked, and her eyes were far away from me, from here.

Her distance gave me the opportunity to study her as I wished. Seraphina had been tall, nearly as tall as I, with long ebony hair that'd trailed down to her waist in a thick straight line. There'd been a tiny cleft in her chin, one I loved to rub my thumb across in our shared, stolen moments. Deep-brown eyes that made me feel as though I were falling whenever I looked into them.

Galeta was the opposite in just about every way. Shorter than me by several inches, and a colorful splash of alternating shades of blue and pale white.

When I'd first met her, she'd seemed as sharp and foreboding as the ice of her gown. But there was a gentleness to her now. The cold, unyielding features seemed more graceful, softer somehow.

She blinked, shaking her head as though to clear away the memories, and I cleared my throat, not sure why I couldn't seem to stop waxing poetic about this woman.

"But I do recall one thing." She looked at me, and my insides suddenly seemed to tumble together.

"And that is?"

A beatific smile wreathed her elfin features. "Flowers. The blueprints for them. All inside of here. Life."

She pressed a fist to her heart.

I frowned. Blueprints implied creation that first wasn't. Was she saying what I thought she was? "What do you mean, blueprints?"

Blue eyes latched onto mine with open frankness. "I mean the very beginning of it all, Syrith. I was there."

What she said was astonishing and made me shiver. "Wait, that would mean—"

"That I am very, very old." She snickered. "Don't remind me."

My lips twitched. Kingdom was several millions of years old. It wasn't possible that this nubile creature before me could possibly be that ancient. The term immortal was used rather loosely in our world, but very few beings actually were. Death could come to us all, be it by a spelled blade or killing curse. There were very few creatures around since the beginning of time.

She sighed deeply, shaking her head. "Truly, I wish I wasn't what I am, dragonborne, but I am what I am. I was an original fae. One of the first twelve. There are no others around, just me."

"What happened to them?"

77

Her chin trembled, and I knew she'd not answer me. Her breathing had hitched, and she made to turn aside. But I tipped my finger beneath her chin.

"You can tell me anything, fairy. I will not judge you."

"How could you not?" She sniffed. "I judge everyone. Even you." Her laughter was sad and miserable sounding.

"Because that's not what I was sent here to do. I was sent here to be here for you. And at first I couldn't understand why. You seemed like a dreadful person, one who I did not want to meet."

A tiny sound between a humph and amusement dropped off her tongue. "Get in line, then, beast, for you would be no different from anyone else. You want to know what happened to the original eleven? I'll tell you, but you will not like it, and perhaps you might even start to hate me for it. I killed them. All of them. To gain their powers. But the colors could never truly be extinguished. That is not how the Creator designed us. Others came after them—some I killed, some I let live."

Her words were indifferent—not cold, but monotone. As though she were merely reciting a weather report. But I saw in the way her shoulders bunched and her jaw muscle clenched that she waited for me to turn on her the same way everyone else eventually had with her.

I did not like hearing what she'd done.

But I was learning there was far more to Galeta than what first met the eye. She was intelligent, she'd wanted their power—or at least that was what she said—but there was more. I heard the unspoken hitch in her words.

"What aren't you telling me?"

She blinked, causing the aloof mask she wore to crack just a tiny bit. "What? I told you already. I killed them for their powers. Nothing more." She shrugged.

But I wasn't buying it. "No, there is more. I hear what you're not saying. You're smart, fairy. There was a reason. So what was it?"

Her mouth parted just slightly, and she stopped walking, turning me around so that she could look at me head on. The fog before us rumbled deeply and was now a deep shade of ebony.

Wherever we were headed, we were close now. I smelled brimstone in the air.

"Stop trying to find some sort of goodness in me, Syrith. Do not turn me into something I am not. You want to know why I killed them? I did it for exactly the reasons I said. I thought that by consuming the colors, I could"—she squeezed her eyes shut—"somehow, I don't know...stop it."

Tears were sliding out of the corners of her eyes, and I sensed she was close to breaking. But whether she'd known it or not, Galeta had just proven my theory correct. There had been more, even if she'd not been aware of it.

"Stop what?"

She laughed, but the sound was frantic and wild. "I don't know. But something awful inside of me."

Her hand landed on her chest, and her fingers clenched, bunching her gown in her fist. "It didn't used to be so bad. But now, it's consumed me. All I am, all I can ever be, is this darkness. And I thought, maybe, maybe with all the colors combined, I could destroy it. Destroy me. So you see, there is nothing redeemable in me, dragonborne."

Grabbing her arms, I squeezed nearly to the point of pain, causing her eyes to snap toward mine. Their whites were wide and flooded with hurt. But not because of me. Giving her a small shake, I shook my head.

"But you can fight it, because you're fighting it now."

"No." She planted her hands on my chest, as though she meant to shove me back, but instead she curled her fingers into it. "Don't you see, beast, intelligent as you are? Can't you feel it? The great magic that pulses in this mirror realm? Whatever it is, it has dampened my darkness, but I know if I leave here I would return to who I once was. And I cannot do that. I cannot be who I was again. She is an awful, wicked being unworthy of anybody's love."

I heard the pain and truth in her words, and though I shook my head in denial, a part of me sensed she was right. There was magic here. Powerful magic.

"I like you as you are, fae," I whispered brokenly.

She hiccupped on a sob. "That is only because you do not truly know me. I fear if you did—"

Framing her heart-shaped face in my big palms, I rubbed my thumbs across the silky feel of her skin. She shivered, and her nails dug into my chest. I hissed and trembled but did not move.

The fog rolled between our legs, and I knew the memories were now upon us. I did not tear my gaze off hers, demanding silently that she do the same.

I scented my blood pooling down my shirt from where she dug her nails into me, and I shook my head.

"I'm with you, fairy. Always."

Chapter 14: In Which a Monster Learns to Love

Galeta

The moment the fog veiled us, I knew what memory would come. I'd smelled the brimstone and fire.

This memory had decided the fate of many.

Trees vanished. The path disappeared.

The fog swirled, coalescing into sharp images. Me seated at the head of a large table, with eleven others sitting beside me. I felt detached from that fairy. She was a part of me, and yet none of this felt quite real either.

I bit my bottom lip, staring at her. Staring at me.

Memory Galeta was cold, swathed in thick sheets of ice. Her hair a bright cerulean. She gazed at the determined fairy godmother flitting before her, clutching onto her star-tipped wand.

The fairy was Danika. And the person on trial was her charge, Gerard—the male whoreson. But he was not there. Danika had sent him packing for Earth before either memory Galeta or her sisters could get their hands on him. Memory Galeta could have brought him back, of course. But then she'd have had to tip her hand that she had the power to open dimensions between realms, a power only godmothers were supposed to possess. So she'd kept her charade in place, confident in the knowledge that she'd still be able to destroy not only him, but his future line as well.

Memory Galeta had gazed into the future, had seen the destruction of his life if she tore his Belle from him. She'd given Belle to the Beast. And Gerard had self-destructed as beautifully as she'd known he would.

Danika, the ever-present blight in her life, had her arms spread wide, her wings flapping angrily as she glared unholy death at memory Galeta. Danika and she went way back. Many hundreds of years.

To another time. Another story, one far more personal to her. Few of our kind remembered the truth of who Danika truly was. To them, she'd only ever been this gray-haired, chubby little fairy. But I knew the truth of it, and so did she.

Danika had never forgiven me for my interference in her life.

All of this, the past and present, collided together within me. Bringing up the memories of what I felt that day, how I'd sneered and laughed in my mind, knowing that I was about to put the final nail in Danika's coffin once and for all. I'd stripped everything from Dani that meant anything. It'd become a perverse game for me. But one I always had to walk a fine line with too.

None could know just how many strings I'd pulled to ensure her pain. The me of today felt sick about it, but the me of yesteryear gloated, knowing how much my words were about to hurt her.

The Blue smirked at the head of the table, giving her head a slight shake.

My heart clenched as I wished I could take it all back. Wished more than anything that Syrith weren't here.

His fingers squeezed mine.

"You cannot do whatever it is you think to do, Blue. You must give him—" Danika's words were a ghostly echo.

I laughed. Both future and present me laughed. The sound high-pitched and keening and spilling unwanted from my lips. My memories were jumbled and colliding within me now. Making me feel fractured and cracked.

Was I here?

Was I there?

I was losing myself to the past. Floating away. Becoming who I once was. But Syrith was right there. He caught me. Held me fast. Pulled me close and whispered into my ear, "Stay with me, little fae. Stay with me."

And so I did. I clung to his shirt, buried my face in his chest, and squeezed my eyes shut. But I could not drown out the words I'd spoken to her that night.

"There will be no more chances. He has been sentenced to death."

All gasped, and I cringed, wishing I could burrow into the earth, hide away from everyone and everything.

"You cannot do that!" Esmeralda the Green cried. *"I am the judge of fate, not you, Blue."*

I didn't need to see to remember the White looking at me, her eyes radiant and lambent, her mouth opened in shock. *"What have you done, Blue? What have you done? You've altered the fates...you cannot—"*

"And yet it is done!" The Blue cackled. *"You cannot undo the words I have wrought."*

"This cannot be!" Danika shrieked. *"You have broken faith with our laws. With our—"*

"Silence!" The Blue shrieked. *"You wish to save your pathetic charge?"* The Blue laughed deeply, the sound chilling. *"Fine. If he falls in love within a month's time, his destiny shall be spared."*

I'd not passed that verdict to please anyone. I'd passed it because I'd known the infamous Lothario could never truly love again. He'd given Belle his everything, and she'd shredded his heart to ribbons. It'd been my way to prove to everyone that I wasn't so bad. But I'd known Gerard could never pass the test. And then I had another, even more destructive idea in mind. On the very off chance that Danika actually did manage to find him a match, I would make it so that love could never sprout from the union.

I would tell no one of my duplicity, not yet. But without sex, could there ever truly be love?

My lips had twitched, and the whites of Danika's eyes had swallowed her gaze in fear. She hadn't known what I'd had planned, but she'd suspected.

Again, past and present tumbled together, and I went from feeling bloated with pain and regret to squeezing down on the diabolical laugh that filled my throat.

"It's gone, Galeta. The memory is gone."

Sucking in a sharp breath, I looked up, trembling as the blessed darkness of nothingness enveloped me. I'd never thought I'd like to see the black as much as I did now. But before I could get a chance to express that sentiment, memories swirled in on the fog once more.

A castle in the clouds.

A desperate man seated on his throne. A child locked in a cage deep below and howling out with madness.

Rumpelstiltskin, blond. Deadly. Beautiful.

Syrith's arms banded tightly around me. His jaw grazed my temple. Inhaling deeply his rich dragon's scent, I tried in vain to get my breathing under control.

The Blue walked into the scene. As cold as ever. Smirking with a secret only she knew.

Rumpel looked up, his fingers digging into the skull affixed to his dark throne. A warrior of old from a land not of Kingdom. He was a demon. A monster. And the old Galeta had been rather fond of the darkness in him.

Until he'd begun meddling. Until he'd gone looking into bloodlines.

"I win," Galeta taunted him.

He scoffed. His cultured voice, barely rising as he said, *"For now. You might believe it so. But I always get what I want. You think I didn't notice your keen interest in putting that French whore down? Why the sudden interest in him, Galeta?"*

Memory Galeta's smile didn't slip, even as her insides trembled. There were few in Kingdom as capable as she, but he was one of them. Heartless. Mercenary. And a bastard.

They'd shared their bodies and beds once before. Attracted, both of them, to the caged power and raw darkness inside of each other. But there'd been no love—there couldn't be between ones such as them.

Memory Galeta shook her head. *"I know not what you mean, devil. Just know this—you'll never free him of his curse. Or yours."*

"You know, fae, I always thought myself the biggest bastard in this land, but no, I don't think so anymore. I'm going to discover what it is you don't want me to know about Gerard. And when I do, you'll sorely regret your interference."

She laughed. The sound cold and menacing. *"Do it, and I vow to the darkness that I'll kill that thing you call your son..."*

"Enough!" I screamed, shoving away from Syrith. I could take no more of this. "Mirror, stop!"

That shout of power exploded from within me, causing the memories to shatter like a glass tossed to the ground. Suddenly, I was shoved out of that castle, back into the dreary, awful mirror realm.

I stood once more on the path, the trees gently swaying around us.

I felt Syrith's eyes all over me, but I couldn't look at him. Not like this. Not so raw. Covering my eyes with my hands, I crumpled into a heap upon the forest floor, laying my head upon the dust-covered ground.

Just a moment later, his hands were upon me. I was weak. Pathetic. I didn't deserve kindness. I didn't deserve him.

I could not stop the tears. They came and came and came and never would stop again, I just knew it.

"Please, Syrith. Please don't." I wasn't sure what I was asking of him.

But when his hands curled around my body and he hefted me straight into his arms, bringing me tight to his chest, I buried my face in his shirt and shuddered.

Syrith

The next two nights were brutal for her and me.

I'd thought we'd made some headway, but after the memories of that day, Galeta had once more retreated into her shell.

I'd wondered if that might affect the magic transforming this land, but it hadn't. The glow of the hearth was still as strong and beautiful as ever.

I sat on the couch, studying the door, wishing I could enter in there and hold her. Tell her she would be okay. All right.

But the truth of it was, what she went through now, she had to go through alone. Redemption never came without pain.

I was beginning to see just how devious Galeta truly had been. And it hurt me, I wouldn't lie. I did not like knowing that the woman I was beginning to fall madly in love with could be anything other than what she was when she was with me.

And it was hard not to judge her for it. Just as she'd told me it would be. I was ashamed of my feelings. Ashamed of feeling ashamed. But it was honest, and it was true. And I needed to work through my own doubts as well.

I wasn't here to make the fairy fall in love with me. Though I was falling quickly for her. No, I needed to be here for her. I needed to be that strong shoulder she could cry on.

And I couldn't do that right now.

The air squeezed with power, and I didn't need to look up to know the goddess had returned. I scented verbena and lavender in the air.

"How is she?" Aphrodite asked.

I shook my head. "Not well. Not well at all." Finally looking over my shoulder, I acknowledged her with a flick of my lashes. "I worry that perhaps this place isn't good for her. That perhaps reliving the past might fracture what tiny bit of good remains in her."

Dite sighed, glancing over my shoulder to the door. "Who can say, Prince? All I know is I taste the Fates' movements on the winds. Change is coming. And whatever you're doing, you must keep doing it."

Heavy hearted, and weary from not sleeping the past two nights, I ran my fingers through my thick hair, causing the tips to stand on end.

"I hate to be the bearer of bad news, Syrith, but today you meet with Baba Yaga. And your head must be in the game. Do you hear me? That witch will pull no punches."

I shrugged, rubbing my palms forcefully together. My mind was not on that stupid love tournament. I cared not what happened in that arena. I was consumed by my need to fix Galeta, but I also understood this was part of the package deal.

"I rather loathe that clone," I muttered.

Dite nodded slowly. "Yes, as do we all."

But she seemed distracted as she said it. As though her mind were far away and on other matters.

I frowned. "Are you okay, Love?"

"What?" She blinked then huffed and batted my words away with a roll of her wrists. "I'm fine. Fine." Her smile was weak. "Let us go, before we are missed."

She held out her hand to me. I stood. Looked back one last time at the door before nodding and following the goddess into the time portal.

Aphrodite didn't linger when we arrived at the tree world.

I called it that because the behemoths towered into the heavens, with their canopies far above me.

Birdsong trilled all around, though I could spy none of them. The clone, rather than lying at my feet, as she'd been last time, already hovered before me.

Her eyes were cold and the color of ice. Except around the rims. There they were a deeper azure.

Her gown too looked a little changed. Rather than ice crystals dangling down, the danglers appeared more like clear gems.

She frowned. "You're here?"

I cocked my head, not sure what she hinted at. "Where else would I be, Galeta?"

Her frown pulled down even harder, hard enough that even though I didn't care for this version of my fae, I began to worry. "Are you okay?" I asked after another few minutes of silence.

At any moment, Baba and her mate would show, and I knew we'd not be able to talk, but the clone was acting strangely.

Taking a deep breath, she gazed at me with icy, hard eyes. "Last time, did you spare that horse? You threw yourself in her path, didn't you?"

Her words came out sharp but also filled with curiosity. I wasn't sure how sentient this clone truly was, and I wondered if somehow it knew.

"Why do you care?"

"I don't." She was quick to answer, shaking her head so forcefully, her twisted curls bobbed around her slim shoulders. "I. Don't." That last word trailed off, as if she were deep in thought.

Up until now, I'd only ever received hate from this wee thing. The gods had warned me that this wasn't truly Galeta, and yet...my heart rate kicked up, and I couldn't help but lay a hand against her shoulder. "Fairy, I—"

Hissing, she rolled out from under my grip and in that same instant had her wand pointed directly at my face. "Touch me again, *be-beast*, and"—she shook her head, looking as confused as before—"and I'll eviscerate you."

Holding up my hands in a posture of submission, I lifted a brow. She'd called me beast. The same way Galeta would. Soft and sweet. Was the clone changing too? Did they know?

Did she know?

"I won't touch you again," I said steadily.

She blinked. "I don't. I can't—"

"Aw, isn't this touching. Looks like the fairy's about to do my job for me. What say you, Freyr?"

Spinning, I rolled out from beneath the clone's wand, twisting sinuously as I used the speed of the dragon so that I shielded the clone from Baba's gimleted stare.

Her male, whom I could only assume to be said Freyr, snorted. "Sure looked like it, witch."

Baba was a stunning woman and a far cry from what I'd been expecting. Stories spoke of a hag who ate children for her lunch. Before me stood an average-sized woman with porcelain skin and long brown tresses. She dressed in a most peculiar manner. Black combat boots, flesh-toned underwear, and a brown leather vest with its pockets full to bursting.

"Baba?" I asked slowly, still not completely certain this wild, eccentric thing was the woman of legend.

The blond-haired Freyr chuckled deeply and shook his head. "Well, I suppose I'll leave you to it, hag. Though remember my words, will you?"

He'd called her a hag, but even I heard the note of fondness in his words. The witch must have too, because her lips pulled up into a brief but exultant grin. "Whatever you say, fatty."

My brows lifted. Those two were very strange.

"All right, I'm tired of you two already." Baba rolled her neck from side to side, causing it to crack loudly. "If I were you, Prince, I'd just step back a tad. It'll only take me a minute to end the miserable, pathetic creature hiding behind your back."

My spine went rigid at the threat. Not because I really cared about what happened to the clone. But I did care about what happened to Galeta. I had no idea if injury to this one could affect my female.

I grinned, feeling the heated surge of battle coil through me. There wasn't much dragonbornes loved more in this world than a good bloody carcass and a violent tussle. Sex or otherwise.

Cracking my own neck, I called my magic to me. I'd not shifted in two days, which meant the shift this time would be excruciating. And bizarre. But perhaps I could use the latter to my advantage. It was said that there were few species alive in Kingdom more knowledgeable than Baba Yaga. If she knew what I really was, she'd know how to end me.

So better to never give her that knowledge.

A roar ripped from my throat, a sound that seemed dragged up from the very bowels of the Underworld. And then the shift started.

Shaping and forming into monstrous visions of creatures I'd taken in the past. Wings for arms. A snake's tail for legs. Bloody, red eyes. Canines longer than a panther's.

Baba's eyes went wide, and she looked stunned for a moment. But a moment was all I needed. I would not kill her, but I would stun her into submission and somehow figure out a way to get the clone away from here so that Aphrodite could whisk me back as soon as could be to Galeta.

But the witch wasn't as old and crafty as she'd come to be by being weak. A flash of her hand shoving inside her vest was all the warning I got, and then my world was suddenly rocked. Lights distorted my vision, and the clanging of cymbals deafened me. Disoriented, I dropped to my knees, putting my hands to my temples.

I expected another death shot. I was a Prince. I'd been raised to battle as a warrior; it was the way of my kind. But even I was helpless when it came to the wrathful magic of an enraged Queen.

Hearing a scratch of movement different from the cacophony to the left of me, I batted out wildly, catching something. With a whoosh of breath, I heard Baba fall with a thud.

And then more lights blasted around me. This time, a sizzling spark of mighty power.

Stories would lead one to believe fairy godmothers were weak and matronly. But I'd already seen the clone fight once. She was deadly and wicked.

Baba howled.

The lights that'd blinded me began to slowly abate, and I managed to catch Baba scrabbling to her feet for purchase. The battle was on then. Intense and magnificent as I watched two powerful women fight it out.

Last time, the clone had seemed possessed, intent on killing the centauress. This time, she battled fiercely, but a part of me rather suspected she held something of herself back too.

In the way she'd sometimes seek cover rather than parry. The clone had been distracted by me during the previous battle. This time, she seemed determined and focused. Casting me furtive glances now and again, as though to assure herself that I was well.

I frowned.

How was that possible?

Was Galeta so changed in the mirror realm that somehow she was affecting even the sliver of soul up here? Anything was possible with magic, but if she could do that, then wasn't it also possible that perhaps Galeta wouldn't be doomed to spending her eternity in that gray world?

Could she come into the above again? Could she control whatever darkness held her gripped? I was lost to my thoughts, watching as the clone kept Baba on her heels, forcing her back so far into the tree line that at one point the witch tripped.

Galeta raised her wand, and I growled but then hesitated. The fairy would kill her now. I couldn't allow that, and yet something inside of me stilled. Waiting. Maybe hoping.

The Blue looked at me. Her thin brows were furrowed and full of questions.

We were locked in one another's sights, never noticing Baba getting to her feet.

"Hey, you! Blue bug. Miss me?"

Both the clone and I glanced up. Baba twirled on her heel and, in one swift movement, pulled her drawers down, exposing the very pale globes of her bum and wiggling it back and forth at us.

She slapped it, causing it to jiggle distractingly. "I can crush walnuts with this thing!" She giggled wildly.

And while we'd been diverted by her absurd antics, neither the clone nor I had seen the vial whip out in her hand before it was too late.

"No!" I roared, racing toward Galeta.

The vial landed with a violent *thunk* against her forehead. The fairy gasped and then crashed to the thick branch beneath her. Eyes closed and looking as though she did not breathe. I grabbed up her slight form, cuddling her tight to me. Releasing a shuddery breath when I heard her slight inhalation.

"Freyr, bloody hell, get us out of here!" Baba snapped.

In the next instant, a strong wind blew through the trees, revealing the bow of a massive wooden ship. Standing astride was her male beaming down at her.

"Did you really—"

She lifted a finger. "You're never to speak of *that* again. Go!"

They flew into the winds, and I looked back down at the clone.

Immediately, that same darkness rolled between us, Aphrodite's cover to help me get out of this realm.

I felt the squeeze of air and the return of the goddess's power. But my eyes were for the clone alone. Brushing a tight curl away from the corner of her mouth, I shook my head.

"Did you see it? Did you see it, Love? Did you see what happened?"

"The clone is changing." The voice was feminine but not Aphrodite's.

Still clinging tight to the now no longer breathing clone, I stared into the golden eyes of the harpy.

"If she can change up here, then surely—"

Her eyes were soft and sad as she said, "No, dragonborne. She cannot. Yes, Galeta's soul is changing, but that does not negate the fact that she remains who she is."

Feeling angry with the harpy, though I knew none of this was her fault, I growled. "What is she? Who is she? Why will no one give me a straight bloody answer?"

She stared down at her sandaled feet, and I felt an immediate wash of shame at my outburst. Clenching my jaw, I muttered, "You did not deserve that. Forgive me, Harpy."

Shrugging but giving me a wimpy smile, she nodded. "It is okay, Prince. I think I'm beginning to understand what is happening between you two. If you want to know who she really is, then I'll tell you. She is a good woman who has borne a terrible burden for far too long. Within her heart beats the seed of darkness. She is the protector of all of Kingdom. The Pink, as she was once known, sacrificed herself to keep that darkness away from all of Its creation. What you are seeing now is the soul of the female who once was and who could maybe be again."

Trembling, because I'd never expected an actual answer, and also terrified because this seemed far greater a burden than merely someone preoccupied with madness, I asked, "Take it out of her, then. Make her whole again. If it's true that she's borne this burden for so long, then doesn't she deserve to be free of it now?"

She nodded. "Yes. There is another vessel."

"Where is it?" I snapped, growling with frustration. "Give it to me. Let me fix her."

Harpy shook her head. "I cannot. The vessel is not yet here. But it comes. It has assured me it comes."

"When?"

She blinked. "Soon. I hope."

That answer wasn't good enough for me. "End her torments. Stop those hated memories. Leave her in peace."

Again she shook her head. "Would that I could, Prince. But the darkness has been so long a part of her that she must be purged."

"So making her relive that pain..."

"Yes." She nodded. "Believe it or not, it is healing her. Slowly maybe, but it is. Trust me, Prince, I did not bring you here to watch you fail. I believe in the Creator, and so should you. If It says that the vessel comes soon, then the vessel comes soon."

None of what she said made much sense to me. All I knew was I was being told to wait. And so I'd wait. My kind was good at that.

She glanced up. "I must go now. But a few things I must tell you. Galeta knows nothing of this past sacrifice. She knows only of the darkness in her soul, and before the games began, she was trying to end herself. To end that darkness. She cannot, though. She never can. If she kills the body, she releases the seed into the world. Tread lightly with her, Prince. And wait on me to hand you that vessel, for I vow I shall soon." Her feathers plumped and fluttered as though she meant to wing away, but she paused. "One last thing. In case you doubt her. Don't. None could have fought the darkness as long as she. Those memories you watch, they may seem vile, but she's prevented so much worse."

When she said that, her eyes looked haunted, and I saw the same sort of look cross her eyes as I sometimes saw in Galeta's own. That of a being who'd seen too much. She gave herself a slight shake before giving me a soft smile.

Harpy vanished. And I glanced down at the fairy in my arms. No longer an exact match for the one in my mirrored realm. I stroked my thumb down her soft cheek.

I had been doubting. But the moment Harpy mentioned Galeta trying to end herself, my heart had given a painful squeeze.

Dear gods above, the sacrifice my fairy had made. I had no reason to doubt Harpy's words. All the questions I'd had began to make sense. Why there'd been such an effort by so many to bring Galeta back. Because of fate or some Creator that Harpy had spoken of. Whatever it really was, it no longer mattered to me.

All I knew was, I would go to the ends of the world and back to ensure Galeta's eventual victory. If anyone deserved redemption, it was her.

The air squeezed with the scent of verbena and lavender.

The clone in my arms vanished, returned to her dark and lonely realm, and it was stupid that I suddenly felt bad about that. She wasn't the real Galeta, and yet somehow from the last time to this one, my feelings for the she-devil had begun to alter irrevocably.

"Are you ready to return, Prince?" Aphrodite asked gently.

I finally looked up at her and nodded. "I am."

She covered her parted lips with her fingers, letting out a tiny gasp. I frowned. Her hands landed on my cheeks as she stared deeply into my eyes.

"You know now, don't you, dragonborne? You know why this happened. Why this all happened. You know the truth now."

Her clear blue eyes sparkled, and I wondered how it was that she'd figured that out merely by looking at me.

I nodded, saying nothing.

She nodded too. "Who are you really, Syrith? Why have the Fates brought you into this?"

I wished I had an answer to her question, but I did not. "I am just a man, Love."

Her lips twitched upward. "A man in love. I see it very clearly now. You will save her, Prince."

I clutched at her wrists, hearing pain behind her words. "What are you telling me, goddess?"

Her look grew haunted. "I wish I knew. I only know this—when it's all over, there will be tears."

My heart turned to a rock in my chest. I didn't want tears. I didn't want Fate interfering in any of this. This was about me, about Galeta.

She shook her head, causing her golden cascade of hair to undulate captivatingly. "Too late for that, my boy. Far too late for that."

Chapter 15: In Which a Fairy Meets a Bird

Harpy

"Show yourself, little one," Ty said.

I frowned. I hated that I could never seem to hide from her. Appearing by the stables, I threaded a stalk of wheat between my fingers. Her keen gaze studied me.

"You are not well. Tell me why." Ty took a giant bite from her pear, smearing the juices upon her lips as she wiped down her chin with her fingers.

I gave a one-shouldered shrug. "I am not unwell. I simply am beginning to suspect all is not as I'd imagined."

Her lips pinched. But she asked me nothing. Ty didn't need to; she wasn't like most other people. She thought matters through first before speaking, and sometimes when she did, she said nothing at all that I expected.

Brown-eyed gaze flicking down to the wheat stalk, she studied my hand hard, and I knew she saw what I'd seen this morning.

A marking.

A tiny birthmark that'd not been there before.

The picture of a tree in bloom.

The mark of the vessel. But I couldn't be the vessel. Surely, it wasn't me.

My heart had sunk when I'd noticed it. Maybe I was only holding onto it for a time. The vessel still came, surely.

But something inside of me squirmed.

Coming down here—it wasn't simply to learn about humanity, but to gain my own too. I didn't want to believe this could be, but I worried that I might be acting willfully obtuse too. Surely, though, the Creator would have told me if I were the one.

Right?

I swallowed hard.

"Talk to me, Harpy."

I sucked my bottom lip between my teeth. I'd come to Ty because I'd known I could talk to her. Could tell her what I was feeling. And she was so smart, so brilliant, maybe she could help me to understand what was truly happening. Maybe I could still save Galeta, and myself too.

"What if you've discovered that you are supposed to be the hero, but you don't want to be? Even if that means the death of another?"

My words were quiet, almost a whisper of sound, and it killed me to even think it. But I didn't want this. I couldn't be the vessel.

I simply couldn't.

Though I now understood what it meant to be part of this world and the fabric of this universe, I wasn't ready to become the darkness. Wasn't ready to lose myself.

And yet even as I thought it, how could I possibly condemn Galeta to death? Because choosing not to accept that seed meant there'd be no escape for her.

Ever.

"And you are that hero?"

"No!" I was quick to correct and then shuddered. "No," I said softer. "I-I don't know."

A tiny neigh spilled off Ty's tongue, and she shook her head, closing her eyes briefly. "That is truly a terrible burden to bear, little one. And I am sorry for it. But however briefly we've known one another, I can say this with all truth of heart—you will make the right decision, Harpy, because that's who you are. And whatever choice you make, I vow to you that you will not be alone in this. Petra and I, we will help you."

Sniffing, I swiped at the heavy tears that'd fallen unbidden down my cheeks and nodded slowly. Throat too full of words and pain, I could no longer bear her gaze.

The Creator had given me a task. I was the messenger. I still had a job to do. Today, I would visit Galeta face to face. Today, I would look into her eyes and she into mine, and maybe, hopefully, I would know what to do.

Galeta

I felt someone watching me.

My heart gave a painful lurch, imagining for a moment it was Syrith. That he'd been unable to bear my solitude another moment and had sought me out. With a jerk, I shoved off the bed. Swiping at my tear-stained face.

But it was not Syrith staring back at me. Rather, a woman. A very pretty woman with large white wings.

I sniffed. "Who are you?"

Had I brought more life into this realm?

Had this strange woman replaced Syrith? At that, a terrible gasp spilled off my tongue, and I clutched at my chest. I couldn't lose him. I couldn't—

"Fear not, wee one," she said. Her voice was heavenly and soft but heart achingly lovely. "Your dragon is just fine. He's doing a duty for me."

I frowned. Was Syrith spending his days with her? Was that where he disappeared to every so often?

Studying her harder this time, I noted the shapely curve of her body. Her breasts—far larger than my own—and her stunning face. My heart sank. She was exactly right for my dragon.

Even from my spot on the bed, I could see her purity, her innocence—it sparkled all through her.

"What is your name?" I asked gently. I wanted to be angry with her, but it seemed impossible to do. She was simply too good. Too kind to hate.

Her smile was crooked as she said, "That seems to be a common greeting among your kind."

"My kind? Are you not my kind too?"

"No." She shrugged. "I am not of this world. I'm from one beyond, and I have no name. Although your male has taken to calling me Harpy. So I suppose you may call that as well."

"My male? Syrith?" I hated how my heart suddenly beat like a drum inside of me, how slick my palms suddenly felt, and how light-headed I got thinking of him as actually belonging to me.

But that idea was absurd.

Fairies didn't mate.

We had no need for it.

I wet my lips.

Harpy grinned. "Aye. Syrith. I rather like that boy, truth be told. I did not think I would when I first met him. So jaded. So hurt by his life."

I frowned. That didn't sound like Syrith at all. He was goodness personified and the strongest person I knew. He kept putting up with me, after all.

She pinched her lips. "Anyway, I merely came to see how you were, little one."

It would be naïve to assume that Harpy didn't know what was happening in here. She seemed to know an awful lot as it was. So rather than pretend, I shrugged.

"I don't know, to be honest. It hurts. Seeing my past. What I've done. Knowing that no matter how hard I try, I can never seem to stop being...me."

My brows bunched. I'd told her more truth almost anyone else in my past. But she didn't seem to judge me for it. Harpy merely nodded.

"You'll be okay, wee one. Just trust him not to hurt you. That's all that's really holding you back."

"What? I do trust him."

"Well, if you did, you wouldn't have hidden yourself away these past two days, now would you?"

My mouth opened with my readiness to deny it, but her words pierced through me with their barbed truth. I snapped it shut.

Her look was knowing. "At any rate, this will all be better soon. I vow it. So long as you do what you must."

"And that is?"

Harpy spread her arms. "Stop fighting this, Galeta. Let it be. Accept your past for what it was, and move on."

That was easy to say. But my past was an awful, murky, and bloody place. I had hurt anyone who'd ever tried to get close to me; maybe I didn't have the right to hope for anything better than to bear this pain for the rest of my days.

"But my past is ugly. It's terrible. I can't forget, and it pierces me like a blade every time I'm forced to endure it."

A feather fluttered to the ground when Harpy shrugged her trim shoulders. "That's life, girl. Don't you get it? None of us are all good all the time. Do not place Syrith on a pedestal. Open yourself to him. He's no better than you or I."

I sniffed again, wiping at my nose, which I knew was now a bright shade of cherry red. "I know that's not true. Everyone's better than me. I shut off that vision before Syrith could see the rest of it. My words against Rumpel's son hadn't merely been talk. I did not want Syrith to see me like that."

Her eyes turned sad. And neither of us spoke for several moments. But finally, she said, "Then perhaps do something different tonight. Do not worry about yourself and your past. Learn about his. Discover that you two have more in common than you might imagine."

"I honestly can't see how that's possible."

"He returns in but a moment. And I will leave you, but I had to meet you, fairy. I had to see you and you see me."

"Why?"

Harpy's lashes fluttered, and she lost another downy feather as her wings fluttered prettily behind her. "I like you, Galeta. And I hope that you'll know you have a friend. Though you may not know me, I know you. And I've always been rooting for you. Though I do have one question. Just one. And I hope you would answer me honestly. May I ask it?"

Her words were so timid that it moved me. I sniffed, wiping at my nose, and nodded. "Yes, Harpy. You may ask."

"Does it hurt? The darkness? Does it hurt you?"

I didn't want to answer. The question was far more personal than any stranger deserved to ask, and yet I knew I had to answer her. The way her eyes were so big and curious in her face, how gentle she seemed, and how her voice shook. That question hadn't been an easy one for her.

"More than you could possibly know. I would never wish this kind of pain upon my worst enemy."

She shuddered, and her lashes fluttered like wings upon her cheeks. "Thank you, fae."

"Galeta! Please come out now!"

I froze at the sound of Syrith's deep treble. Twirling, I stared at the door. Feeling terrified of everything and yet also steadied by the strange woman's words. Looking back to where Harpy had been, all I saw were two lonely feathers lying on the floor.

Smiling softly, I muttered to myself, "Trust him. Trust him, Galeta. You can do that. You can do this."

90

Using my magic to transform to human size, I squared my shoulders and forced myself to march out of the safety of the room.

Syrith

I was already staring at the door when it finally opened.

My heart leapt at the sight of her. Her eyes were bloodshot, and her wings appeared nearly wilted behind her. Even her hair seemed far more limp, now barely even showing a trace of curl to it. And the color was far paler than ever.

Now I could no longer even call it blue. More like an ivory, white with hints of gold.

Galeta gripped the doorframe so tight, her knuckles whitened, and she reminded me of a terrified rabbit the way she stood so still, barely even daring to draw breath as she held my steady gaze.

Her mouth parted just slightly on an inhalation, and I tipped my chin forward, waiting on her to speak. But then she shut her lips and gave a tiny shake.

"No," I said. "Say whatever it was you were about to say."

I was physically exhausted and mentally drained. I didn't want to try and guess anymore what was going through her mind. I simply wanted Galeta to be honest with me no matter where the truth led.

Licking her top lip, she took several deep breaths before saying, "I feared you'd left for good this time, Syrith."

Her words were reticent and soft. As though she was forcing herself to speak. After all the progress we'd made, I hated knowing we were back to this. I'd been prepared to fight, to tackle the door down if need be, but now that she was out here, I was almost too exhausted to keep on my feet.

Taking the few lumbering steps back toward the couch, I settled onto it with a plop. "I said I would not leave you, fae, and I meant it."

Dropping my head into my hands, I closed my eyes. I'd hoped after what I'd seen above that the world down here might have transformed again, might be different. But it was still gray, still depressively gloomy.

I didn't hear her approach until her small hands landed on my knees and she gave them a tiny squeeze.

"Prince," she said softly, "look at me."

Unable to resist her when she lowered her walls between us, I did look and saw something in her eyes that caused my heart to swell.

Hope reflected back at me.

"All I ask," she said softly, "is that you try not to judge me too harshly for how I react. My past isn't pretty, and it shames me. But I do not wish to fight with you. You and I are connected somehow in this strange realm, and—"

Galeta had no idea how weak I was today. After the softness shown me by the clone and the way she'd fought... Her words to me now, they tore down my own defenses, and without thinking, I tipped her chin up with my forefinger and swooped in.

Not giving either of us time to think.

She gave a tiny gasp but didn't pull back. And then my lips found hers, and I pressed down tight. Softly, gently caressing her mouth with my own. Tasting, nipping at, and learning her, imprinting her all over me.

I knew what I was doing. I was jumping into this with eyes wide open. I was letting her in too. For so long, I'd shielded my heart, built defenses around me, letting no one in. Determined to forever be alone, consumed by my unrequited love.

This step I took now, it was dangerous for me. For her. For us. We were both walking a fine line, and though I knew how ill advised this was, I was helpless to control my feelings.

Galeta squirmed, dropping several breathy moans and enflaming my own passions.

I'd not felt this discombobulated in a long, long time. I wanted the fairy. Wanted her lying nude beneath me as I worshipped and feasted on her body. As I made love to her and bound her as irrevocably to me as I already was to her.

But not like this. Not now. Not after all the pain and hurt she'd suffered. All Galeta knew was pain, hate, and duplicity. I would rather die alone than ever have her believe I was no different from everyone else in her life.

As painful as it was, I finally broke the kiss. But I couldn't pull back completely. My hands had tenderly cupped her shoulders as my thumbs stroked her petal-soft flesh. Her eyes were wide and lips swollen.

"Syrith." She breathed my name like a prayer.

My lips twitched, and my heart swelled.

She swallowed hard, letting me see her vulnerabilities. Letting me in. And it humbled me to know that she'd likely never done so with another in her life.

My fairy was a prickly pear. Tough and sharp on the outside, but inside, she was sweet and fragile.

It had bothered me this morning, knowing the depths of her darkness, but now I felt honored to know that with me at least, she was willing to be exposed. Her nails curved into my pants.

"Spend the day with me." Her words were shy.

"You won't lock yourself back in that room? Galeta, perhaps I shouldn't say this so soon, but—"

She pressed a finger to my lips, silencing my words. My heart twisted painfully within me.

"Then whatever it is, don't say it. Let us only live in this moment. I am tired, my beast, and wish only to spend the day with you. Inside these walls, where it is safe." She gave me a weak smile, as if begging my forgiveness for her rudeness.

I hadn't been about to profess my undying love to her, because I wasn't even certain that was what this was. All I knew was I felt far deeper for Galeta than I had even my beloved Seraphina.

Mother had always told me that in Kingdom, the very truest kind of love was a magic all its own. I'd never believed her. I'd loved Seraphina, and still, she'd killed herself.

But my feelings for my old lover were but a drop in the bucket compared to the all-encompassing sensations sweeping through me when I thought of my fairy.

"Lead me, fae, and I will follow."

Chapter 16: In Which a Powerful Truth Is Revealed

Galeta

We'd been talking the past hour. Me still kneeling before him, and Syrith staring down at me with his perpetual smile.

I was awed by my Prince.

Awed that he genuinely seemed to care for me. True, we hadn't known one another long, but I'd seen the gleam of kinship aplenty in my time as headmistress in Kingdom.

There were souls that, upon first meeting, simply clicked. As though they'd been fashioned one for another.

Not always lovers. Sometimes the best of friends. But there was an immediate soul bond, and I felt that now. With him.

Anything I said, he smiled, or laughed, or chuckled, or nodded politely. Telling me that he truly was listening to everything I said. The old me might have been jaded, wondering what it was he wanted.

Except for the fact that I also did the same with him.

He fascinated me, my Syrith. My cheeks hurt from smiling so often. And I didn't think I'd laughed more in my life than I had the past hour.

His silly stories of Wonderland. His exploits growing up with the Hatter and Cheshire. Learning how to handle his gifts.

"Mother always did hate when I'd meet up with that mangy cat, as she'd say." He winked, and the region of my heart melted just a little bit further.

"You were a bad boy, Prince. I rather think I might have liked you."

He snorted. "Cheshire taught me many forms. He can shift also, just not like me. Did you know he has a human form?"

I raised my brows at that. No, I hadn't known the cat had a male form. Made me wonder whether he'd been cat or man first.

"Hm." I chuckled softly. "So if you aren't merely just a dragon"—I waved a hand down his body—"or a man, what is your true form? I confess I haven't come across shifters such as you often in my long life."

The sparkle in his blue-green eyes suddenly burst, and his body went rigid. I knew somehow I'd asked something that was a sore subject for him.

I frowned, pulling back into myself almost immediately. I'd grown careless and comfortable with him, laughing and talking and imagining that we were at the point where he'd share such intimate details with me.

What a fool I'd been.

"I'm sorry," I stuttered.

Grabbing one of my hands, he yanked it toward him. Opening my palm and placing it tight over his chest, holding me fast and shaking his head. The strength of his body felt like corded steel beneath my hand, and I trembled.

"Do not shut me out, fae. I will not allow it. Not anymore."

His words were quiet but also resonant.

I blinked and confessed, "The truth is, Syrith, I'm badly out of the practice of knowing how to interact with others. I've always simply told them what to do. There was no friendly banter or back and forth between us. I am trying, but—"

The touch of his knuckles upon my cheeks was featherlight and made my lashes flicker.

"And you are doing a great job of it. I've never been so thoroughly amused as I have this past hour. But your question touched on a matter very painful for me. And one I've rarely shared with others."

I frowned, intensely curious but also willing to give him his privacy. "I will not push you, Syrith. I did not know. My apologies."

He shook his head, rejecting my apology. "No, you're correct. You did not know. How could I blame you for asking what seems like a simple and straightforward question? I can't."

His eyes grew distant as he looked at the wall over my shoulder. I could practically read the memories scrolling past his mind's eye. If I really wanted to, I could pluck those memories straight from him. Few knew just how powerful I truly was.

Within the very tip of my finger rested life and death. I could have crushed Kingdom beneath my wee palm if I'd really wanted to.

That thought made me realize that though a part of me really was evil, another side, buried so deeply I rarely felt it anymore, had tried at least to keep me grounded.

It was a revelation I'd not expected. There'd always been a war inside me, one I thought the darkness had always won, but what if there was actually more to me? What if I hadn't been born to be this...thing? What if I'd been born to be more?

Something inside of me fluttered, and warmth began to spread through my bones. My brows twitched. Was that even possible?

"Her name was Seraphina."

Syrith's deep timbre cut through my epiphany, causing me to shake my head and scatter the strange thoughts like marbles.

"What? Who was Seraphina?"

Leaning his head back on the couch, he stared up at the ceiling. Exposing the long line of his thick neck and the bulge of his Adam's apple. It rolled with his swallow, and I was absurdly mesmerized by the flex and pull of the tendons in his throat. The light dusting of bristles upon his flesh.

Syrith was a potent male, and in the quiet of my mind, I was willing to admit that he drew me in more and more.

"Come up here and sit beside me, fairy. If I must tell this tale, then I wish to feel your body pressed against mine."

My brows shot up to my hairline. I'd never asked him to speak of his past. And yet I was more than willing to listen if it meant I got to sit closer to him. Hopping quickly to my feet, I sat beside him. Tucking my feet beneath me and resting my thigh against his.

The transference of his heat through me was immediate and sparked through my blood like lightning.

I sucked in a deep, shuddery breath as my insides rioted and my nerves strung tight.

Casual as could be, Syrith draped his arm across my shoulder. The comforting weight of him, his scent, and his nearness—it made me feel weak and tingly everywhere.

Was this love that I felt? Was this the power I saw in others? Was this feeling of being infinitely bigger than oneself what I'd destroyed with my careless and unrepentant evils?

I trembled, swallowing hard as a thick knot banded around my soul. I was beginning to understand in a way I never could before just what I'd destroyed, and it wounded me.

His fingers brushed deliciously against my skin, breaking me out in a wash of goose pimples. Feeling both brave and weak, I placed my hand upon his upper thigh.

His muscle bunched tightly, and I wasn't sure whether that meant he liked it or not. I went to move, but he said, "Don't. Leave your hand there. Your touch soothes me."

Biting onto my lower lip, I nodded weakly, feeling suddenly sick to my stomach. But not because I was ill.

I felt very odd right now. Weak and fluttery but also strangely mighty. I curled my fingers into his pants, and he trembled beside me.

At first my posture was tense, uneasy. But after several moments, I began to relax. Giving him most of my weight as I leaned further into his side.

And then my head leaned against his shoulder, and Syrith kissed the crown of my forehead. I smiled.

"I loved her for years. We'd been betrothed as children," he began slowly.

My heart clenched when I heard him admit to loving another, but I was no fool. A man such as Syrith couldn't have remained alone long. He was too beautiful. Too kind.

"What happened?" I asked gently.

His nose began to track through my hair as he inhaled. And I nearly squeaked at the intimate touch, but I liked it too. It made my body burn and caused things between my legs to tighten and throb.

Good gods above, had I really just confessed to a throbbing? I almost groaned at that stupid thought. I'd once heard a maiden confess to such. I'd cursed her to celibacy after that, laughing through my nose at the absurd notion of throbbing anything.

I wondered what had happened to that maiden. I'd not even known her. I'd simply cursed her and flown on about my business. Never giving her another thought. With a heartfelt sigh, I fluttered my fingers over my gown that was no longer built of ice, but now of spider silk.

Maybe if I ever escaped this prison, I'd find her again. Fix her. I sighed.

But Syrith didn't seem to notice my sudden depressive mood. His gaze was unfocused and stuck in the past.

"Seraphina was all I'd ever wanted. We'd grown up in neighboring realms, but our fathers were both Kings, and we didn't often get to meet up. But when we did, we spent all our time together. When we were children, I loved nothing more than to play by her side and explore the wilds of Wonderland. As a man, I would steal her away to woo and romance her. She was my everything. And I knew as surely as the sun would rise the next morning that Seraphina was all I'd ever want."

My body stiffened up again. It wasn't that I wanted him to stop telling me of his past, but I'd be a liar if I said hearing this was any fun for me.

To imagine Syrith touching another. Kissing her as he did me. Doing other things. It killed a part of me to think there'd ever been another. There'd been a first that hadn't been me.

Of course, I knew he and I were nothing now. We merely shared a few kisses now and again. It'd been rare, but I'd done so with a few others in my life. More curious than anything. None of it leaving a lasting impression upon me. In fact, I'd once bedded Rumpel to satisfy that same sense of curiosity. It'd done nothing for me, and I'd never thought of bedding another since.

But the slightest touch of his hand to mine, and it completely undid me. Made me feel weak and strong.

He turned my chin toward him. "Look at me, Galeta."

I did, fighting a ball of tears gathering in my throat. What a stupid woman I was.

"I will never be anything but honest with you. It is a vow sealed in truth between us. But she was a part of my past."

"Past? As in no longer?"

I didn't believe he was still with the female, but even now I heard the love in his voice when he spoke of her.

"No." He shook his head. "Seraphina died three years past."

I sucked in a sharp breath. So not only had he loved her, but she'd passed. I would forever battle the ghost of his first love. Not that it should be a contest, but that was a wretched position to be in.

My lips thinned. I felt crushed by his words even as I also felt stupidly relieved by them. I hated myself for feeling this, but I didn't know how to stop it either.

"She killed herself because of me, fae," he whispered brokenly.

"What?" My head snapped up. I hadn't expected that at all.

That hurt that would sometimes flash through his gaze was back now, burning intently and making me want to take that pain away from him, want nothing more than to erase a past that seemed such a torment to him now. I was crushed by his obvious hurt. My heart beat hard in my chest. My stomach hurt. For him.

I wanted to ask him why. Wanted desperately to know all the sordid details. But after how he'd reacted when I'd asked him about his true form, I knew that truth and this story were somehow intertwined.

Syrith had used many forms around me. But I'd never sensed any of them to be his true one. Not even the one he wore now. The one he seemed most comfortable in.

Grabbing his free hand, I brought his knuckles to my lips and kissed them. Rubbed my thumbs across his calloused hand. His breathing suddenly turned erratic, and I felt his hot eyes drilling into me.

Tilting my face, I rubbed my cheek across his knuckles like a kitten and breathed, "It's okay, Syrith. You don't have to tell me. I won't judge you for it."

The hand he'd casually draped across my shoulder moved to the sensitive tip of my wing, and I sucked in a sharp breath.

"You asked me who I really was, Galeta," he said deeply. "I showed her. One night, beneath the bloodred moon. I showed her who I truly was. The next morning, she was found dead. Leaving behind only a note that read—"

"Ssh." I shook my head. "Don't speak it."

His thick brows twitched. "Don't you want to know?"

"No." I stood on my knees, looking him deep in his eyes. "No, I don't. Because there are some things in life that aren't worth revisiting. She hurt you, Syrith. Don't let her keep doing that."

He was quiet for a moment. "Aren't you curious? If it were you, I would be."

My grin was weak, but my words were strong. "Of course I'm curious, but not at your expense. Digging up the past, it brings the demons out with it. What's the point, beast? Sometimes in life you simply have to accept what was and let it go."

He stilled. "Have you?"

I knew what he was asking. And he knew that answer. But I answered him anyway. "No, I haven't. And so I lock myself away in that room, dying inside, because these memories wound me. I cannot change who I was. But I can change who I want to be. The Blue was a terrible person." I framed his beloved face in my palms, squeezing gently. "But you don't make me feel like her. You make me want to be a better version of me. Someone I know exists, but I've buried so deep, I'd forgotten she was ever even there. I don't know what Seraphina told you, Syrith, but it doesn't matter to me. All I know is that when I see you, I feel whole again. You did that, and no matter what your true form might be, I will never forget it."

I stilled, realizing just how much of myself I'd stripped bare before him. But I'd needed to make him see, needed to somehow make him understand that it didn't matter to me if he had one head or twenty—he was still special to me.

"I'm monstrous, fairy. You say this to me, but you've never seen me as I truly am."

I laughed. "What does it matter the skin we wear? It's the heart should matter, Prince. And mine is just as monstrous as you claim yours to be."

Turning his face, he pressed a tight kiss to my palm, making my skin burn. Involuntarily, I crawled closer to him. Pressing my small breasts tight to his chest, putting our faces so close that our lips shared breath.

His entire frame shook, and it thrilled me.

"You're not a monster," he breathed.

I shook my head. "And neither are you. Would you do me the great honor of allowing me to see you?" I asked into the still hum beating between us.

The whites of his eyes overtook his irises—a sure sign of his terror, and it pained me to see it. I wanted to hurt Seraphina for hurting him as deeply as she had. The old beat of that darkness whipped through my bones that someone as good and kind as Syrith could have ever felt such pain.

If he didn't matter to me, I would drop it. But he did matter. Very much. Pressing my forehead to his, I rubbed my nose with his.

"Whoever you really are, whatever you look like, I don't care."

"Then why see me at all? It will ruin you, Galeta. You say it won't, but it will. Even my own parents have a hard time gazing upon me."

"I could force you to if I really wanted to. If I were the old me, I'd have no qualms about doing just that, but this matters to me, Prince. You matter to me. I want to see you because I want to prove to you that not everyone is like Seraphina. We are friends, you and I. You've helped me more than you can know. So let me be your friend now and help you back."

His hands gripped my wrists hard, rubbing the bones together and causing me to suck in a sharp breath. But I knew it was fear that gripped him, and so I stayed my tongue.

I saw the play of emotions cross his tight features. The rage. Pain. Hurt. And finally steely determination.

He stood, slipping out of my grip easily, and I missed his warmth already. Taking several steps back, until his back was nearly to the hearth, he gazed longingly at me.

"I would say something to you first, Galeta. No matter what happens after this, it's been an honor knowing you."

My heart broke. He was so sure I'd reject him that he'd already said his good-byes. I shook my head.

I imagined a monster drug up from the very pits of the Underworld. Maybe with skin that looked like melted wax, red and raw. A dragon's head and serpent's body. Maybe he was green, or blue, or black. I shook my head.

"Do it, Prince. Do it before you lose your nerve."

His hands curled into fists by his side. I thought that maybe he might decide to walk away, maybe beg me for a stay of execution, as it were. But Syrith was dragonborne and made of sterner stuff.

His chin notched, and my heart grew in my chest, threatening to overwhelm me with pride for him. He did not want to do it, but he would because I'd asked him to.

Magic tightened the room. Curls of glowing red cascaded over him. I flinched at the bright light, shading my eyes with my hands. When the light faded, I took a moment to breathe deeply.

Whatever happened, I would not react. Not in front of him. Whatever he was, whoever he was, I would remember who he really was. Syrith was seeing me at my worst, and yet remained. I could do no less for him.

My stomach a twisted mass of razor-tipped butterflies, I dropped my hand and looked.

And there he was. As he'd always been.

My Syrith.

Tall. Strong. With a chest as broad and powerful as any male dragonborne's. His legs were thick and powerful looking. His hands flinched as he awaited my verdict.

I looked up at his face. At where it should be.

I'd heard of the legend, the headless horseman. But Syrith did have a face. It was ghostly blue and barely there, but it was there. I grinned, exposing the long curves of my fangs.

His eyes were still wide, and fear etched an indelible mark around them. His lips were thinned and pinched.

"I see you, beast." I grinned. "And here I thought you'd be a monster. I'd been prepared for the very worst. I feel rather let down, all in all."

He chuffed, the sound a mix of a whiz and a huff. "What?" Looking angry now, he jerked his hand through where his head should have been. Coming in contact with nothing but air.

Were I anyone else, I doubt I'd be able to see his face. In truth, Syrith would be a macabre sight to most anyone not built of magic.

"Do you not see what I am? The twisted deformity of a man and ghost? Were I missing a limb or two, it would be one thing. But to have no face—"

Getting up and feeling ridiculously more at ease than I'd thought possible just moments ago, I walked over to him. My wings flitted excitedly behind me.

I grinned. "Syrith, have you forgotten who I am?"

His nostrils flared. "I'm beginning to think I know very little of who you truly are."

I grinned. Because I'd forgotten a long time ago too. But I was remembering now.

"I'm magic, my boy. And you are so beautiful."

Then, flitting my wings, lifting off my feet until I was eye level with him, I leaned forward and pressed my lips to his.

A spark passed between us. And though at first I felt nothing, I poured a wave of that golden magic into him. But I would never give him back his head. Because this was who Syrith truly was. And shockingly, I rather liked it.

Knowing I'd somehow managed to tame a beast such as he—it was a heady, intoxicating thought. He'd tamed one too. Though he might not know it.

What I did do was make him feel me. Feel the breadth of my mouth move against his own.

He sucked in a powerful breath. "Galeta, I—"

"I know, beast," I murmured against his mouth. "Now kiss me."

And he did. His hands gripped my biceps, holding me fast. Gods, he was powerful. I sighed. Losing myself to his heady touch.

When we finally broke apart, both of us breathing heavy and staring deep into each other's eyes, I knew our world had changed again.

Taking my hand in his, Syrith marched to the front door.

Once I might have balked, but I trusted him completely. I stepped through that door and gasped.

"Flowers, Syrith. They bloom in color."

The path that led away from our door was bursting with them. With violets, poppies, daisies, sunflowers, bluebonnets, petunias, dragonsnaps, scarlet orchids, and so, so many more.

I covered my mouth with my hands as tears rolled down my cheeks. But this time it was joy that brought them.

He touched the backs of my hands. I looked up at him. He'd changed again, returning to his familiar male form. But I didn't care.

Heart bursting nearly to the point of pain, I whispered the words that'd been seared upon it. "I love you."

The trees shook, the clouds parted, and a bright-golden beam of sunlight washed over us.

Chapter 17: The Heart Knows

Syrith

I loved her. Though the words had frozen on my tongue two weeks ago, I knew it with every fiber of my being. I worshipped this fairy before me.

Seraphina had been nothing compared to this.

Galeta loved me too. Truly loved me. She'd seen me, and she'd never once flinched. But more than that, something about my true form had broken down that final wall between us.

I'd felt it. The fall.

Her touches were more frequent now. Soft. Sensual. In many ways, she was still a novice, but she learned quickly. Her kisses weren't so hard or punishing. They were soulful, deep, and penetrating.

We'd stayed out of the hut for the rest of the day, holding tight to one another as we'd watched the sun track westward until, finally, the bright jewels of starlight had filled the navy-blue sky.

Animals now gathered in this realm. Birds sang in the trees, and lumbering beasts marched over the ground. The world was a strange mix of grays and bright, vivid colors.

We'd stayed within the shelter of the hut, not straying too far. But I didn't sense it was fear that kept us here this time. Rather, Galeta and I both felt our time in this mirror realm slipping away.

I'd not seen or heard from Harpy for some days now. And apart from the occasional moments I'd been whisked away to do battle in the games above, it was just Galeta and I.

She slept with her door open now. And I'd begun to crawl closer and closer to her bed each night. Until this morning—I now rested upon the foot of it.

Watching her with my heart in my throat.

She was in miniature, with her arms crossed in front of her and her cheek resting upon them. Her breaths were soft, her face at peace.

Her colors were changing. There wasn't a hint of blue on her now. Just her eyes, but they weren't unnaturally cold. They were warm and filled with laughter.

She teased me so easily now.

I love you...

The words echoed in my head. My cat's tongue twitched with the need to get them out.

Aphrodite had told me that today would be my final day in the tournament. It was obvious now to one and all that the clone too had altered. She was softer. Still Blue, and still played dirty, but when she looked at me, love burned through her gaze.

Whatever was happening to Galeta down here, a sliver of the real her was also in that clone up there.

I love you. I love you. I love you...

How the words burned for release. I'd sworn a long time ago that I would never again say them. That I would never again give in. But I'd fallen so deeply and so completely, I couldn't not feel this either.

It was fear that held my tongue and nothing more.

Her chest inflated and deflated with her even breaths. Reaching out a paw, I gently rubbed my fur against her back, and she smiled.

How was it that I'd never realized what true love should really be? How was it that Seraphina's beauty had so addled me that I'd actually believed myself happy with her?

Looking back, I could finally recognize her indifference to me. The way she'd lean away when I'd move in for a kiss. How at times she'd tease me with cruel, cutting words, and yet I'd been so blind as to believe she'd honestly felt as I had.

Not once had Galeta made me feel ashamed of myself. Not once had she made me feel I wasn't enough.

To her, I was.

She might not say it. And though I knew that fairies didn't love, I also knew that for the farce it was. This fairy, at least, did.

The world had lit up when she'd uttered those three words. And each night before sleep, she'd say the same to me.

I'd thought at first it was only Galeta with her walls up, but I now knew I'd had them with her too.

Galeta's breathing pattern shifted. Going from deep to shallow. She was waking. This was my favorite time of day, watching her rise. Waiting until she spotted me, and seeing that slow burn of love blaze across her face.

I would tell her today.

I would open my mouth and simply say the words.

The room popped with a tightening of magic. I knew immediately that Aphrodite had returned for me. My heart sank. I wasn't ready to leave yet. But the sooner I left, the sooner I could return.

"Your love blazes through my heart, dragonborne," Love said deeply.

I nodded, not tearing my eyes from my woman. I would follow her to the ends of Kingdom if need be, but I would never leave her side again. No matter where the Fates took us.

"Why have you not told her yet?" Aphrodite asked softly.

Imprinting every swell and curve to memory, I finally turned. Hopped down from the bed and shifted mid-jump into my familiar form.

Using a bit of dragon's breath, I cleaned myself off then dusted off my vest before smiling broadly at the goddess staring quizzically at me.

"Because I was afraid, Love. Afraid that by saying it out loud, I'd somehow ruin it all. Afraid that by confessing the truth, I'd discover this dream to be nothing but a nightmare. But I'm not scared anymore. And I will tell her everything."

Aphrodite was dressed in a gown of swan feathers that looked painted upon her tight body. Blond hair flowed down her shoulders. She might be beauty personified to every other male in all of the worlds, but her beauty paled in comparison to the woman who gripped my heart fast in her wee hands.

Looking back at Galeta one final time, I whispered the words that'd imprinted themselves on my heart.

"I love you."

Lush lips tipped up in a sleepy smile. I wasn't sure if she'd heard or not. But I would never stop saying it to her.

"Come, Syrith," Aphrodite said deeply, "we must not tarry."

Galeta

I love you...

The ghostly echo of Syrith's words wrapped around my heart like a string. With a cry, I sat up looking around my room in a daze.

When I'd first come this world, there'd not been much life. But life was blooming, even within the confines of these four walls. My bed, which had once just been a lumpy mattress, had begun to turn into the softest, lushest mound of rich moss. The bare walls were now crawling with vines whose leaves were as broad as a large man's palm, and were dotted with a colorful array of miniature flowers. Saplings had sprouted from the ground, with the promise of soon becoming deeply rooted and mature conifers.

It wasn't just me changing things. It was him too.

"Syr? Are you here?" I whispered.

The memory of those three little words continued to hammer away at my heart. Shoving thick curls of hair out of my eyes, I only gave it half a thought that this morning it appeared far blonder than ever before.

"Beast?" I said tightly, nerves stretched taut as I awaited his response. He'd said he loved me. Those words hadn't been a mere dream, right? Two weeks ago, I'd unburdened my heart to him, and though he'd still yet to say it to me, I felt his adoration in everything he did.

Every stolen look. Every casual and not so casual touch.

My heart sang.

But as I blinked the sleep from my eyes, I realized with a sinking heart that he wasn't here anymore. He'd vanished, as he was often prone to do.

I trusted Syrith implicitly. And did not doubt that he cared for me. But through the weeks, I'd begun to wonder just where it was he'd go off to in such secrecy.

The Harpy?

Nibbling on my bottom lip, I shook my head. No, I wouldn't go there. I'd choose to believe in him, not allow doubts to poison my mind. With Syrith, I was determined to start anew. To be different from whom I'd been. For him, I would try to be a better person.

Hopping to my knees, I bunched the comforter in my hands. I did not need to search the hut to know he wasn't in it any longer. I felt his absence as keenly as the sharp strike of a blade.

Looking at the open door of my bedroom, I began to think thoughts. Where was he? Was he safe? Did he need me?

Sometimes he'd return from wherever he'd been looking bruised and sore. His eyes shaded by exhaustion. Today when he returned, I would finally be brave and ask him.

Sucking my bottom lip between my teeth, I bit down sharply, causing my fangs to pierce the soft meat. I hissed as my blood tingled upon my tongue.

"Do not worry, Galeta. He is well. He must be." My voice quivered.

I no longer thought he'd leave me. I no longer worried about that. Of one thing I was absolutely certain—my Beast needed me as deeply as I needed him.

Deciding it was past time to get up, I hopped from the bed. I would try to keep up some form of normalcy. I took time with my appearance today. And who knew, maybe by the time I'd finished, he'd return to me.

Stomach twisting from a mass of nesting butterfly wings, I grabbed hold of it and forced myself to breathe in and out. I'd never really cared before what anyone thought of my appearance.

Yes, I'd been vain, but in my own way. Before, my looks had been geared more toward intimidation than wanting to attract any member of the opposite sex. I'd purposefully kept my appearance deceptively youthful with those ridiculous corkscrew curls and young features. I'd made myself appear like a living, almost demonic-looking doll, knowing just how off-putting that persona was for others.

Flicking my fingers over my face, I called my true features to the fore. Gone was the face of a youth. I was a woman true. Appearing to be in my midthirties now. There were slight wrinkles around my eyes, frown lines I'd developed over the eons. No laugh lines, though, which tended to happen when one rarely found humor in life.

Mouth parting just slightly, I studied the face of the woman before me. Seldom had I indulged in truly looking at myself. My features were softer, prettier than I remembered. My eyes, a deeper blue now, sparkled with hidden wonder. Blooms of first love. My stomach quivered, and I forced myself to breathe slowly in and out.

I'd given Danika such grief for her choices. What a hypocrite I was. And yet—I smiled softly—I would never take it back.

My nose was petite and perfectly situated. My lips, fuller on the bottom than the top, fangs sticking out a very little even when I did not smile. I had plump cheeks, and was rosy complected. I was pretty, but it felt as if I stared at a stranger.

I did not know this woman standing before me. For so long, I'd been the malicious youth, and I'd grown used to that image. It was my armor against the world. But, for better or worse, Syrith had changed me completely. My gaze landed on the buttery gold of my hair.

When had it stopped being blue? Picking up the thick hank over my shoulder, I studied the tips of it. So much of me had changed in so little time, I wasn't quite certain how to handle this.

Heart hammering painfully in my chest, I squeezed my eyes shut. What would happen when I finally left this place? Would I become who I once was again? It'd been many days since I'd thought of my hysteria and desperation to end my life. But I did now. The vial, which had never left my pocket, now felt suddenly heavy and branding. I could never become that monster again. But I knew my time here would come to an end.

I felt the magic of this realm fracturing more and more each day. The broth yesterday morning, for instance, hadn't tasted as rich and delicious as previous days. It'd been water with seasoning. And though there was more color now, it wasn't as saturated as it'd been when the flame of the hearth had first turned red. Life bloomed, but it was also slowly dying.

I hadn't told Syrith this, because I'd not wanted him to worry. A part of me began to suspect that the moment all color returned to this realm might also be the moment I ceased to be.

I didn't know for certain—it wasn't as if the Harpy had returned to me and confirmed this. But I knew magic, and my inner core felt a great disturbance rubbing like an agitated hornet's nest within me. Something dark and bleak was coming, and I wasn't sure I would survive it.

My eyes flashed open. Best not to go too far down that depressing path. *Focus on something else, fae.*

Dropping my hair, I called forth a brush. A task. That was what I needed. Something to help me focus less on these rapid changes overcoming me and simply lose myself in the mundane of the day to day.

Brushing out the thick knots in my hair I'd allowed to form after days of not taking good enough care of myself, I began to slowly feel better. I thoroughly brushed my teeth, not once but twice.

Standing before the mirror, I decided to alter my gown too. A wand was good for big magic; it helped me to channel my focus. But rearranging my wardrobe was hardly beyond the realm of my meager abilities.

What to wear had always been an easy decision for me before.

Ice.

An outward reflection of my inner torment.

But I no longer felt so conflicted, so torn. Flicking my wrist, I fashioned a gown from the magic pulsing around me. I didn't take much, but I grinned, feeling good and clear headed as I worked. It'd been so long since I'd created anything.

Fashioning a gown based on memories of others I'd always secretly envied, I had to take a step back and grin happily when I'd finished. It floated before me, beckoning. It was glossy, a soft blue color, and sparkled from tiny clear gems that'd been looped through the threads.

"To me," I whispered to it. And, instantly, I'd swapped out dresses.

The cut of the dress was daring. Held up only by a neck strap, accentuating my small breasts so that they appeared plumper than usual, and framing my slender waist prettily. But it was the back of the gown that caused my wings to flutter in anticipation of what he might think when he saw me in it.

Many years ago, I'd stumbled across a woman I'd found lovelier than almost anyone else I'd ever known. Her name had been Siria, but most of Kingdom had simply known her as the sun.

Once, she'd been an innocent.

Though I'd not destroyed her as I had so many others. I'd rather liked Siria. She'd been doomed to love the moon, but he'd never returned her affections. She'd sought out my counsel now and again.

And I'd given it.

Though it'd come to nothing, because in the end Danika had turned the Moon's head, and he'd never looked back.

But one of the things I remembered most about Siria were her gowns. Creations crafted of sunlight and imagination.

Drawing from the memory of one I'd particularly enjoyed, I twirled on my heel and studied the long, smooth form of my bare back. My wings were on full display. I fluttered them gently, feeling slightly scandalized to be wearing something that covered so little.

But I wanted him to see me for who I really was.

The long strands of my hair slid down my back, but it was distracting, hiding my curves. Thinning my lips, I decided to go all in.

Touching the barest tip of my finger to a slight curl, I murmured, "*Menus.*"

Instantly, my hair shortened, going from waist length to chin length, revealing the smooth, long lines of my neck and keeping my back on full display.

My pulse pounded thick in my veins at the drastic change.

What if he didn't like short hair? What if I'd been wrong? Perhaps I shouldn't have cut it. Maybe I should have braided it, or—

Galeta! Where are you?

Sucking in a sharp breath, I twirled at the sound of my name.

Help. Help!

The voice hadn't sounded like Syrith, but there was panic laced throughout. I shook my head as dread slithered through my gut.

"I'm coming, Syrith! I'm coming." I raced from the shelter of my hut. My heart pumping so violently within me, it was painful. Forgetting about such trivial nonsense as gowns and hair, I raced for him as fast as I physically was able.

I didn't think where I went. Didn't stop to question what I was doing. All I knew was he needed me, and I would never let him down.

Please! Don't do this...

What was happening to him? Was someone hurting him? To hurt him was to wound me. I would kill anything that dared. That old hate, old violence rode me hard. It would be so easy to surrender to that darkness again.

So, so easy.

Blinded by my tears and panic, I stopped running and flew. Losing myself in one twist after another. Not giving heed to where I headed. Moving deeper and deeper on the path of shifting, rotating colors. Sweat coated my brows. My wings. My body.

Every inch of me trembled. My muscles ached. My mouth tasted of cotton. Blood pounded through my ears.

But I would not stop.

Not until I found him. Not until he was safe again.

The forest began to twist around me. Images formed, memories of the past that came flooding in. I shook my head.

What was this?

I stopped flying when a scene coalesced before me. A man with hair of black and skin of ivory stared back at me. He shook his head. Fear scrawled terrible lines across his normally handsome face. He stood alone upon the stern of his ship, clinging to a red crushed-velvet gown.

His eyes looked haunted, dark. The silver hook of his hand glinted in the night.

I trembled, for I did not remember this memory at all. What was this madness?

The male looked up. At me. Directly at me. His eyes burned like flame. And a slick sense of unease slithered through my belly like the tight coils of a snake's undulation.

A terrible feeling of foreboding took me. Where was Syrith? I'd heard his voice. Hadn't I?

"*What have you done?*" Tears streamed down the vision's cheeks, and a look of utter desolation had scrawled itself upon his expressive face.

I glanced over my shoulder, wondering if perhaps the rest of the memory were behind me, but there was nothing there, not even trees. It was black, barren, empty.

"*I speak to you, fae,*" he snarled, the sadness now replaced by a rage so thick, it was a palpable stench in my nostrils. I began to shake, cupping my hands to my arms and denying what it was I was seeing.

This was no memory of mine. But the breeze kicked up with the scent of salt and the brine of the ocean deep. Hook's face contorted with madness. "*Say something*! *Tell me something. Tell me you did not do this, or so help me gods, I will skewer you like the rat that you are,*" he spat.

Surely he wasn't talking to me—memories couldn't do that. But when I looked back at him, he'd walked closer, until now his face was so close to mine, I could practically feel the wash of his breath tingle upon my flesh as he growled, "*You swore to do right by us all, and still you failed. Selfish creature that you are, you stole my happy ending, and now I'll steal yours.*"

His hook slammed into my gut, and I screamed, dropping to my knees. Murderous rage was all I saw.

Chapter 18: In Which a Fairy Is Finally Ready to Let Go...

Syrith

I arrived not too long after in a world bathed in darkness. Aphrodite had vanished already, but my clone awaited me.

Her corkscrew curls were no longer. Her hair was now thick waves that fell to her waist in a shower of malleable gold.

Her face was pale, her eyes wide. She gripped her wand tight.

"Syrith," she said softly, and I nodded.

These were two different women, both sharing one soul. But one wasn't real. And yet my heart beat with love for each.

"Fairy," I said deeply. "What is the matter?"

She shook her head, tiny fangs nibbling on her bottom lip. "We haven't much time before the last couple arrives, but I wished to say something to you. I've been dreaming of a world of mirrors and gilded colors. You're there. And you love me."

Her words were soft. A statement, but also a question. Her stare was quizzical, curious. Asking me to please tell her she wasn't crazy.

I swallowed hard, not sure what to say. Unsure whether the clone was even allowed to know who she really was. Wondering if maybe by telling her I'd be breaking some laws of magic. Unwittingly causing a future catastrophe. I simply didn't know enough about magic to know what I could and couldn't do. I bit down hard on my bottom lip, pleading silently with my eyes that she not question me further.

She thinned her lips. "You don't have to tell me anything, beast, because I already know. I know who I am and who I am not."

I stepped closer to her. Her electric-blue wings fluttered powerfully, causing a caress of wind to gently beat against my body. As I remembered the fairy I'd left lying on the bed this morning, my heart could no longer distinguish between the two.

"I love you, Galeta the Blue. With all my soul and all my heart," I whispered. "Whoever you are, it matters not to me. You, every part of you, is precious to me."

I trekked a finger along her jaw, and her lashes fluttered prettily. "I may be merely clay and magic, dragon, but I love you too. Whatever you're doing with me, it's working."

My lips parted. I'd told this clone nothing, and yet she'd managed to work out the truth of it on her own. Tiny sliver of soul or not, I recognized the imprint of the woman I loved, and groaned deeply.

Leaning forward, she gave my lips the merest of kisses. Just a whisper of touch really, but I felt that touch whip and flex through my bones with the force of a violent wave.

We were so caught up in one another that neither of us noticed the couple had arrived until we felt the heated blast of flame spiral our way. Time suddenly seemed to slow to a crawl, and I noticed things I wouldn't have otherwise.

Fiera, the elemental goddess of fire, floated a few yards away.

Dressed in a gown of living flame, she mouthed two words to me.

I frowned. Instead of moving away, I stayed where I was. My feet rooted to the nothingness beneath me.

I'm sorry.

It was what she'd said, but I couldn't understand it.

And then time spun forward, moving in a dizzying blur.

"No!" Galeta screamed, shoving me away. Moving into the very spot I'd been occupying. That bolt of fire, it'd been coming directly at me.

But instead of hitting me, it hit her. Square in the chest, heaving her back violently. Tossing us both down.

"Galeta! Galeta!" I scrabbled for her. Reaching out blackened fingers to her. Only just realizing the goddess's flames had licked at me too.

My beautiful fairy was no more.

Her body lay in a sizzling heap before me. Her chest was concaved and steaming, and her flesh was blackened. The wand was gone.

Roaring toward the heavens, I shifted into a beast. But Fiera was already gone.

It'd all happened so fast.

The clone had saved me.

That thought hammered at my skull like cannon fire. The clone who couldn't love. Who couldn't be more than what she was. She'd sacrificed herself for me.

My hands shook. A mixture of pain, humbled gratitude, and shock.

"Galeta, my beauty. My love, open your eyes." I gathered her crumpled form to me. But her eyes were closed, and the light had left them.

Soul feeling fractured within me, and sick at my stomach, I dry heaved. The anger beating inside of me was full and vengeful, but there was no escape for it. The world became a watercolored canvas. Dragon tears could heal.

I dripped one after another onto her form, but nothing changed.

"Syrith, release her now and come with me." Aphrodite was back and holding out her hand to me.

"No. No! She can't be dead." I forgot that she was simply a clone. I forgot that this Galeta was not my Galeta, because she was. There'd been a sliver of soul in her. What'd happened to it? Was it lost forever?

Every part of her was mine.

"*She* is not dead. The clone is. But you need to come with me now, dragon. Your true fairy needs you!"

Hissing, I stared at the goddess of Love with blind rage and hatred as tears leaked uselessly from my eyes, only giving her words half an ear. Shock kept me rooted where I was. I shook my head, trying to clear the webbing of watching the woman I'd loved die before my eyes.

"Syrith! Snap out of it!" She rushed forward, kneeling before me and grabbing hold of my vest and giving me a firm shake. "Listen to me, boy. Your woman is dying. You must get to her. Now!"

Finally, her words penetrated my agony.

"What?" I gasped, confused and disoriented, feeling as though I'd just watched my woman perish, and yet my Galeta still lived.

"She's not truly dead, Prince." Aphrodite pleaded with wide eyes. I frowned. "Just this clay. Just this bit of soul. But if you don't want to lose the rest of her, you need to get up now and come with me! Galeta will respond to no other but you. Now come!"

Desperate to avert the same fate twice, I reverently and gently laid my clone down. Closing her eyes with two fingers.

"Where is she?" My humanity rumbled with the echoes of my beast.

"Lost in the memories. She went in search of you, Prince. She is lost and in grave danger of losing herself to the past."

Without a moment's hesitation, I snatched her hand, jumped to my feet, and ran across the threshold of time and realms Aphrodite had already opened for us.

Just as the tunnel began to close behind us, I saw Harpy appear. Her eyes were sad. Haunted. Her normally immaculate gown looking rumpled and wrinkled. Her hair was in wild disarray around her head. That was when I realized I'd neither seen nor heard from her in days.

Harpy looked ill. And while I was curious in an abstract sense, none of that mattered right now. Because she was reaching for Galeta, taking her slight form into her arms, and my heart clenched powerfully in my chest at the thought of the clone's destruction.

"No! No! Leave her. Don't touch her!" I roared, reaching impotently toward Harpy, but it was too late—the portal had sealed shut, separating us. I grabbed at my chest, feeling the echoes of my heart thump powerfully against my palm, sick at my stomach.

I was smart enough to know that wasn't truly Galeta, but it also had been.

I'd just watched the woman I loved die. Memories of my past began to churn and bubble up, tormenting me. Mocking me. What if my Galeta had died too? What if I was, once again, too late? What if...

Aphrodite gave me a strange look. "Whom did you yell at, Prince?"

I cocked my head, looking at her strangely. Had she truly not seen the bird?

She blinked, grabbed hold of her temple, and rubbed deeply. "It doesn't matter. No matter. We're very nearly there. Find her, dragonborne. Save the fairy. Save our world."

My breathing hitched, and madness burned through me as I fought not to drown in my panic. How much longer would I be forced to endure this separation? What was happening to Galeta now?

Aphrodite tried to engage me in further conversation, but my thoughts were inward. I didn't hear her. I thought of nothing other than my fairy. Of stopping what'd just been done once.

Finally, the damned portal opened, and I rushed out, stepping directly into chaos.

Memories crowded all around me. Galeta swinging a blade through a kneeling serf's neck. Galeta laughing and sentencing man, woman, and beast to death. Galeta screaming.

Galeta crying.

Galeta swearing to the night that she would do it. She would finally end her suffering.

A massive golden dragon pleading with her to not do this. To listen.

Memory after memory after memory crowding one on top of the other, threatening to crush me. I was disoriented, lost to these memories.

Before, there'd only ever been one memory to battle, but now there were so many, I didn't know where to start. Where to go. My fingers clenched.

"What is this madness?" I gasped.

Aphrodite, who I'd thought had left, came up to stand beside me. "This is the end, Syrith. Find her, before her past destroys her completely."

I ran. Not knowing where, only knowing I *would* find her. I'd grown up in Wonderland, a land filled with lunacy and insanity. I'd learned to navigate that place—I would learn this one.

My dragon had claimed her. She was mine. And within my soul beat the pure inner core of hers.

"Find her," I commanded my beast.

There was now an impenetrable tether between us. The tug of her pulled me to the left. Shifting into a blazing phoenix, I flew toward her, crying out with the loud shrill of the powerful bird that I was coming.

But the memories were crushing me. Crowding me. Anywhere I looked, anywhere I turned, they were there.

"You cannot do this!" Danika cried. "You cannot do that to Jericho. You know I love him. How could you?"

Tears dripped from her eyes. Her long brown hair hung limp around her slim shoulders.

Galeta sneered. "You stole my flower. You had no right. He doesn't belong to you, Danika. No male does!"

I tore through that memory, shattering it to ribbons. Closing my ears and eyes off as best I could to Galeta's past.

I already knew it wasn't pretty. But I would not be the one to judge Galeta for it.

I'm coming my love. I'm coming. I blasted the thought at her. Hoping that somehow, maybe, our bond meant she'd hear me. She'd know she was not alone.

Your choice, my child. Two paths. One of light. One of darkness. What do you choose?

107

A voice far deeper than any I'd ever heard in all the worlds echoed through the pandemonium of Galeta's memories.

And there she was. My wee, lovely fae. But she wasn't The Blue. She was pink. Her features were soft, lovely. Her eyes completely innocent.

I watched the scene before me, entranced, hypnotized by it.

Galeta floated on a cloud of starlight. Surrounded by eleven other fairies. But none burned as brightly as she. She was a beacon in the night.

And I knew this was the beginning of it all. The start of Kingdom. My soul trembled as I realized what it was I was seeing.

They'll all hate me. They'll never know, will they?

Tears burned my eyes at the pain in her words. This was the story Harpy had told me. All the darkness, all the pain Galeta had brought upon others, she'd not been born to be that way.

This was the true woman.

This was the love of my life, willingly sacrificing herself so that others might live.

I will never forget or abandon you, my daughter. If you choose to bear the seed of darkness, I vow to you that someday I will return and free you of this curse.

I did not see the voice that spoke, but the fire burning through me rose higher. Even my soul shook. That voice belonged to something far greater than anything known.

Harpy had spoken of a Creator.

And now I felt It.

My heart beat with a powerful rush of love for my fairy as tears ran thick and free down her cheeks.

Then do it...

And then she screamed. Body twisting and contorting as agony scrawled heavy lines across her lovely face. Pink fading into Blue. Darkness crowding her bones.

Changing her.

Even I could see it.

I shook my head as if I could stop it. But I couldn't. Because this had been her past. Her sacrifice.

And all for people who'd never appreciate it or know. Claws shot from her hands. Her face contorted into a scream that ran and ran and ran into eternity as that seed of darkness claimed her.

With a cry of fury, I tore through the image that I knew would haunt me all the days of my life, and that was when I finally found her. She was kneeling, head hanging forward. Alone and surrounded by a fog bank of darkness. Her tiny shoulders shuddered. Her short golden hair covered her face like a curtain.

Sobs wracked her tiny form as she clutched tight to her chest.

"I'm sorry. I'm so, so sorry. I will never do this again, I vow it," she whispered over and over, the sound so broken and heartrending that it crushed my soul to hear it.

She lifted her hand.

Sunlight glinted off the green glass she held. Galeta shuddered, lifting the tiny vial to her mouth, and I screeched. The Phoenix's cry was a bloodcurdling agony ripped from the depths of my soul.

Shaking her head, she looked up. Her eyes were bloodshot, her pupils nothing but tiny pinpricks within.

"You're not really here, my Prince. You're a mere figment of my heart. I love you, but I cannot hurt anyone else. Forgive me, Syrith. Please forgive me."

Tucking my wings in tight to my sides, I barreled to the ground. My heart a raging, panicked thing inside my chest. I would be damned if I lost her again. Landing just as she tipped the vial over, I shifted and slapped it so hard out of her hand that it knocked her backward. She landed with a hard thud upon the ground and groaned, and I grimaced.

Her eyes were closed, and she was clutching at her stomach.

108

"My love." I raced to her, grabbing her tight and holding her to me, both grateful I'd arrived just in time and impossibly angry.

The glass and its contents had shattered upon the forest floor. The thick jewel-green blades of grass that'd been beneath it now withered and curled in on themselves. Anywhere the liquid touched, life died.

Grabbing her shoulders, I gave her a swift shake. "How dare you! How dare you try to kill yourself! How dare you—" My words shook, and tears stung my eyes and clogged my throat, making it so that my words were broken and shattered as I whispered, "I saw you die today. Don't you ever do that again. You, you who knows how deeply Seraphina's death wounded me. How could you? How could. You?"

Shock scrawled through her deep-indigo eyes. "Syrith? Is it really you? But I thought you'd...you—"

I slammed my lips to hers, my heart a twisted, mangled mess in my chest at the thought of how close I'd come to losing her forever. I was furious. Angry. And not gentle.

But neither was she.

Her hands curled into the nape of my neck, clawing me. Drawing blood. I hissed, but the pain was exquisitely grounding.

I nipped at her lips with my own fangs. Tasting. Touching. Inhaling her heart, her soul. Wanting every inch of her inside of every inch of me. I'd cracked myself open completely to this fairy. Seraphina's death had broken me. But Galeta's would end me.

"I love you, you silly, wonderful, awful, beautiful fairy," I moaned brokenly against her lips.

I needed more of her. Needed to be inside of her. Up until now, I'd been patient, gentle with her. But I'd watched her die once and nearly do it again. Gentleness wasn't a choice I possessed anymore.

Letting my dragon loose, I tipped her chin up forcefully so that I could slide my tongue in deep. She accepted me with a heady moan, and I lost myself completely.

To her touch.

Her sighs.

I loved her. With every part of me.

Every fractured, broken part of me was hers completely.

Galeta was just as violent with me. Her clawed hands tore at my vest, ripping it straight down the middle.

I'd had no thought of making love to her this day.

I'd merely wanted to return to her, to hold her. But I would die now if my beast did not claim her completely.

In every way possible.

Her movements were almost angry as she shoved first my tattered vest off, then my shirt, popping the buttons in every direction. I was just as manic.

Barely taking notice of her gown, only knowing I needed to get it off her now. I tore the damned thing straight down the middle. Exposing her completely. Revealing her tiny breasts. Her impossibly flat, impossibly smooth stomach. Her skin color was a pearlescent ivory, beckoning for my touch. And on the tip of her right breast was a birthmark in the shape of a tree.

I grinned. Loving every inch of her.

I tightened my fingers into her hips. Jerking her, somehow now she was straddling me. Her long, lean legs had wrapped around my middle.

Her kisses were punishing and bruising, and I gloried in them all.

Small, clawed fingers raked across my skull, making me hiss, making my blood boil. The magic within me went wild, causing me to flicker between forms. I couldn't control myself.

One moment I felt the press of her mouth like a hot brand, and the next it was just a whisper of pressure. I growled, shaking my ghostly head.

"Stop," she hissed as I tried to pull away. "I can still feel you, Syrith. Every part of you. Your lips singe me with flame. Your eyes bore straight through me. I can feel you."

She framed my face in her hands. A face that should not be, and yet I felt her touch burn through me.

"How do you do that, Galeta? How do you still see me?"

Her thin brows drew down, and a look of raw pain touched her fine features. "Because you are mine, beast. All mine. Every inch of you. Can you not feel this? The burn of true love? Does it not beat inside of you as it beats within me?"

Forcing myself to breathe through the battering ram of my emotions, I locked down on my magic, taking back control so that I was whole again. I nodded. She did beat inside of me. She had almost from the very first moment I'd met her.

"I must confess a truth, my heart."

She blinked prettily, her chest heaving for breath as her breasts brushed against my bare chest, causing the embers within me to stoke and heat and coil tighter.

"What?" she breathed.

"My dragon has already claimed you as mine. I am sorry; I didn't give you the choice. I didn't ask you fir—"

She laughed, but the sound was high-pitched and manic. "I knew that already, Prince. And I want so desperately to be good for you. But I confess that I would do a great many terrible things to keep you with me always."

Her eyes looked as if she were shattered, and I knew she hated her weakness for violence, but what I would never tell her was that she could have spoken no other words to me that would have caused my heart to sing as violently and swiftly as it did now.

She was mine.

And I was hers.

I'd finally been claimed, and by one of the most vile and cursed of creatures to have ever lived, and I loved her even more because of it, because I was one of the few who truly knew why.

"I would burn entire villages down for you, my fairy."

She gasped. And without a word of warning, leaned forward, stealing my lips with her own. Sliding her wet tongue along the seam of my lips. I opened on an exultant growl.

Our tongues tangled, dueling fiercely. Tasting of one another, branding our scents so deep within each other's souls that there'd never be any excising it.

I tried to sit up, to move so that I could get my damnable laces undone on my pants so that I might finally free myself. But she shook her head violently.

"Galeta, I need to—"

She flicked her wrists, banishing the rest of my clothes. With a stunned chuckle, I opened my mouth to tease her, but my wild fairy was having none of that.

Wrapping her hands around my shoulders, she pressed me down into her. Holding me fast with the supernatural strength of her kind. But I didn't mind her savageness, because I was savage too.

With a snarl, I claimed her lips. She sunk her fangs into my bottom lip, and I thrilled at her dark touch. Coming alive for her.

Seraphina could never have handled my beast.

"More, Syrith. Give me everything," she moaned.

And I did. Latching a hand onto her outer thigh, I notched her knee, opening her wide to me.

"Are you ready, my fairy?" I grunted, so hard and stiff that every inch of me ached.

If she told me to stop, I would, but goddess help Kingdom if she did. Because I think I might have truly done something terrible to some innocent village somewhere. Dragon myths existed for a reason.

Her eyes turned soft and dewy, her smile seductive yet innocent. She nodded. "I'll always be ready for you, my Prince."

With a cry of satisfaction, I sheathed myself deep in one swift motion. She stiffened beneath me, and I thought I'd hurt her.

Trying to pull out, I planted rows of kisses along her brows, her cheeks. "I'm sorry, my beauty. So sorry."

She laughed, the sound deep and shivery. "Never apologize for such pleasure." Then, slamming her claws down on my arse, she shoved. "Move."

Laughing from deep inside my soul, I did as my fairy commanded. The first slick glide of me touching deep within her caused her to shiver. The second caused her to gasp.

"Good?" I asked between heated kisses.

All that left her lips was a fiery grunt. Galeta met me thrust for thrust. Moving as one, we were lost in the synergy of our bodies, the song of souls.

"Always, my beast, always," she said on a languid sigh.

And then the strangest thing began to happen to her. Her body began to burn in mine. Growing hotter, deeper, fuller. Magic poured out of her, the glow of it permeating every inch of our realm, and everything it touched, everywhere it went, the world began to glow with life.

Leaves sprouted from the trees. Vines covered in roses slithered through roots. Great birds cawed through the sky. The breeze grew redolent with the wash of millions of flowers, bathing us both.

And though my body moved by rote, my gaze was astonished by the creation and life she birthed. I looked down at her, awed, moved by her beauty, only to realize I held a woman aglow in flame.

She burned like the sun, and I gloried in it. My beast roared its approval. A smile wreathed her lovely face.

Deep-blue eyes peered up at me. We moved as one unit, one body, one soul. Her slender fingers framed my face.

Love burst through every inch of her.

"I love you." I finally said it. Her eyes widened for a fraction of a second, then they turned soft, lovely.

"And I you."

My form shivered as I began to draw closer to the pinnacle of our shared pleasure. Her fingers sparked against the phantom flesh of my face. I still felt her. And I knew now, I always would.

"Tell me you're mine," I said as I rocked my hips harder moving deeper inside of her.

Her lashes fluttered, feathered against the tops of her cheeks. She wanted to close them, but I wouldn't let her.

"Look at me, fairy, and tell me you're mine," I commanded.

"I'm yours, dragon. Only yours."

With one final grinding of our hips, we both exploded into that little death.

Chapter 19: The End Is Only the Beginning

Harpy

The wind rolled with magic, and I felt the call of my Creator.

It is time. The vessel is now come...

With a gasp, I twirled, lips curving upward with joy, ready to embrace the sacrifice of the pure innocent come to take her place. I knew it couldn't have been me. I'd worried over nothing.

The mark had faded this morning. I had indeed been hanging onto it for another.

Galeta had forever transformed herself down here. Her time as The Blue was now no more. I'd not watched them make love, but I'd felt the pull and sway of the mightiest of magics.

But when I gazed behind me, there was nothing but trees. Life that'd sprouted from their union. No more gray in this world. Color had leeched into everything.

It was beautiful.

It was pure.

It was lovely, and my soul trembled with a deep and terrible knowledge.

"The vessel is—"

You, It said simply.

The trees trembled, and wetness trekked down my cheeks. I shook my head. "But...but my mark faded," I breathed.

Touching my fingers to my cheeks, I pulled them away, staring at the wetness glistening upon them. Tears? I'd never cried before.

It is you, my little golden flower. I sent you to her to watch her. To learn and grow. To mingle amongst the peoples of that world. To learn what it was to love, to sacrifice, to hurt.

I sniffed. I did not want to do this. I'd seen the madness that'd been borne through that seed. Galeta had been a pure soul before it had taken her. My fate would be no different.

But it would, my little harpy. For I have learned things myself. Growth never stops, even for a Creator.

"But you know all."

It laughed, and lightning struck the tops of the trees. *Not even I know how things will turn out until they happen. The Pink could have told me no, but she didn't.*

"Can I tell you no?" My voice quivered.

Of course. The choice has always been yours.

I wanted to say no. I wanted to plead with him to create another vessel, another creature to bear this burden. And in that moment, I knew a sad truth. Galeta had surely wished for the same.

I swallowed hard.

She'd been brave. I was weak. But I didn't have to be. A lonely tear slid down my cheek.

The breeze around me stirred, drying up my tears. My body pulsed with warmth, with love. The Creator was holding me. Showing me Its regard and loving kindnesses.

I felt Its hope, but also Its love. It would not judge me or reproach me either way. I truly was free to do as I willed.

I bit my bottom lip.

"If I do not take this seed from her, what will happen?"

She would die in this place. Even now, the magic is breaking down.

An idea sprouted in my head. "The clone. Could the clone's form not protect her from the ravages of that darkness? It is another shield. A piece of armor. It changed in the world above. Surely—"

But even as I said it, I knew it could not. The clone had been destroyed by Fiera's fiery blast. A blast I myself had whispered into her ear as command.

I'd been the instrument of the Creator all along.

You know as well as I that it could not protect her. And you know why. Within these walls, her mind has been restored, but outside this realm, she would revert to who she once was. And worse than ever. I made her a promise long ago that her torments would one day end. I know her heart; she is soul weary, my beautiful one. Galeta has no intentions of leaving this realm, ever. And once the magic of the mirror is destroyed, it will end her too, releasing that seed into Kingdom.

I was outside the purview of this magic. I could choose to walk away and suffer no consequences from my actions.

"If I take the seed, what will happen to her? To this world?"

She will be saved. But you are right to ponder, my dear. I am not quite certain about all that will transpire—those choices have yet to be made—but there will be great change in store for all.

"Good change?"

It paused, and I bit my bottom lip hard.

In the end... yes. Though it will not come without its fair share of pain too.

I swallowed hard. "And me, what of me? Will I be doomed to walk the same path as she once did?"

I've learned a great many things during Galeta's tenure. And I will make a vow to you, my precious one, just as I once did to her. I will never forsake you, I will never leave, and I will always be there for you.

I bowed my head, and every limb in my body pulsed and throbbed. Deep down, I'd known the day the marking had appeared on my wrist. I'd rejected the idea outright because I hadn't been ready to accept it.

Biting down on my back teeth, I looked up at the sky. Savoring its beauty one final time, knowing my mind and heart would be twisted by the darkness soon.

"I am ready."

Galeta

When I blinked my eyes open, I wanted to laugh to the heavens. Shout his name and claim him for all the world to know he was mine.

But his strange look caught my attention, and I swallowed hard. "Syrith, what's the matter?"

"Galeta," he whispered, but I heard his love, and my lips twitched into a ghost of a smile. "Look at yourself."

Frowning, I shook my head. "What?"

"Look at yourself, fairy. Look."

Feeling a tad panicked, I called forth a looking glass and pushed on his chest to get up.

He did, but his movements were wooden and stiff.

Heart hammering painfully in my chest, I sat up, but I didn't need to stand to notice the immediate changes.

I touched a hand to my cheek. The face staring back at me was the same. The hair, so deeply blond it appeared golden, but my body sparkled. My flesh glowed. As though some mighty hand had taken a pile of diamonds, crushed it beneath its fist, and doused me in it.

And the dress I'd discarded not long ago was now back on me. Spilling down around my body like a living wave, it clung to my every curve.

My wings, always electric-blue and broad, also glowed. Like neon. I gasped, shaking my head. I was...beautiful. "What is this sorcery?"

113

"It's you," he said deeply.

I blinked. Feeling. Strangely. Whole. The darkness burned within me, but it no longer controlled me. I was free.

With a giggle, I rushed to him, framing his beloved face in my palms and kissing him soundly. "I love you. I'm free, Syrith. We're free."

He nodded. Kissing me back hard. But then a tight growl tumbled from his lips, and a flash of hurt crossed his eyes.

"I have not forgotten what you nearly did, Galeta. You must vow to me now, in all honesty and truth, that you will never again try to harm yourself. I could not bear it."

Feeling terribly ashamed of myself, I shook my head. "Syrith, I was mad with grief. The burn of that darkness has been a blight in my life for so very long. I could not bear it another day. And then I saw Hook."

He frowned hard. "Hook. James Hook?"

"Yes." I nodded, recalling that vision. The pain of his hook embedding into my stomach had been so real, until Syrith had appeared and banished it all. "I've never meddled in his affairs, so far as I'm aware. And yet he was here"—I gestured to the ground before me—"glaring at me with pain and hate. Blaming me for destroying his happy ending..."

I shivered, remembering how real it had all been. How visceral. I clenched my jaw. Not at the memory of my pain, but at his.

That recollection hadn't been one of mine. But it'd been very, very real. Why? What did it mean? When I'd stolen the Gray's powers lifetimes ago, I'd stolen her power to "see." What many didn't know was that the Gray hadn't simply seen the past—she'd also seen the future, and now...so could I.

Had that been an omen of things to come?

A terrible black chill of foreboding zipped down my spine, causing me to tremble.

Syrith's grip was warm and grounding on my hands, helping to yank me from terrible thoughts. He squeezed my fingers tenderly. "I do not know or understand the magic in this place, my beloved, but perhaps what you saw was an image of your own demons. Your own fears and doubts. You've destroyed happily ever afters for others. Perhaps it was an image to make you think—"

"Maybe it wasn't a portent." I desperately latched onto the idea. "Maybe it wasn't really him at all, but my subconscious way of acknowledging what I'd done and a reminder to never do this again. To fix what I've broken?" My words sounded unsure because they were.

I didn't believe any of what I was saying, but I was frantic to make it so.

His hands were so tender on my face that I melted into his touch, loving him more than I'd ever thought I could love anything.

He shrugged. "Mayhap. I know not. But it's a good place to start, no?"

My smile was wimpy. "Aye. It is, Syrith."

Nodding, he gazed at me as if I was his world. In a way no one ever had before. I was unlovable to all but my dragon. Love was a strange and powerful thing. Magic I'd never understood before. But it was deep, and it was sure and all-encompassing.

"I will fix our world," I said, my vow trembling with truth. "I will undo what I've wrought. Somehow, but—"

I wet my lips, not sure how to tell him of my suspicions. Tipping his head forward, he lifted his brows, as though waiting on me to finish speaking.

Nibbling on a corner of my lips, I sighed. "Syrith, I am not certain I can leave here. And I'm not sure I even should. Though I am free of this darkness in here, and I sense great magic in this realm, it isn't stable. It is fleeting, and I am scared."

"Then we'll figure this out. Together. And we will make our world right again, Galeta. You and I, side by side. No matter how long it takes, I will never leave you again. Do you hear me, fae?"

I nodded swiftly.

"And you must vow never to do the same."

Ashamed of myself, for how he'd found me, but also glad that even at my lowest, he'd not turned away from me, I wrapped my arms around him. Syrith truly loved me. I knew now how much that mattered. I'd never been truly loved before.

Buttons had cared for me, in his own way, but in the end, he'd left. I suspected that should I ever become the monster again, Syrith never would.

He'd stay.

He'd suffer.

But he'd stay.

"I love you, beast. And I will never again try to hurt myself."

Syrith embraced me tight, and I knew he never meant to let me go. And that was quite all right with me, because I never wanted him to either.

Syrith

I'd rutted her like a beast on the road. I planned to take my queen back to our hut and make love to her all through the night. To whisper of my love, to be tender and gentle, as I hadn't been the first time.

I stroked her back, smiling into her hair at how responsive she was to my every touch. It hadn't been light that'd pulled me out of the shadows, but darkness. I loved my fairy with everything within me, and I meant to prove it to her all the days of our lives. Soon, we'd figure out a way to bury that darkness forever so that she need never suffer again. But not right now—right now was a time for loving and healing.

I stood, bringing her with me. And we held onto one another for several long moments.

Sometime between the thirtieth and fortieth breath, the squeeze of power pulsed through the air. I twirled us in unison, expecting to find Aphrodite standing behind me, but it was not.

Harpy looked at me then at Galeta in my arms. "Galeta," she said, dipping her head regally, "good to see you again."

Galeta's hand pressed into the small of my back, and she shivered. Worry scrawled a tight line across her thin brows, causing my own nerves to pinch.

"Harpy," she said softly, and I had to wonder when the two had learned of one another. "Why are you here?"

"Because I found your replacement," she said with tears sparkling in her eyes. "You are free, little fae. Free now to live and love. As you so richly deserve."

Galeta blinked. "Replacement? Replacement for what?"

That was the moment I realized Galeta still didn't know the sacrifice she'd made.

Harpy's smile was gentle. Walking toward us, she gently laid a hand upon my woman's shoulders and said, "It is time, Galeta, to learn who you truly are."

The pulse of great and powerful magic encased us like a vice. Galeta's jaw dropped, and I knew that Harpy was showing Galeta everything I'd seen as a Phoenix.

Galeta gasped, shaking her head. "No. No. No," she whispered over and over, sounding stunned. Shocked.

Finally, Harpy stepped back, clutching her hands to her breast and nodding sadly. "Yes, fae. All true."

Her pretty gold eyes shimmered with unshed tears. I frowned. Dragons were highly emotional, sensitive creatures attuned to the emotions of those around them. And I sensed something great and heavy weighing down Harpy's shoulders.

Galeta covered her mouth with her hands. "I wasn't always a villain?"

The first tear dripped from Harpy's eye. "No, wee one. You weren't. And you won't be anymore. When you return to your world, you'll be who you always should have been."

Galeta blinked, digging her fingers into my arms. It was only then I realized I was still nude. Thankfully, with whatever Harpy was going through, she hardly seemed to notice or care.

"Harpy, who's the replacement?" Her words were barely a pinprick of sound in the now hushed realm.

Harpy's watery grin was sad.

And all the pieces finally clicked into place.

Harpy's visits.

Why she'd built this world. Why she'd lingered to learn. She'd watched Galeta, and I'd never understood why. Until now.

The replacement vessel, it was her.

I shook my head.

Galeta cried. "No, Harpy. You can't do this. You've been a good friend. I'll live in the mirror. I'll stay put. Nothing has to change."

A single tear tracked down the lovely bird's face. "The mirror's magic can't contain this darkness forever, fairy. You know this as well as I do. We finally got you back. What kind of friend would I be if I let you—"

Sobbing violently now, Galeta touched her forehead to my chest. "I can't lose you, Syrith. Not now. Now that I can remember, can breathe again. I know who I am. I'd rather die than go back to what I was, but I could never force this upon another."

My heart shattered because I knew she'd chosen, and she was right. I could never ask Galeta to sacrifice another just so that we could be happy. It wasn't fair. Especially not to a creature as innocent and kind as Harpy.

I leaned down, kissing her with all the passion in my heart. Letting her know that even in death and beyond, I'd love her forever.

I'd thought I'd known love. But I knew the truth now.

Galeta wasn't just my love.

She was my soul.

And when you loved something, you set it free.

"I'll stay locked in here with you until the mirror shatters. If you go, my fairy, then I go with you."

"Forever?" she whispered.

And I nodded, tucking a stray curl of golden hair behind her slightly pointed earlobe. She smelled of raspberries and sunshine. Gods, I loved her. So much that it was an ache.

"Forever," I whispered right back.

We were kissing again, and I was drowning in the pure and sweet essence of her. The evil still dwelled within her, and it was only a matter of time before it consumed her soul once more, but for now, I had my woman, and I would never let her go.

I was so lost in her touch and taste that I'd not heard Harpy's approach until she was upon us. Galeta froze, gasping painfully and going still in my arms. Heart hammering in my chest, I shot my gaze upward, only to spot Harpy with her hand extended and her claws dripping blood. Between her fingers, she held a tiny black seed of power so dark it rocked me to my core.

I felt the evil.

The stain of violence. War. Destruction.

It lived and breathed and beckoned to all.

The colors that Galeta had brought back into this world began to leech through again, turning dank, gray. Gloomy.

The seed destroyed all it came in contact with.

Harpy's eyes looked shattered and tight with pain.

Galeta's flesh instantly brightened, flushing with blood. Her colors began to swirl. Her eyes turned golden. Her skin a shade of burnished peach. Beautiful wings dipped in bright beams of glowing magenta stretched out from behind her back.

Her eyes were wild, frantic. She twirled in my arms, swishing the scent of wildflowers through the air with her.

She stared at Harpy, who now sobbed silently. "I will leave. I promise. Go far away from peoples. I will never hurt a soul. I saw your fight, Galeta, and I can only pray I'll be half the vessel you were. You deserve your peace now."

Her smile was watery but brave. I shook my head. Galeta tossed out her hand, reaching to snatch that darkness back, but it was too late.

Harpy had shoved her fist deep inside her belly, and tipping her head back, she howled. Screaming with the agony of a wounded and dying animal.

Beams of fire covered her, and she flung her arms out. Wings spreading. And with one mighty heave, she shoved off the ground, flying away as far and as fast as her wings allowed.

Galeta and I stood there in numbed silence. Shocked and unable to understand that we were free. That she was free.

After what felt like hours, she turned slowly toward me, eyes wide, and shaking her head.

The bright flush of her flesh had paled out. And her lips were pinched tight. She grabbed at her chest. "Syrith? I don't feel wel—"

I had just enough time to reach for her before she collapsed in a heap. Roaring, fearing my bride had died, I shook her suddenly lax body as a deep glow of gold began to pulse through her form. Growing brighter and brighter and brighter until...

That pulse shot out of her like an explosion. Rocking the world around us, causing the mirror to rumble. Trees toppled. The land fissured, ripping open violently and dragging everything down with it.

If I didn't do something now, we'd die here.

Gathering her into my arms, I shifted into that of my dragon form and flew as though the hounds of hell were at my feet. A minute later, the land we'd been standing upon vanished. Simply ceased to be.

Pumping my wings harder, I fought the dizziness of moving at such high speeds. Swallowing my panic. I had to get us out of here before we were forever lost to this madness too. I exited the mirror only a second before it shattered completely, shooting slivers of glass like missiles in every direction, some of them piercing through the thick hide of my wings. I roared, tilting midflight.

With a growl of determination, I clenched my fist, clinging tight to Galeta's slight form. I dared not stop. I was headed for Nox.

But where the clone rested her head each night was now no more. There was no land. No trees. Only the infinite void of space.

Eyes wide, I shook my head, rejecting the reality of what I was seeing.

All of it was gone.

The peoples. The games. The gods.

There was nothing left anymore.

Galeta moaned. I kept my clawed foot banded tightly around her, terrified of losing her now. Shifting directions, I headed for Kingdom, praying to the Gods of every pantheon that it remained. That it hadn't been lost too. Wondering what in the devil had just happened but feeling an unsettling disquiet as I recalled the fear in Calypso's eyes at the start of the game.

She'd sensed something terrible would happen.

Was this it?

And if so, what exactly *had* happened?

Slowly, I became aware of another presence nearby. There was nothing ahead or to the left or right of me. Craning my long, sinuous neck over my shoulder, I spotted the gigantic shadow of another dragon.

Even in the depths of night, I caught the glint of gold.

Realizing immediately that this had been Galeta's familiar, I slowed my flight to allow the beast time to catch up to us.

Buttons—which I'd always found to be an odd name for such a massive animal—sniffed his broad nostrils at me, as though tasting my scent and taking it in deep. Naturally, being half dragonborne myself, I knew it was taking my measure.

Burning, intelligent eyes studied me.

I did not ask how Buttons had found her after so long a time apart. The bond between familiar and master was a powerful one, even if the master rejected the familiar, as Galeta had. His burning eyes zipped down to the tiny bundle of precious pink gripped in my talons.

"I knew the moment time had collapsed that Galeta had succeeded," he said slowly. The crack of his voice echoed loudly in the vastness of space.

"What do you mean time has collapsed?"

Shaking his massive shoulders, Buttons grunted in obvious agitation, causing a ball of flame to shoot from both nostrils.

"Follow me," was all he said.

The massive beast veered toward the right, toward a shimmering veil that parted realms.

I didn't understand how any of this was possible. How we were in space. How we could breathe. Because nothing made sense anymore. Buttons soared through the veil, and I followed. If it was a trap, we had absolutely nothing to lose at this point. We needed to find land. That was all that mattered now.

The moment I broke through the barrier, the familiar sights and sounds of Kingdom assailed me, and the breath I'd not realized I'd been holding spilled from my mouth.

Buttons hurtled toward land like a blazing comet. Knowing that if my woman were aware right now, she'd be telling me to follow close at her dragon's heel, I did just that.

We tucked in our wings at nearly the same moment. The whistling of displaced air from our rapid approach shook the large, rooted trees around us. Seconds before touching land, I shifted, transferring Galeta from my claws to my arms.

She felt like a feather in my arms. I touched down gracefully, jostling her only a little.

But it was enough to get her to groaning again. In moments, she was blinking her eyes open and rubbing a hand over her brow.

"What...what's happened, Syrith?" she asked in sweet confusion.

Loath to release her, I very gently sat her on her feet, keeping a firm grip on her arms to make sure she'd not collapse on me again.

"Where are we?" She blinked. Looking around and then gasping as she finally caught sight of her dragon. "Buttons!" she said in a shocked gasp. "What are you doing here? How did you find me?"

Glancing from the corner of my eye at the dragon, I watched his serious countenance temporarily transform into one of worry and care.

Dragons and dragonborne rarely gave their hearts into the keeping of another, but when we did, it was forever. Buttons loved her as surely as I.

A ghost of a smile whispered across my lips. She'd always thought herself unlovable, but there had been one who'd cared all along. It made me feel more bonded to the beast for it.

"I will always find you, Galeta, whether Pink or Blue," he said gravely, "but now is not the time for sentimental fluff. A serious problem has developed in Kingdom."

Worry pinched her pretty features. As she looked around her, her wings began to beat in earnest. "Why are we in the Enchanted Forest?"

I wasn't sure how or when she'd done it or when she'd found it. I'd had my eyes on her the entire time, but from one moment to the next, she was suddenly gripping tight to her wand, its tip glowing like star flame.

Buttons nodded. "Yes, you are right. In the games, I was given into the care of Fable. It is why I even came here, to ascertain all had gone accordingly for her and she'd received her happily ever after."

A bad feeling began to worm through my gut. The same must have happened to Galeta, because she was gripping my hand tight, squeezing the fingers so hard, the bones ground together.

"And? What's happened, Buttons? You're worrying me."

"I wish I had better news for you, my queen. But all is not well. One second, Fable and Owiot were trying to undo the curse upon the sleeping form of Snow White, and the next, a massive blast ripped through the very fabric of this universe. Time has altered somehow. Snow White is gone. The castle is void of peoples, save for the Dark Queen and her mate and...one other."

She shook her head. "Buttons, please stop stalling. You're frightening me. What's happened? What has—"

Suddenly a wail of heart-rending pain swept through the woods, the cries of a tortured soul echoing all around. Galeta shuddered, and my blood ran cold.

"What is that?" I asked.

Button's eyes turned downcast. Dragons were proud, some would even say vain creatures. To see one looking so obviously dejected and forlorn made me feel physically ill. I grabbed hold of my stomach as a sudden, violent feeling washed over me.

"That tortured cry you hear is Fable. For she has just discovered that in this new reality, she does not truly exist. But more than that, her grandmother and grandfather, Hook and Trishelle, have never met. Her mother, Nimue, was never born. And worse still, Calypso no longer knows her own granddaughter. Hades is a brooding, silent figure in the Underworld, and magic has betrayed us all."

Chapter 20: In Which a World Goes Boom...

Galeta

"*What?*" I shrieked, half mad with stone-cold fear and confusion. "This can't be. This can't be! If none of that happened, then how is Fable even still here? You must be wrong, Buttons. This cannot—"

The tortured cry of that dying animal raised all the hairs on my arms, and without stopping to think, I raced toward it.

Entering a castle that'd once been bustling with life and beauty. Now a decrepit, blackened, and ruined thing. As though a great fire had swept through it, leaving only the hull behind, eradicating all life with it.

Standing at the center was a weeping Fable, with her dark magic swirling about her like a funnel. She was still a thing of unmitigated dark beauty.

Dressed all in white, she'd altered so completely in the games. Turning from a woman with a heart as dark as Galeta's own into one soft and gentle, capable of loving again.

Hook's ghost taunted me. I hissed, recalling the kiss of his blade through my gut with vivid intensity all over again. Fable couldn't lose her happily ever after.

This couldn't happen.

I wouldn't let it.

A tower of water in the shape of a cell held Fable fast. Owiot was reaching toward her, trying in vain to approach the jail, but every time he would, a wave would reach out and slap him aside.

"Owiot, no!" Fable cried. Her face was splotchy and swollen, her eyes bloodshot as tears rolled down her face. "She'll kill you. By all that's holy, I demand you stay back. Stay away from me!"

But the brave male wouldn't listen. He was running back toward his dark queen, trying desperately to rescue her from the chaos keeping her kneeling and screaming out in agony as water swiftly covered her form.

Using my powers, I commanded the waters to cease. But it was no use. The tower ran higher and higher, until once more the queen screamed, struggling and fighting against the swift current that rushed down her throat. Giving a violent jerk only a second later, she went absolutely still.

Eyes wide, mouth open. Dead.

I heard a scream, and I realized it was my own. "She can't be dead. This can't be happening."

"Fin!" I pointed my star-tipped wand at the water. And cried with relief when suddenly it dispersed, melting in a puddle at her feet. I rushed toward Fable, intent on saving her.

But this time it was Syrith who pulled me back, his strong arms wrapping like steel bands around my waist and hugging me to him. "Do not touch that cursed water!" he snarled.

And my joy at imagining I'd somehow saved her soon turned to horror as I witnessed the water begin to rise again. Fable was awake. Not dead as I'd thought. But she was sputtering. Choking and gasping. Looking longingly at Owiot. And then the water rose to her waist, and the screams of the wounded began in earnest again.

"What's happening?" I screamed, at a complete loss as to how I could fix this. Change this.

Owiot was the one to look at me then. "Calypso did this. She went insane. Cursed Fable when she said she was her granddaughter. I've never seen the goddess so mad. That magic flew through us. One second, she and Hades stood beside Fable, and the next, Hades vanished and Calypso turned into...a monster."

Unable to bear the sight of Fable's suffering even another second, I did the only thing I could. I remembered my time as the Blue. Knew the dark spells even still. Light magic had done nothing for her, but maybe dark could.

"*In morte,*" I whispered, voice breaking as tears slid down my cheeks and I pointed my wand at the suffering queen.

Fable was on her knees, hands thrown up, neck squeezed tight in her obvious agony. Her face was flushed with terror, and her mouth parted in a permanently silent howl.

The waters, which had risen to waist deep, stopped rising. The vortex of Fable's shadow also ceased.

"You killed her!" Owiot shouted, then with a violent shake of his head, he ran toward Fable. This time, he was finally able to reach through the bars of her cage and touch her. But she was locked in place, a still, lovely statue.

My heart shrank at the sight. The dawning dread of what I'd done simply by allowing Harpy to carry the seed was beginning to impress itself upon me with horrific clarity. Somehow, when the seed had been released from me, magic had run wild. With nothing to stabilize it, it'd gone out of control. Changing not just happily ever afters, but the very fabric of Kingdom itself.

"She is not dead, Owiot, I vow to you."

Weeping openly, he turned his shocked brown eyes toward me. "What's been done to my female? Can this be undone? What has happened to everyone?"

"Yes," I nodded. "It can be undone, but only once Calypso releases her from the curse. Fable sleeps. But were I to unfreeze her now, the tortures would only resume in earnest."

Syrith grabbed me by my shoulders, but I couldn't rip my eyes off the grieving husband before us, clinging to a statue that did not breathe or move with life.

"Did you feel that magic too?" I asked my lover.

The tight clench of his jaw said it all, and I began to shake violently. Fable existed in a world that no longer knew her. Her entire family tree had been wiped out.

"Oh gods, Syrith. Your family. We have to find your family."

The whites of his eyes overtook nearly all color, and his dark skin blanched as if all blood had leaked out of him.

Taking him by the hand, I called forth a traveling tunnel and shot through it. Clutching him tight to me. Why had Fable remained when her family had vanished? If time had altered, then how much of it had altered?

I'd soon have my answers, and I knew, deep down, I'd like none of it.

We barreled out of the other end of the starlit tunnel like cannon fire.

"Don't let me go, Syrith," I commanded, wondering if maybe the reason why he remained was because somehow he'd been with me. Maybe my magic had kept him here. I didn't know. I simply didn't know anything.

The castle was a bustle of peoples and familiar faces. Which went miles toward easing my fears.

"Go to their rooms. At this hour, they'd be enjoying a repast of tea," Syrith said, voice more serious than I'd ever heard from him.

We were high up in the air and noticed by none below us. "Which one is their room?" I asked, facing the massive gray-stone castle of the King and Queen of Hearts.

He pointed, and I zipped toward it. I wasn't gentle; when I got to the opened window, I flew in, yanking him in behind me. He hissed, and I felt his large body catch in the frame.

"Did I hurt you?" I asked.

He shook his head, and though I spotted a gash in his cheek leaking blood, he didn't seem to notice. His eyes were scanning the rooms. I was watching him and knew the instant my worst fears were confirmed by the sudden flare of panic that twisted up his handsome features.

"They're not here, Galeta! They're not here."

I grabbed the corners of his jaw, squeezing tight and forcing him to look me in the eyes. "We'll find them, Syrith. Do not—"

The chamber door was suddenly tossed open, and a rotund woman dressed as a scullery maid stepped through, brows twisting quizzically. "I thought I'd heard noises. Why are ye scuttling about and making such a ruckus, Prince Syrith?"

My mouth dropped in shock.

Syrith's did too. "Boylena! You recognize me?" He sounded ready to pass out.

Planting strong hands on her wide hips, she gave Syrith and I a stern look. "Well, a'course I do. Ye've only been Prince all yer life. And well you ken, your folks don't like you traipsing through here in their absence—"

"Absence!" He hissed. "Where are they? Where'd they go?"

His fingers dug into my shoulders painfully. Boylena suddenly went from looking annoyed to baffled. "Why, to Olympus, a'course. Prince, are ye well? Shall I go fetch the—"

Wilting against me, he lowered his head onto my shoulder, breathing heavily and deeply. I rubbed at his back, staring at the maid with a tight smile. Until I knew what had happened, there wasn't much I could tell anyone.

"Boylena," I said slowly. The maid finally looked at me, suspicion evident in her eyes.

But there was no time to slowly ease the staff into the knowledge that I was now the Prince's mate. They'd learn soon enough.

"And '*oo* are ye, fae?"

I didn't take it personally, hearing the immediate dislike and distrust in her tone. We fairies hadn't developed the best of reputations through the centuries, but again, there'd be time for chitchat later.

"I'm his mate true," I said. She gasped. I ignored that too. "Listen, it's imperative that you answer my questions right now. I promise to you that I'll answer all I can for you when I have time. Did you feel a pulse of wild magic roll through here not some—"

Suddenly, her eyes grew wide. "I did." She nodded vehemently. "Made me trip down the stairs, it did. Frightful, powerful blast."

So magic had rolled through Wonderland too. This was not good. Had all of Kingdom been affected, then? Oh gods, the ramifications of what this might mean made my knees tremble.

"Boylena," I said slowly, "do you remember anything? Anything at all before that happened?"

She frowned. And even as she shook her head, I spied a flare, a glint of pure, unadulterated terror race through her dark brown eyes.

"Nay." She said it slowly but with a voice grown unsure. "I recall nothing." But one glance down at her hands, and I spotted what she did not seem to be aware of.

Her knuckles had paled to bleached white, and her hands visibly shook. Boylena had lost something precious to her. She might not know it, but some visceral awareness deep down inside of her did, and the horror of that loss had only just begun for her.

My soul shriveled within me.

"Thank you, Boylena. You've been very helpful."

Turning my back on her, I looked at Syrith. "Where would your parents be? Do you know?"

"At Father's family estate." He shook his head, still looking dazed.

The sinking feeling of before only intensified. If his parents were in Olympus, then I had a terrible idea I knew what'd happened today. And by all that was holy, I could only pray I was wrong.

"Call them," I said.

He nodded as I created a bubble that would be able to call through dimensions and time.

The glistening orb floated before our eyes.

"Mother!" he said sharply. "Father! Come to me now."

In seconds, the lambent sheen turned thick with coalescing color. And then the image of a fearful queen filled the screen. She was blond haired and blue eyed. Her features were exotic and lovely, and I could see parts of Syrith in her.

"Syrith? By all that's holy, what's the matter with you, boy?"

Zelena's eyes turned immediately toward me. There was a quick frown and then a moment of clarity. "Ah, I see. You won our boy's heart after—"

There was absolutely no time for exchanged pleasantries. Holding up my hand, I cut her words short. "Listen to me, Queen, and listen well, for I haven't much time. Do not return to Kingdom, whatever you do. Do not step foot inside this realm."

"What?" Suddenly, the face of Ragoth filled the screen. The King looked not only confused, but also angry. Swarthy skinned, with shaggy black hair, he had definitely passed his traits down to Syrith.

This was not the first impression I'd wished to give my in-laws, but it was imperative they stay where they were.

"Terrible magic has been unleashed upon this world," I said, speaking slowly but concisely. Syrith's fingers dug into my lower back. I knew shock still kept him quiet.

"*What's happened?* Is Syrith all right?" the queen asked in a fearful rush.

I shook my head. "For now, yes. But time has altered. People have vanished. If you come back, I fear that the same could happen to Syrith. Somehow, he's still here, and I think the reason is because you were not. You were not touched by the magic, ergo, the magic left him be."

"What? That makes no sense. Who's unleashed this magic?" Ragoth again. The dragonborne literally had smoke curling out of his nose.

"Me," was all I could say. And then I began to shake. I couldn't lose it. I had to hold myself together. I had to fix this.

"You! You!" Ragoth was screaming, but the bubble suddenly vanished.

Syrith had popped it, silencing the rage of his father in an instant. Then he took me in his arms and held on tight.

I clutched at his back. "What have I done, Syrith? What have I done?"

He shook his head. "You did nothing, Galeta. This wasn't you. This is wild, unstable magic unleashed. Not you. Do you understand? Not you."

His words were growled, and his fingers were desperate as they gripped me tight. My stomach heaved. I knew he was trying to soothe me, but I didn't feel soothed in the slightest. This was my fault. Just as everything else had been.

I'd destroyed all of Kingdom, and this time without even trying.

"How far back does this go? Where does it end?"

"*What! Have! You! Done?*"

A shrill, piercing screaming filled my ears. I didn't need to turn to know who it was. I felt the pressure of magic as a travel tunnel sealed tight.

Danika Moon glared furious daggers at me. "My head!" she screamed, grabbing hold of her temples and squeezing tight. "Memories that aren't real. Families in chaos. Ruin. You!"

I'd never seen the beautiful fae so angry, not even the day I'd cursed her nubile form to freeze into that of a hag. Her spider-silk dress was in tatters. Her nut-brown hair full of brambles and weeds, as though she'd raced through anything and everything in her path to get to me.

"My brain has been consumed by two memories of lives that cannot be real! And there is an aching emptiness within me. What have you done, Galeta? What have you done?"

Tears ran down her face unchecked, but I was given no chance to respond back. For another figure had appeared.

"Bring her back to me!"

Rumpelstiltskin appeared before us. His eyes were wild, and he appeared more demon than man, his image flickering from something dark and deadly to the mask of the man I'd always known.

"Who?" I asked, but I already knew.

"My world! My life."

He was tossing furniture around, blasting out magic in his madness. "I felt the touch of your hand in this. None remember her. Her father is with another. Her mother does not exist in this world. I am not mad! I am not crazy. My woman, my Sh—"

"Shayera's gone too?" I whispered, but the way he suddenly stilled, it was as though I'd screamed it.

Twirling on me, heaving for breath, and face contorted with both madness and shock, he rushed me. Gripping my forearms. Syrith tried to stop him, but I shook my head, telling him I was okay.

Rumpel shook me so violently, my neck whipped back and forth.

"You know her! She is real! She is mine." His beautiful face was contorted into one of madness. "Give her back to me, fairy. Give her back."

Danika was suddenly there, wiping her nose. "Shayera...carrots?" She blinked. "She's not real." She blinked again, eyes running over with heavy tears as she looked at Rumpel and me. "But she is." She tapped her head. "I remember. There are two worlds. In the other, she was there. And I loved her too."

At those words, Rumpel released me, sinking to his knees and curling his head upon the thick carpet. His body shaking powerfully. And though I heard nothing, I knew he sobbed for the wife he'd lost.

How was it that he remembered? How was it that some could and some couldn't?

A thought suddenly came to me then. "What year is this?"

"What?" Syrith asked, sounding more sure and less shocked now. "What do you mean?"

Danika was on her knees, trying to comfort Rumpel, who seemed to want none of it. They were both lost to their own misfortunes, and I had a terrible thought, that just like Rumpel, Danika too had lost her mate. Only she hadn't realized it yet. In fact, she might never know at all.

I trembled and shook my head. "I'm not sure. But it matters, somehow. I don't know how, but it... Hatter!"

He'd know. I knew he'd know. His and Alice's romance had been powerful magic. They had to still be together. They had to be. Grabbing Syrith's hand, I flew, dragging him with me.

"Where are we going?" he screamed into the wind.

"The Hatter's cottage. To find him. To find Alice. I have to know how far this disruption has gone."

Syrith didn't speak the rest of the way, for which I was grateful. It gave me time to think. Harpy took the seed, and magic erupted. In the trials for my soul, I'd been forced to endure the pain of seeing all the happily ever afters I'd destroyed. Gerard and Belle. The Wolf and his wolf bride. Jinni and his Queen. Hook and Talia. Hatter and his first Alice Hu. The Moon and the Sun.

Oh dear gods...

Time has reset. Button's words echoed back at me.

Spying the Hatter's cottage, I flew as fast as my wings would carry me. Breathless when I landed, my fingers felt numb and cold as I knocked on the door.

The devilishly handsome madman answered only a moment later, smiling broadly, and I suddenly couldn't breathe right. Either he was happy because he was with his Alice, or he was happy because he'd never known her at all.

"Hatter," I snapped, "what year is this?"

"Well, that was rather brusque," he said in his deeply accented voice. "But if you must know, it is the year twenty-o-two. And just who are you, pretty fairy? Would you care for a spot of tea? I've got plenty."

Suddenly, a steaming pot and a cup and saucer appeared in midair.

"Twenty. O. Two," I mouthed. Dear heavens above, I hoped he was lying. Otherwise, time had just sent us back nearly to the very beginning of their happily ever afters.

Syrith touched my lower back, and I leaned into his hand, needing his strength. I nodded.

Kingdom time and Earth time were vastly different, but if I wasn't mistaken...Alice quite possibly already existed on Earth. I could still fix this, although he seemed oddly content for a man who'd just lost everything. So perhaps he hadn't lost his Alice at all?

"Hatter. May I speak with Alice?"

He shrugged. "Sure, why not?

"Alice," he called over his shoulder. "A strange fairy wishes to speak with you, my little lotus blossom."

My lip curled. Since when had he begun calling her that?

And then Alice came to the door. Long black hair. Smooth brown skin. And a sensual smile. This was Alice Hu all right, but the wrong one.

"Hello, fairy," she said, and her voice made me shiver with its undertones of ice and calculation. "What do you want?"

Eyes going wide, I said nothing back to Alice 1.0. Grabbing hold of Syrith's hand, I opened a portal of time and returned to the Heart's castle.

Everyone was as I'd left them.

All who could looked up at me with emptiness and devastation written in their eyes. I notched my chin for the biggest test of my life.

"It's time to restore our happily ever afters. Now, who's with me?"

Love my books? Then make sure to sign up for my newsletter or follow me on FB, or better yet, do both. I know Kingdom seems bleak now, but believe in the magic of happily ever afters, and don't lose heart. Our little fairy might surprise you yet. If you enjoyed this book, please make sure to leave a review—those things are golden in my world! Also, if you want to know more about Kingdom, specifically many of the popular characters referenced here, did you know I wrote many books under the name Marie Hall. You can start with book one, Her Mad Hatter and work your way through.

Author's Notes

The next queen is coming soon, though it's a mystery who she'll be. If you want to know, stay tuned to either Jovee Winters's FB page or sign up for her newsletter, which is probably the best way to keep up to date.

The next queens, in no particular order, are as follows:

The Centaur Queen

The Fire Queen (Fiera's Story)

The Mesmerizing Queen (The Pied Piper's Story)

And if you want to start at the beginning, make sure to pick up your copy of The Sea Queen!

About Jovee Winters

Jovee Winters is the pen name of a *NY Times* and *USA Today* bestselling author who loves books that make you think or feel something, preferably both. She's also passionate about fairy tales, particularly twisting them up into a story you've never thought could be possible.

She's married to the love of her life, a sexy beast of a caveman who likes to refer to himself as Big Hunk. She has two awesome kids she likes to call Thing 1 and Thing 2, loves cooking, and occasionally has been known to crochet. She also really loves talking about herself in the third person.

Want more Kingdom?

Did you know I also wrote a slew of Kingdom tales featuring many popular characters such as The Mad Hatter, Robin Hood, and Captain Hook—to name a few. I wrote them as Marie Hall. Below you'll find the complete listing for those stories.

Kingdom Series (Fairy Tale Romance)

Her Mad Hatter (Free everywhere! Book 1, based on Alice and the Mad Hatter)
Gerard's Beauty (Book 2, based on Beauty and the Beast)
Red and Her Wolf (Book 3, based on Little Red Riding Hood)
The Kingdom Collection (Books 1–3, with bonus deleted scenes)
Jinni's Wish (Book 4, based on Arabian Nights)
Hook's Pan (Book 5, Based on Peter Pan)
Danika's Surprise (Book 5.5, novelette and first introduction to the upcoming Dark Princess Series)
Kingdom Chronicles (Books 4 & 5, and includes Danika's Surprise)
Moon's Flower (Book 6, based on the legend of the Man in the Moon)
Huntsman's Prey (Book 7, spinoff Dark Princess Series)
Rumpel's Prize (Book 8, loosely based on the legend of Rumpelstiltskin and Beauty and the Beast)
Hood's Obsession (Book 9)
Her One Wish (Book 10)

10806918R00077

Made in the USA
Lexington, KY
30 September 2018